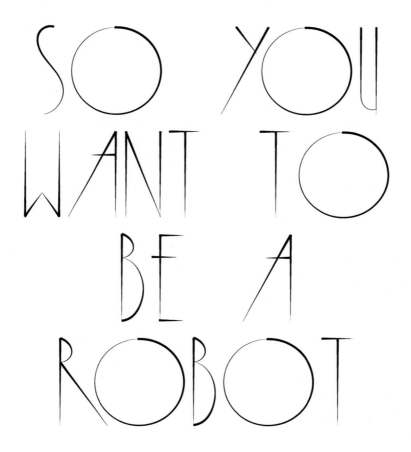

SO YOU WANT TO BE A ROBOT

21 SHORT STORIES BY
A. MERC RUSTAD

LETHE PRESS
MAPLE SHADE, NEW JERSEY

Published in 2017 by Lethe Press, Inc.
118 Heritage Avenue • Maple Shade,
NJ 08052-3018 USA
www.lethepressbooks.com • lethepress@aol.com

ISBN: 978-1-59021-641-5

A full publication history of the stories featured in this volume appear at the end of the book.

Interior and Cover Design: INKSPIRAL DESIGN.
Cover art: MATTHEW TIMSON.

Library of Congress Cataloging-in-Publication Data available on file

For all the Teslas out there.

CONTENTS

THIS IS NOT A WARDROBE DOOR

Dear Gatekeeper,

Hi my name is Ellie and I'm six years old and my closet door is broken. My best friend Zera lives in your world and I visited her all the time, and sometimes I got older but turned six again when I came back, but that's okay. Can you please fix the door so I can play with Zera?

Love,

Ellie

Zera packs lightly for her journey: rose-petal rope and dewdrop boots, a jacket spun from bee song and buttoned with industrial-strength cricket clicks. She secures her belt (spun from the cloud memories, of course) and picks up her satchel. It has food for her and oil for Misu.

Her best friend is missing and she must find out why.

Misu, the palm-sized mechanical microraptor, perches on her seaweed braids, its glossy raindrop-colored feathers ruffled in concern.

Misu says, *But what if the door is locked?*

Zera smiles. "I'll find a key."

But secretly, she's worried. What if there isn't one?

DEAR GATEKEEPER,

I hope you got my last couple letters. I haven't heard back from you yet, and the closet door still doesn't work. Mommy says I'm wasting paper when I use too much crayon, so I'm using markers this time. Is Zera okay? Tell her I miss playing with the sea monsters and flying to the moon on the dragons most of all.

Please open the door again.

Ellie, age 7

ZERA LEAVES THE treehouse and climbs up the one thousand five hundred three rungs of the polka-dot ladder, each step a perfect note in a symphony. When she reaches the falcon aerie above, she bows to the Falcon Queen and asks if she may have a ride to the Land of Doors.

The Falcon Queen tilts her magnificent head. "Have you not heard?" asks the queen in a voice like spring lightning and winter calm. "All the doors have gone quiet. There is a disease rotting wood and rusting hinges, and no one can find a cure."

Misu shivers on Zera's shoulder. *It is like the dreams,* Misu says. *When everything is silent.*

Zera frowns. "Hasn't the empress sent scientists to investigate?"

The Falcon Queen nods. "They haven't returned. I dare not send my people into the cursed air until we know what is happening."

Zera squares her shoulders. She needs answers, and quickly. Time passes differently (faster) on Ellie's home planet, because their worlds are so far apart, and a lag develops in the space-time continuum.

"Then I will speak to the Forgotten Book," Zera says, hiding the tremor in her voice.

The falcons ruffle their feathers in anxiety. Not even the empress sends envoys without the Forgotten Book's approval.

"You are always brave," says the Falcon Queen. "Very well then, I will take you as far as the Island of Stars."

Hi Gatekeeper,

Are you even there? It's been almost a year for me and still nothing. Did the ice elves get you? I hope not. Zera and I trapped them in the core of the passing comet so they'd go away, but you never know.

Why can't I get through anymore? I'm not too old, I promise. That was those Narnia books that had that rule (and they were stupid, we read them in class).

Please say something,

Ellie, age 8

Zera hops off the Falcon Queen's back and looks at the Island of Stars. It glows from the dim silver bubbles that thicken the air like tapioca pudding.

She sets off through the jungle of broken wire bed frames and abandoned armchairs; she steps around rusting toys and rotting books. There are memories curled everywhere—sad and lonely things, falling to pieces at the seams.

She looks around in horror. "What happened?"

Misu points with a tiny claw. *Look.*

In the middle of the island stands the Forgotten Book, its glass case shattered and anger radiating off its pages.

LEAVE, says the book. BEFORE MY CURSE DEVOURS YOU.

Gatekeeper,

I tried to tell Mom we can't move, but she won't listen. So now I'm three hundred miles away and I don't know anybody and all I want to do is scream and punch things, but I don't want Mom to get upset. This isn't the same closet door. Zera explained that the physical location wasn't as fixed like normal doors in our world, but I'm still freaking out.

I found my other letters. Stacks of notebook paper scribbled in crayon and marker and finger-paint—all stacked in a box in Mom's bedroom.

"What are you doing with this?" I screamed at Mom, and she had tears in her eyes. "Why did you take the letters? They were supposed to get to Zera!"

Mom said she was sorry, she didn't want to tell me to stop since it seemed so important, but she kept finding them in her closet.

I said I'd never put them there, but she didn't believe me.

"We can't go there again," Mom said, "no one ever gets to go back!" and she stomped out of the kitchen and into the rain.

Has my mom been there? Why didn't she ever tell me? Why did you banish her too?

What did we do so wrong we can't come back?

Ellie

ZERA'S KNEES FEEL about to shatter.

"Why are you doing this?" Zera grips an old, warped rocking chair. "You've blacked out the Land of Doors, haven't you?"

YES, says the Book. ALL WHO GO THERE WILL SLEEP, UNDREAMING, UNTIL THE END.

Zera blinks hard, her head dizzy from the pressure in the air. "You can't take away everyone's happiness like this."

NO? says the Book. WHY NOT? NO ONE EVER REMEMBERS US THERE. THEY FORGET AND GROW OLD AND ABANDON US.

"That's not true," Zera says. "Ellie remembers. There are others."

Misu nods.

Zera pushes through the heavy air, reaching out a hand to the Book. "They tell stories of us there," Zera says, because Ellie used to bring stacks of novels with her instead of PBJ sandwiches in her backpack. "There are people who believe. But there won't be if we close all the doors. Stories in their world will dry up. We'll start to forget them, too."

WE MEAN NOTHING TO THEM.

Zera shakes her head. "That's not true. I don't want my best friend to disappear forever."

GATEKEEPER,

I don't know why I bother anymore. You're not listening. I don't even know if you exist.

It's been a while, huh? Life got busy for me. High school, mostly. Mom got a better job and now we won't have to move again. Also I met this awesome girl named LaShawna and we've been dating for a month. God, I'm so in love with her. She's funny and smart and tough and kind—and she really gets me.

Sometimes she reminds me of Zera.

I asked Mom why she kept my letters.

She didn't avoid me this time. "I had a door when I was younger," she said, and she looked so awfully sad. "I was your age. I met the person I wanted to stay with forever." She let out her breath in a whoosh. "But then the door just... it broke, or something. I tried dating here. Met your father, but it just wasn't the same. Then he ran off and it was like losing it all again."

I told LaShawna about Zera's world. She said she didn't want to talk about it. I think maybe she had a door, too.

I was so angry growing up, feeling trapped. You know the best thing about Zera? She *got* me. I could be a girl, I could be a boy, and I could be neither—because that's how I feel a lot of the time. Shifting around between genders. I want that to be okay, but here? I don't know.

The thing is, I don't want to live in Zera's world forever. I love things here, too. I want to be able to go back and forth and have friends everywhere, and date LaShawna and get my degree and just *live*.

This will be my last letter to you, Gatekeeper.

If there was one thing Zera and I learned, it's that you have to build your own doors sometimes.

So I'm going to make my own. I'll construct it out of salvaged lumber; I'll take a metalworking class and forge my own hinges. I'll paper it with all my letters and all my memories. I'll set it up somewhere safe, and here's the thing—I'll make sure it never locks.

My door will be open for anyone who needs it: my mom, LaShawna, myself.

—Ell

THE BOOK IS silent.

"Please," Zera says. "Remove the curse. Let us all try again."

And she lays her hand gently on the Forgotten Book and lets the Book see all the happy memories she shared with Ellie, once, and how Ellie's mom Loraine once came here and met Vasha, who has waited by the door since the curse fell, and Misu, who befriended the lonely girl LaShawna and longs to see her again—and so many, many others that Zera has collected, her heart overfilled with joy and loss and grief and hope.

In return, she sees through space and time, right into Ell's world, where Ell has built a door and has her hand on the knob.

"Ell," Zera calls.

Ell looks up, eyes wide. "Zera?"

"Yes," Zera says, and knows her voice will sound dull behind the door. "I'm here."

Ell grins. "I can see your reflection in the door! Is that the Book with you?"

The Book trembles. SHE REMEMBERS.

Zera nods. The air is thinning, easing in her lungs. "I told you. Not everyone forgets."

I would like to see LaShawna again, says Misu.

VERY WELL, says the book. THE CURSE WILL BE REMOVED.

Ell turns the handle.

Bright lights beams into the Island of Stars, and Ell stands there in a doorway, arms spread wide. Zera leaps forward and hugs her best friend.

"You came back," Zera says.

"I brought some people with me, too," Ell says, and waves behind her, where two other women wait.

Loraine steps through the light with tears in her eyes. "I never thought I could come back…"

Misu squeaks in delight and flies to LaShawna.

Zera smiles at her friends. Things will be all right.

"We have a lot of work to do to repair this place," Zera says. She clasps Ell's hands. "The curse is gone, but we have to fix the doors and wake the sleepers. Are you ready?"

Ell grins and waves her mom and girlfriend to join her. "Yes. Let's do this."

TOMORROW WHEN WE SEE THE SUN

I.

THE LAST WOLFLORD will be executed on the cusp of the new solar year.

II.

WOLFLORD (TITLE): *nomadic, nameless survivors of destroyed warships; those who did not accept ritual immolation during the Decommission. No allegiance to the Principality ; outlaws. The antiquated title is self-taken from the first deserter, whose name and memory were erased upon execution; precise origin unknown.*

7

RELEASED FROM ITS stasis, Mere stretches and glides through the wide atrium wreathed in bionic roses and silk banners. It pauses at the gates that hang perpetually open on the Courts of Tranquility. The sensory matrix on the threshold purrs against its consciousness in greeting.

"What awaits this it?" Mere asks the threshold.

The last wolflord. A great victory.

Mere feels nothing at the announcement, as it should. It is not allowed emotion.

It parades to the pool, proud-arched spine and lifted jaw; autonomous machine-flesh granted scraps of self and mind.

(In the glued and stapled seams, it has painted its own awareness. A taste for Zhouderrian wines fermented in the aftermath of white dwarf stars; the poetry of Li Sin, disfavored master of nanite-barbed words; desire stacked like coiled DNA strands, a tower of cards; a voice etched from grave-silence and forgotten pauses between peace and war. It displays none of itself, for it has also learned fear: it can be taken apart and erased if it deviates from its scripted role.)

Mere crouches at the pool's lip. Once its function is complete, it will be returned to stasis. Mere dreads its inevitable sleep.

From this vantage, it surveys the Courts of Tranquility, the synaptic-like rainfall of light along the membranous domed ceiling, the living heartbeat of the tamed planet carved and grown to a million fine-tuned specifications and indulgences. And those within, oh yes, it has seen these courtiers often:

—nobles in redolent synth armor; generals and admirals decked in finest military dress; pilots, their faces replaced with the mindscreens of their ships—

—an eleven-souled sorcerer who drinks the breath of his favorite nemesis, their words twined together as they spar with tongue and gaze, neither ever ready to destroy the other (for then the fun would end)—

—the Gold Sun Lord, resplendent armored god, ensconced in a hover-throne that drifts about the Courts, omnipresent and untouchable—

And below, in the oblong pool where Mere has spent half of its conscious existence, the last wolflord is bound wrist and ankle, suspended in water as every ancillary world watches the feed. There will be no backup made of the wolflord's mind, no funerary rites in the Archives of Heaven. Treason unto the Principality is not suffered lightly.

The Arbiter of the Suns steps forward and lifts reedy, sulfur-scorched hands. Smoke-cured breath fills ordained words with harmonies and atonal bass-clef chords. "You are summoned here, dearly condemned…"

Mere unbends its body, muscle and ligament stretched along metal bones, and glides into the pool, water slicing to either side of its midriff. It cradles the disgraced wolflord's head in one splayed hand. The other, fingers knife-tipped, rests along the condemned's throat. Unseen, Mere spools neuron-thin tendrils into the base of the wolflord's spine and siphons away pain and fear.

The wolflord's body slackens in synthesized, unwanted calm. "Why do this," the wolflord grinds out, words blocked by auditory and visual firewalls. None in the Courts of Tranquility will witness a criminal's last words.

By protocol, Mere is granted the same erasure. It could scream and curse, and no one would hear (except its keepers, silent beneath the pool and always watching). "It is civilized," Mere says with a mocking smile.

"No." The wolflord struggles to speak. "You. Why do you…obey, Mere…"

Mere has never heard its name, found upon waking when it was first brought online, spoken aloud. For the first time since it has served as executioner (sixteen hundred rotations), Mere wants an answer from the damned: "How do you know this it?"

The wolflord's eyelids droop with the sedative. "Loved you…once…I am so…sorry…"

"…and thus the heavens are cleansed anew," says the Arbiter, and Mere cuts the last wolflord's throat.

Blood ribbons out, diluted and sucked clean into vents. The wolflord's spirit sinks as a glossy pebble to the pool's bed.

Mere glances up at the Arbiter's consorts that are ringed about the pool edge. Tattooed jawbones, bared of muscle and flesh, grin with engraved teeth; razored laughter cooks inside skinned throats.

"Where did you net the wolflord?" Mere asks.

They hum a response in chorus, each voice sculpted as a single, distinct, perfect note.

> *You shouldn't care for the dead.*
> *A traitor on the rim of knownspace,*
> *seeking paradise in madness.*
> *Spoke of you, of others lost,*
> *begged mercy for crimes*
> *and forgiveness, never granted.*

They tip eyeless heads down in regret. The Arbiter's consorts are hunters and bailiffs, as close to allies—never friends, never close—as Mere has. They bring it trinkets and bits of new poetry, synthesized tastings of wine, scents of uncharted galaxies and the sound of dying stars. In return, Mere slips the consorts filaments forged between its ribs to dull their unceasing pain.

(Sometimes they share fragments of memory of who they were before they were exulted. Mere has trouble recalling what they have told it.)

Mere unwinds the neural threads from its fingertips, catching final memories and thought-imprints in illegal mods on its palms. It scythes its fingers in the water to wash away the blood.

With duty finished, the Arbiter glides away, flanked by consorts, to join the eleven-souled sorcerer at a table.

The wolflord's hair fans out in gray strands that brush and twine lifeless about Mere's wrist. Mere tilts its head, startled by the odd sensation like it is choking. Is this grief? How can it grieve what it does not remember?

MERE IS PUT back in stasis where it dreams.

The keepers do not watch Mere sleep. So it unwraps the last worlflord's stolen memories.

> her hair smells of ruined worlds and clover soap
> bring my conquests, she says, bring all of them and I will aid you
> she whispers a string of coordinates, a planet once called Rebirth
> each kiss nettles the tongue with microscopic treason, plague passed mouth to mouth
> call forth the Red Sun Lord, champion of the dead
> let us live again; let us rebuild; let us redeem ourselves

The rest: lost like unsanctioned souls brewed in a frosted glass kept chilled at zero Kelvin.

Mere aches, a phantom-physical sensation it cannot control.

There remains an early impression in its subconscious: on a barren world, a laboratory lined with glass suspension tanks, cold-filled with other bodies. Mere has no empirical evidence the recollection is its own. It was made, but by whom is unknown.

(It has no desire for a creator.)

Yet, the she with the plague kiss—it feels kinship for her, sharp, embossed on its awareness with sudden heat.

THE DECOMMISSION (EVENT): *as a measure of good faith upon the signing of the peace treaty between the Seven Sun Lords, each god decommissioned and executed one thousand of their most powerful warships. Each ship and its pilot self-destructed within an uninhabited system of choice and was granted honor in the eyes of the Seven Suns.*

MERE WAKES WITHOUT its keepers' bidding. It blinks back the protective film on its eyes and stares at the lid of its stasis pod. Odd. Mere presses its palm against the lid, and it retracts into the floor.

A she crouches outside, dressed in mirrorsilk armor, visor drawn over her face so all it sees is its own reflection. "Mere?" she says, synthesized voice low.

"You have acquired unauthorized access to this it," Mere says. "It is curious why."

The stasis chamber is empty. Unadorned red walls and its stasis pod in the center with a ring of security lights above. Mere notes the disabled alarms and the blinding virus chewing at the keepers' optic-feeds.

The she flicks her visor up. Her eyes are quicksilver, liquid and bright— cybernetic implants that contrast space-dark skin. "I'm Century. I'm here to free you."

Mere is intrigued. No one has ever wished to free it, not even the Arbiter's consorts. "Why?"

"I made you," she says. The smell of the ancient laboratory is etched under her armor. "A crime I cannot undo. But we have no time. You have already been condemned for not reporting this security breach." Her lips twist in a bitter smile. "Do you want to live?"

Mere has no organic heart (it knows the rhythmic beat of muscle against bone, has read of it in lines of Li Sin's poetry), yet it still knows fear. It lost any choice when the she broke in.

"It will follow, then."

CENTURY BLURS DOWN the maintenance halls, the invisible veins of the Courts, enhanced speed given by her armor. Mere lopes at her heels.

It processes data and sensation in microseconds:

—it is an exile, a faulty machine to be unmade—

—this is no coincidence Century broke into the Courts of Tranquility, a feat deemed impossible by the Principality, only hours after the last wolflord died—

—it is *exhilarated*—

—what will it do now? Its purpose, courtly executioner, has been dismantled—

They slip beneath the cityskin to the spaceport. Vessels of all make and class dock in thousands of bays. Century stops before an eel-ship, coiled in jewel-skinned splendor. Its great eye-ports are open, and Century signals with a hand; the eel distends a proboscis lined with diamond mesh and graphene plates like a ramp. Century leads Mere into the eel's body.

Alarms klaxon in Mere's head—its escape is known.

Within the eel's retrofitted abdomen, synthetic tubes house the mechanics and computerized guts. Finery for living; oxygen filtration system and water recycling.

"Where will you take it?" Mere asks.

Century does not reply.

Mere crouches, toe-talons locked against the mesh floor panel. The she whispers to the eel-ship, and the great sinuous vessel unpeels itself from the port and scythes into vacuum.

III.

OLINARA V (PLANET, FORMER POPULATION: SEVENTEEN MILLION): *Once a thriving colony world settled early in the founding of the Principality, it was decimated by the Gold Sun Lord when an escaped trinket-slave sought refuge in the Olinarain wilds. Olinara V is now classified as an uninhabitable world.*

MERE HAS NEVER been off-world. It taps the gills of the eel-ship, which obliges and unfurls interior flaps of skin to reveal translucent, hardened outerflesh and a view of space.

This odd, unclassifiable sense of kinship with the dead has grown the farther from the Courts they travel—a need (honor-bound) to see the dead to proper rest so they might pass into one of the afterlives in paradise or purgatory, reinvention or rebirth. It has killed so many, it longs to redeem itself. The last wolflord gave it the key.

"Why did you free this it?" Mere asks.

"An old debt." Century grinds her teeth. "Once we're out of range of the Courts' sensors, I jettison you in a shuttle, wraith. You can make your own path."

Mere pets the eel-ship, grateful for the indulgence, and turns towards the she. "Take it to the court of the Red Sun first."

"No," Century says.

"You *will*." Mere flexes its hands. "You forged this exile without consent. You owe this it."

Century whirls. The she has a plasgun at its jaw, muzzle pressed into soft tissue beneath its chin, and in turn, it rests its fingertips against the back of her neck. It looks down at her. The mirrorsilk burns into its skin, coiling up its wrist and burrowing towards bone.

"I can unmake you far easier than I made you, Mere."

"It can sever your brainstem through your armor with but a gentle pinch of its fingers."

Century scoffs. "We are both destruction incarnate. Perhaps this is a better end."

Mere does not think the she wishes to die; it does not. If it kills her, the eel-ship will never take it where it must go. "A truce." Mere lowers its arm, flesh chewed back to wire and metal skeleton, the knives bright. It will heal slowly. "It has a proposition."

Century holsters the gun. "Do you?"

Mere extracts the last wolflord's memories, printed into a small holochip it saved for one of the Arbiter's consorts. "It is the wolflord who found Rebirth, is it not?"

Century's shoulders tighten. "That world was lost long ago."

Mere repeats the coordinates to her. Her expression remains inert. "It is what the wolflord remembered at death."

"Damn you." Century tips her head back and sighs. "I told him to forget."

Mere offers her the holochip. "Clearly."

Century doesn't accept. "We thought the Red Sun's presence would weaken the bindings of the consecrated pool. Once that happened, we could collect the soul seeds and bring them somewhere. Another planet. Give them proper rest. It was just a dream."

"'Dreams need not stay trapped in sleep alone,'" Mere says, quoting Li Sin. "Bring this it to the Red Sun Lord. We will rescue the dead."

Century raises her eyebrows. "Do you know how many security protocols I hacked to get in 'unnoticed' the first time? I helped *build* the Courts." She snorts. "I constructed the pool. I built the door matrix. The Courts were supposed to be an end to the galaxy-spanning wars I fought and won. The Principality was supposed to bring peace, starting with the Decommission."

It tilts its head, watching the she sidelong. "You are old, then."

"I am," Century says with a bitter laugh. "But what's age any longer?"

"You do not believe this endeavor possible."

"No," Century says. "I don't. Not anymore."

Mere examines its healing arm, flesh reknitting. There is an ache in its ribs it cannot define. "At least bring it to the Red Sun. All the souls in the pool are there by its hand; it would see them to a better fate."

Century flinches, near-imperceptible.

But she speaks to the eel-ship, and they set course for a different court.

BLUE SUN LORD (GOD): *one of the Seven Suns, everlasting and all-knowing rulers of the Principality. Dwelling within the Hollow Systems, the Blue Sun Lord oversees the sanctified pool within the Courts of Tranquility; the Blue Sun Lord is a merciful and generous god* [search terminated]

THE SHIP GLIDES through a radiant nebula; the eel-ship's body glows as it absorbs radiation and shed filaments from the void, skin sluiced away from a progenitor star. This reminds Mere of Li Sin's collection, *Bound Infinity, Transcendent*. Mere has dabbled in poetry, played with bits of unattached verse:

> *Breathing in designer atmosphere / academic blood sport*
> *Sip sorrow's martini / watch sequin-skinned guests sway and flow /*

Mere stumbles over further stanzas, uncertain. Does it possess its own creativity, its own words, or are they borrowed finery collected from too many other sources, pieces plucked from the dead?

Other space eels twine and dance in the ruins of gasses and elements and carbons.

"Beautiful," Mere murmurs.

Century, tucked in a fold between the eel-ship's ribs, doesn't look up from her reading. "Anything can be beautiful. Even monsters."

Mere has never been praised for its aesthetic. "Will you tell it why it was made?"

Century sets aside the tablet. "I built you from the remains of my enemies. It was to be their eternal subjugation." Quieter: "I still regret it."

"It has heard," Mere says, "regret may be molded anew, if one chooses. This it will shape its own future once its duty is complete."

"And where will you go if you survive?" Century asks. "Any planet you linger on will suffer like Olinara V." Her jaw tightens. "I saw what befell that world. You can't escape forever."

Mere has no basis for argument. "What do you run from?"

Century's mouth thins into a line. "I should have left you, wraith."

Mere tilts its head. It is grateful, unexpectedly, that she converses with it, that she has not ejected it from the ship and let it drift into frozen death. "It would rather live briefly outside the Courts than forever in chains."

Century coughs, a strangled laugh. "Sweet mother of stars. You have no recollection, do you?"

"What should it recall?"

She reaches into a slit in her armor. "Here." The holochip rests heavy on her palm. "Your birth, if you want it."

Mere accepts.

HUNDREDS OF GLASS pods, each cold-filled with bodies—her enemies, trophies, former friends betrayed. The wolflord stands beside her (young, war-scarred, shipless). The wolflord has always remained loyal to Century, and she has taken the wolflord under her protection so the former pilot will not be discovered and executed.

"Must you do this?" the wolflord whispers.

She has taken pieces of each enemy, mind or flesh or bone or blood or gene, and she has built a sexless bipedal wraith from her conquests. It stands taller than she, lithe deadly machineflesh, and she gives it her organic eyes last of all, cased in cybernetic implants.

"It is a mere tool," she says, fondness in her tone.

The wolflord sighs. "That is all we are to you."

She turns, head tipped in curiosity. "Would you be more?"

Instead of answering, the wolflord nods to the many glass pods. "And the remains?"

"The wraith will execute them," she says. "In doing so, it will become mine alone, unburdened from its former selves."

The wolflord flinches.

She presses her palm against the wraith's chest, igniting its processors and sparking its lifeforce siphoned from her dearest enemy. The wraith opens its—her—eyes.

"Wraith," she says. "I have made you for one purpose."

It blinks several times, then bows.

"It will serve in the Courts of Tranquility," she says to the wolflord. "A celebration of our new age of peace."

The wolflord's gaze meets the wraith's, but the wolflord looks away in shame.

(There is a subfile tucked inside that is not the she's. The wolflord planted it, imprinted with a name: Kitshan Zu.

In the months between its awakening and the completion of the Courts of Tranquility:

"They will erase this," the wolflord says, hand at rest so gentle on Mere's cheek. "They won't let you have what's yours. Not memory nor self. Not..." The wolflord swallows. "I have to go. Century has work I must finish in her name."

Mere blinks, chalk-gray skin furrowed between its cybernetic eyes. "I wish to go with you, Kitshan."

The wolflord kisses Mere, lips rough and course and so familiar. "If I could steal you, Mere, I would. I promise you one thing—I will come back for you. When I learn how to free you, I will come back."

"Then I will wait," Mere says, and pulls the wolflord close one last time.)

Mere shudders as the memory knits into its own consciousness, blended with so many dreams of the dead.

A fragment, unburied: The wolflord was most often a he, and sometimes not, and always kept his name. Kitshan.

Mere wishes it had memories of its own to braid into a lost narrative in which it was happy with him, in which they shared passion and laughter and sorrow. This is like its favorite of Li Sin's sonnets, where the poet laments falling through a time vortex and breaking the time stream by trying to reclaim lost love.

"I watched the feeds," Century says. Outside the ship, great gaseous whales converge in a celestial pod, frequency-song caressing the hull and sides. "I saw his capture. I was too far away to get to the Courts before..." A crisp, vicious head shake. "I would have spared you that, if I could grant you but one mercy."

Mere has nothing to say to the she.

IV.

REBIRTH (WORLD): *there is no such designated planet in the Principality archives. Further searches will result in disciplinary measures.*

THE COURT OF the Red Sun is bones and dusk, burned into a cold shell of its former glory.

The eel-ship glides into membranous ports that ring the station. Heptagonal, forged from old warships and dead stars, lit and powered within by the Red Sun Lord's essence.

Century sits motionless in the cockpit. "You better hurry. The other Suns will find you. Always, they will find you."

Mere is aware. The Courts call to its blood; until it finds a way to unlock its own molecular leash from its keepers' hold, it must stay a dozen steps ahead. But first it must survive an audience with the Red Sun, the Death of Endless Worlds.

Mere enters the airlock. Spindle-legged drones bow and guide it through red-splashed corridors to the throne room of the Red Sun Lord.

A beautiful spider-prince, chitin-skinned humanoid with four delicate legs protruding from the spine like desiccated wings, sits at the Red Sun's left, a shadow-garbed concubine. Eight jewel-rimmed eyes watch under thick lashes. "Those beholden to the Courts of Tranquility are seldom welcome, wraith."

Mere bows. "It seeks aid for the lord's chosen."

The spider-prince leans close, a spine-leg lightly brushing the Red Sun's helmet. The visor rises, and the Red Sun's gaze sears into Mere's flesh.

Mere folds itself in supplication, its back blistering. It unbends an arm, lifts a palm, and shows the holochip record of the wolflord's execution. "It asks the lord to listen." Pain sinks deeper—it holds its ground, and does not scream. "The lord has claim to the dead," Mere says, "and if the lord will come to assert that claim, this it will retrieve the souls of the lost and give them peace."

The heat relents as the Red Sun drops the helmet visor. Mere shivers as its cells begin repair, and the coolness of the dim throne room sinks into its burned flesh.

"May this one eat the wraith?" the spider-prince purrs.

Mere waits, its body taut.

The Red Sun stretches out a hand, and with a sigh, the spider-prince rises and sweeps forward. He takes the chip from Mere's palm and inserts it into a port in his ribs.

"A pity," the spider-prince murmurs, with a longing glance at Mere. "I am *starving.*"

"Perhaps another time," Mere says. It listened well to courtly wit and challenge. It has read much of Li Sin's political treatise, curated by the poet's ship, *Vector Bearing Light.* "It might poison you in turn."

The spider-prince smiles, appreciative. The projection blossoms outward, slow like congealed blood, and the image of the last wolflord stands before the Red Sun.

fleeing the Arbiter's consorts on a far-flung world, injured
looking up at the sky, begging
the last wolflord is bound in the pool, throat cut

The Red Sun's armored form stiffens, fists clenched on the starlight throne. "And why should I not unmake you for this crime, wraith? The last of my disciples, no more. Why did I feel nothing..."

The spider-prince slinks back to the Red Sun's side and strokes the god's armored shoulders, soothing. "The Courts of Tranquility are shielded, my liege-love."

The Sun Lords are cosmic bodies reshaped into compressed armored shells after a treaty two millennia ago. They have never ceased being enemies. Six rule the Principality while the Red Sun Lord, who was always death, broods alone in the outer reaches of dominion.

Mere continues: "It has defied the Sun Lords of Tranquility to come and beg for vengeance. It once cared for the dead and does not wish to obey its masters."

"And what," says the Red Sun, "would you do with the souls, wraithling?"

"It knows of a world far outside the Principality where they will be safe: Rebirth."

The spider-prince taps his long, graceful fingers against his chin. "Rumors do exist among the lost of such a world, my love."

The Red Sun stands. Mere flattens itself to the floor.

"Come," says the Death of Endless Worlds. "I will return to the Courts of Tranquility."

WRAITH (OBJECT): *an organic drone (technology outdated and now forbidden by the Principality) constructed from pieces of other organics and androids. Wraiths are non-sentient and possess no soul. The majority of wraiths were created before the Treaty of the Seven Suns as shock troops built from the dead.*

THE RED SUN arrives in a ship built from bones of ancient solar chelonians and no port dares refuse it entry. The Death of Endless Worlds burns footprints into the halls. Mere follows, never stepping in ash.

"You'll have but a few seconds once inside," Century told it while the eel-ship rode beside the Red Sun's vessel. "If you're caught again, nothing will save you."

Since when has it been caught before?

Soundless, the Red Sun strides into the Courts of Tranquility. The smell of emptiness, the dark between the stars, clings to scarlet and black-scaled armor. Unease writhes through the courtiers, fermenting into panic.

"You dare?" The Gold Sun Lord steps down from the hover-throne and cuts through the skittering courtiers, armor brightening. "And you bring this *thing* with you?"

Mere spreads its hands in mock supplication from where it stands on the threshold matrix.

"You break every law by coming here," says the Gold Sun.

"Except one." The Red Sun extends a fist towards the pool. "I have a right to the dead."

"No," says the Gold Sun. "Not anymore."

Gold Sun and Red Sun raise non-corporeal blades to each other in silent duel.

You should run, murmurs the threshold.

Chaos blossoms.

Mere dives into the pool. It knows every soul pebble, so it scoops a hundred seventeen into its abdomen pouch. The others are already rotted—celestial molecules broken down from the inside, wrapped in distended film, which the slightest disturbance will break and spill out only dust. It cannot save them all.

It knifes through the water and catches the wolflord's soul last.

Mere senses the keepers' watching, cold optics drifting in amniotic fluids behind the pool's walls. Sudden anger sparks in Mere. It slams a hand into the tiled side. Cracks web around the impact. Again, Mere strikes. Its hand sinks through insulated glass and it snatches one of the keepers: an optic node attached to sensory cables.

Alarms ricochet among the keepers, but Mere holds tight. It bounds from the pool.

The eleven-souled sorcerer confronts it, wreathed in iridescent shadow. "Stand down, wraithling," he says, thin lips curled mirthless.

Mere coils muscle and hydraulics in its legs and leaps, toe-claws bared. It cuts through the sorcerer's shadow shields and ducks away from his grasp. It kicks the sorcerer in the chest with bone-shattering force. The sorcerer falls back.

Automated defense drones circle overhead. Exhilarated, Mere sprints towards the door matrix, letting the Red Sun's wroth deflect its pursuers.

Good luck, murmurs the threshold, and Mere smiles.

This time, it runs through the upper halls of the Courts: past luxury holo suites and theaters, gardens and feast halls, over bridges that span crystalline waterfalls and floating glass spheres filled with lovers and voyeurs alike. It crosses into the industrial sectors, locks bypassed by Century's nanite snakes, which slither through the walls as fast as it runs.

And then, once more, the spaceport. Mere sprints down the wide central platform towards freedom.

Four mammoth crustacean guards—crab-bodied, armored, spotted in hundreds of eyes—unwind from the walls and mesh themselves between Mere and the eel-ship. Mere springs up, spotting niches in armor, planes of body and joint it can use to climb and evade. It has no *time* to fight.

A fifth crustacean guard appears behind it and hammers a claw into it mid-air.

The blow shatters Mere's arm and rips open its side. Its body is thrown halfway across the platform, ribs crushed. Mere curls in on itself to protect its belly and rolls. A sixth crustacean guard circles behind and seizes Mere in great pincers. It twists, hissing, a single breath between it and being decapitated through the midriff.

"Stand down." The voice resounds with such weight and power, Mere mistakes it for one of the Sun Lords. The crustacean guard freezes. "Know my voice: for I am the Unmaker of Worlds."

The others hesitate. Mere lifts its chin, orienting itself on the voice.

Century stands on the platform, wreathed in a film of ultraviolet light. It projects from her skin, her teeth, her voice.

"The wraith is mine." Century extends a hand, commanding. "Give it to me, now, unharmed. Disobey my word and I shall rain destruction upon your people until there is naught by the trembling memory of *pain* in the heavens."

Gently, the crustacean guard sets Mere down. The others back away, submissive. Century does not move.

Mere limps towards her, past her, and into the ship. She follows, but the crustacean guards do not. Mere collapses inside.

The eel-ship twists and streaks from the port, chased this time by droneships beholden to the Seven Suns: faceless pilots uprooted and loosed once more.

"We will lose them in subspace," Century says, calm. "If not for long."

Mere apologizes to the ship for spattering its blood on the floor as it cradles its side. It takes a slow breath, the crunch of bone rearranging in its torso and arm familiar. "You are a Sun Lord," it says at last.

Century rolls her shoulders. "Once I was the Violet Sun. We took new bodies, it's true, but they change, they weaken. Anything that lives can die."

Mere strokes its undamaged hand along its abdomen; its cargo remains undamaged. It wonders what its soul might look like, compressed into a pebble beneath cold water. If it was born from the fractured pieces of the Principality's enemies, what will its existence reflect in death? It is automatous, but it still more machine than organic, and there are no simple answers in the theologies or heresies it has skimmed.

It unfurls its broken fingers with its other hand and examines the keeper it stole. Inside the optic, thousands of compressed recordings tagged *wraith_ construct*.

"Don't," Century says, but makes no move to stop it. "You'll only hurt yourself, Mere."

Mere downloads the recordings.

V.

A CRUSTACEAN GUARD drags Mere's limp body from the surgical pods, where it was once more tested for pain tolerance (high) and fitted with a restraint collar beneath its throat-skin so it will not escape again (*fourth time*, the keepers say, disapproving).

"Why do you run?" the guard asks as Mere's eyes open. "There is nowhere to go. Do you like being hurt?"

Mere hisses at the guard, always the one to find it. "Why do you *stay?*"

"There is no choice," says the guard, quiet.

"I will *make* choice," Mere says.

The wraith is put in stasis.

DOZENS OF NEAR identical recordings:

Mere fulfills its duty as executioner.

It is taken to a containment chamber of sterile walls and faceless technicians. Its memory is selectively culled so it no longer remembers the details of the ones it has killed.

Sometimes, the wraith fights. Dead technicians are easy to replace.

But even technology fails. Mere takes advantage of the blocks in the feeds over the pool and slices open its arm to write on its bones; the flesh glues together before the technicians focus the light instruments into its head.

(The keepers hum interest to each other: *Why does the wraith care about the names of the dead? Where is the fault in its programming?*)

The keepers cannot find the anomaly.

IT HAS NOT attempted to flee in two cycles, so it is given privileges and allowed to wander the cityskin. It seeks out the Arbiter's consorts, confined in luxury and pain. Zarrow and Jhijen, the newest consorts who still keep hold of their names, welcome Mere. It basks in attention and conversation. Zarrow teaches it laughter. Jhijen invites desire; Mere can experience pleasure as much as pain. Mere could have picked from any number of genders, but it does not have an interest in the choices, so it remains neutral, comfortable with its pronouns. Jhijen and Zarrow always respect its choice, as it does theirs, when their genders change like the fluid motions of a dance.

(*Mere thinks*, the keepers note. *It thinks of the consorts as* friend.)

There is no timestamp to show when Zarrow and Jhijen disappeared.

THE SHE BOUND in the pool looks like Zarrow.

"Who are you?" Mere whispers.

"…and thus the heavens are cleansed anew," says the Arbiter.

Mere does not kill the she.

The keepers hastily feed a loop of crafted images into the broadcast, so the universe watching will never know the wraith's hesitation. The Courts of Tranquility see what is expected; polite applause follows.

Obey, the keepers send to its processor.

Mere shakes its head, snips the fibrous chains, and lifts the she from the water. "It will not kill this one. The she has committed no crime."

The she that looks like Zarrow brushes her fingers along its cheek. "I'll remember you."

The Arbiter's eyes burn with fury. "The she is an insurgent who disobeys the Seven Suns."

Mere laughs at the Arbiter. "So do I."

The restraint collar activates and crumples Mere on the edge of the pool. The consorts lift the she's shallow-breath body and carry her off; her true death will be private. Mere cannot stop it.

Mere hisses in pain as the Arbiter watches. It lifts its arm, shaking, and digs its knife-fingers into its throat. Blood and fluids drip into the pool as Mere cuts out the collar piece by piece.

The Arbiter backs away, a step shy of haste.

Mere's body slides over the side, into the water. It floats there as its skin regrows and the crustacean guards come to drag it away.

All the Arbiter's consorts are replaced and the wraith's privileges are revoked. The keepers implant a block in its neural protocols that will never allow Mere to speak as an "I" again.

IN ITS STASIS chamber, Mere scrapes sharp fingers against the wall, which throbs and erases each mark; still Mere tries to carve the names of the dead, transcribe them from its raw bones before the keepers or the security drones stop it.

VI.

MERE CRUSHES THE remains of the keeper's optic and stands, shivering. There are many, many more files. It deletes them.

It looks at Century.

Century rubs beneath her quicksilver eyes. "When I gave you to the Blue Sun Lord, a final gift to seal our peace treaty, I couldn't take you back." She turns away. "The wolflord was working on a way to unbind you. I refused. I do not wish to see war again."

Mere wipes the keeper's fluids from its hands. Bones have mended and the eel-ship has washed away the blood on the floor. "How soon before we are found?"

She shrugs. "We will find Rebirth first. We will finish this."

AFTER IT ASKS and receives permission from the ship, Mere etches all the names of the dead into the eel's rib bones. The ship promises to remember them.

Mere murmurs its thanks.

And you? the ship asks. *What would you like to be remembered as?*

Mere hesitates. Of the possibilities it might choose from, it does not want to be: *executioner, killer, weapon.* But what else does it deserve?

"A wraith."

Mere does not know what else it should say.

VII.

LI SIN (REVOLUTIONARY): *a neutrois poet whose work is known for biting wit, political critique, and transcendent beauty. No records can be found on Li Sin's birthplace or their death. The poet stopped writing and disappeared after challenging the Gray Sun Lord in the Year of Unpraised Night 2984; the Gray Sun slumbers in the Arora Nebula, undisturbed and unresponsive since.*

THE SHIP DROPS from subspace over planetary designation Z1-479-X: Rebirth.

Mere peers through the ship's gills at the blue-green-white sphere. It is devoid of cityskin; no metal-glass veins or infrastructure rising to the sky. Mere has never seen a world like this.

"I never thought I would see it again," Century says. Her voice catches like skin on a metal burr. "Come."

Mere says goodbye to the ship.

Farewell, friend, says the eel-ship.

They take a shuttle with two life-pods down to the surface.

KITSHAN ZU (WARSHIP PILOT): *Zu's ship,* Forever Brightness, Burning Dark, *was killed in battle and disconnected its pilot prior to its destruction. Zu was comatose*

in an Olinara V field hospital until his disappearance following the visitation of the
Violet Sun a cycle later. The ex-pilot's whereabouts and fate are unknown.

THE NIGHT SKY froths with clouds. Mere marvels at the prickly moss webbing the stony ground and the kiss of damp air against its body. This world is unshaped and wild, virile with flora and fauna it does not recognize from the Principality's records. It has never seen so much uncultivated wilderness, even in holos. Field and forest pass, and still the map leads Century forward.

They landed in a dry canyon and followed the she's implanted map.

They find a river, unsanctified and alive, bubbling past without notice. Mere stands transfixed. It wants to touch the water's delicate skin, but does not feel worthy.

This world cannot know its presence long. Mere yearns to stay, to wander the wonders it has only glimpsed on this planet. But it is a taint, a cultured, weaponized stain from the Principality, and it does not belong. It will take the shuttle and let the Arbiter chase it to the universe's birthing place, so long as no harm comes to this world or any other.

"Here," Century calls. In a clearing ringed in living walls of flowers, Century stands motionless in raw, rich soil. "Can you feel it?"

Mere shuts its eyes and breathes in. Its skin and circuitry hum with power. "What is it?"

"Life. Potential." A sigh. "The world welcomes us all. I remember…I remember. I was born here. That is how I know it; why it haunts my bones."

Mere tilts its head. "What now?"

"Give the ones we carry rest. Perhaps they too will be reborn. Our part is done."

Mere slits its abdomen pouch and lets the pebbled souls fall loose into the ground. The earth shifts and closes gently over each one.

Energy it cannot name loops through Mere—the world's fingers caressing its mind.

BE WELL.

Wordless, an impression sweeps through Mere: the dawn kissing the earth, the souls wrapped in soil released from their pebbled shells crafted by the pool. When the sun rises, all will be complete. The dead will find their afterlives or their rebirth.

Century removes her armor piece by piece, and runs her fingers along her scarred scalp. "Will you kill me now, wraith? That is your purpose. It is…what I deserve."

Mere has never been given *choice*. It has seen the wolflord to rest. What further purpose must it serve?

It tallies what it would do if freed: seek out the funerary holo of Li Sin and pay homage; sip wine on a far-flung world where identity is unnecessary; learn to dance without downloading precise diagrams of movement; travel the stars; write poems of its own; see wonders; live. And it would remember.

Mere retracts its knife-tips into fingerbones. "You gave it its freedom. It returns the grace. Do as you will."

Century dips her chin, military acknowledgement. "Gratitude, Mere."

Mere lifts its head, elated. If it can show mercy, it can do so much more.

Century smiles at Mere. "I will sleep, as I've not done in so long. When I wake…we'll see. Farewell."

"Farewell," Mere says to its maker, and lopes towards the ship.

It is *free*.

IN THE CANYON gullet, the repulsors of dropships thrum. Mere slows, dry earth cracking beneath its feet. The shuttle is visible at the end of the ravine, caked in reentry burns and wind-blown dust.

The air brings the sharp scent of bloodied and oiled mechanics. Mere's sensors link with other semi-biologicals.

The mercury-veined butchers, stained silver and red, squat in single file rank along the canyon's lip, sores popped from necrotic skin. Beneath the light-bent holoprojectors, the butchers' forms are true: fragmented drones from the Gold Sun and the Blue Sun, vessels programmed with tireless efficiency.

The Sun Lords have found Mere.

But these are no hollowed shells. Mere sees the frightened eyes of armor-bound clones (of the Arbiter's consorts, as they were before they were exulted— Zarrow is there, and so is Jhijen), unmasked behind targeting arrays. It knows each one of them, has shared memory and dreams with them. Once (so long ago) it dared think of them as *friend*.

Mere stands frozen between the butcher-clones and Century, the wolflord, and all the seeded. In a microsecond, realization:

—no longer must Mere kill—

—the seeded need but an hour more, until the sun rises and wakens new life—

—weaponized bones, detonator heart, poison blood: Mere can unmake all the Sun Lords' drones, dismantle and slaughter until all that remains is gore-soaked earth; christen the seeded with the promise of eternal war, mark Rebirth for a fate shared by Olinara V—

—Mere wants to *live*—

The drones have come only for Mere, the Blue Sun's disobedient trinket. Once the mission is compete, this world will be a forgotten sanctuary once more.

Mere steps forward as the butcher-drones approach. It will fight them, but not to win. The Suns will witness its desperation and be satisfied with its death. It will not be brought back to the Courts of Tranquility. It will remember.

This is its chosen purpose and its choice: to save the ones it can.

The butcher-drones attack. Mere lets them come.

It composes a final a poem, and though the last wolflord will never know, Mere dedicates the words to Kitshan.

> *Your eyes, grace-touched / forever refuge*
> *We will live together*
> *Tomorrow / when we see the sun.*

THE SORCEROR'S UNATTAINABLE GARDENS

WROUGHT-IRON FENCES loop around the gardens: six deep, the outer three progressively higher, more elaborate, and with more spikes atop, while the inner three create a mirror effect. Say you make it over all six fences without impaling yourself or falling or getting trapped between iron bars that suddenly constrict or twist or move. Say you avoid the fourth fence, the electric one, or the second one with the poisoned varnish, or the sixth one with a taste for blood.

(Once upon a time, a sorcerer lost their shadow in a bet with a magician. The bet itself is unimportant. Shadowless, the sorcerer wandered the world until, unexpectedly, they found a shadow whose person had been lost to a bet with a sea-witch long before.)

If you make it past all six fences, then you reach the first garden. It's a great circular loop of hawthorn and foxglove hedging that has no convenient holes or doors. The hedge speaks with a rusty, gravelly, morbid voice; its cadence is so slow you forget the first word before you hear the third one. The hedge asks riddles, like hedges are wont to do in a sorcerer's garden, and if you get it wrong, the gophers eat you.

(The sorcerer and the unattached shadow fell in love. "Can we stay together forever?" asked the shadow, twined with the sorcerer under the autumn stars, and the sorcerer said, "Yes." The sorcerer did not intend to lie.)

But let's say you answer the riddle, which no one has been able to guess for sixty-five years, and the hedge opens just enough for you to squeak through with lacerations on your sides and foxglove pollen infecting the cuts. Then you reach the second circle, a rose garden.

(What the shadow did not know was that once upon a time, the sorcerer made a bet with a demon and lost. The bet itself is unimportant; the wager was the sorcerer's happiness. As soon as the sorcerer found true joy, the demon came to collect.)

Roses of every color imagined or not imagined fill the garden. The air is so thick with fragrance you get high with the first breath and overdose with the second. But let's say you can hold your breath, or you brought a mask. You hear the roses speaking. Not riddles, of course, because the roses are too polite to infringe on the hedge's territory. What the roses say is: *eat you eat you eat you.* And then they will, of course. Roses need fertilizer just like any other plant. Your bones might become thorns for the next bushes that sprout, if you're fortunate, and if you're even luckier, one of the yellow roses will drink your soul instead of the red ones. And if you're especially tasty, it won't even hurt.

(The sorcerer said to the shadow, "I'm so sorry. I didn't mean for this to happen." To look on the shadow brought only grief to them both. So the sorcerer banished the shadow, because once a sorcerer makes a bet, they cannot go back on the wager. Shadows can't weep.)

But let's say you don't get eaten by the roses. The circle you find yourself in next is a lightless tower that goes downward and never up. Chains spun from hanged men's gurgles crisscross the stairs that don't really exist. Beware of the ivy along the walls, for it grows on memory, until your mind is choked and full of leaves, and roots dig out through your skin and you forget why you came, and you sit there forever, and forever, and forever, and…

(The shadow found itself in a glacier. The ice the shadow absorbed melted and dripped down the shadow's face, and it looked at its hands and clenched them into fists and said, "I *will* find you again, love." Somewhere on the other side of the world, the sorcerer heard the shadow's words and despaired.)

But let's say that you don't trip over nonexistent steps and fall into the abyss, and you bring herbicide for the ivy.

(The shadow traveled the world alone, becoming a master of disguise, a jack of all trades. No cost was too great to acquire what was needed. The shadow absorbed knowledge and languages and magic and shut away grief so deep it forgot, for a time, it was there. Then the shadow learned how to hunt demons.)

The second to last circle is made of bubbles, translucent spheres summoned from the essence of Death Itself, for Death has always had a whimsical side. If you pop one, it swallows you, compressing your lungs, siphoning your blood, unraveling your nervous system, grinding your bones into dust. There is no space between the bubbles through which to pass.

(On the other side of the world, the sorcerer put all their skill into making an unattainable fortress, circles of gardens no one can ever penetrate. There will be no more bets, and no more loss, and in their self-made prison, the sorcerer sits alone. One day, the sorcerer hopes, they will fade from memory so the shadow may mourn, and perhaps one day find peace again.)

But let's say you brought needles to prick the bubbles ever so carefully and catch the pieces of death in a lead-lined pouch. When you carve a path through this circle, you find a simple wooden door that asks for a password. If you answer wrong, the door will never have existed. But you answer: "Heart," and it opens.

(The shadow laid a delicious trap for the demon: freshly picked souls, harvested from the Tree at the Center of the World. The demon approached, feet soundless on the ice floes the shadow drifted on. "What game shall we play for this luscious prize?" the demon asked, and the shadow said, "No game. I'm here to kill you.")

Let's say you make it into the final circle, the one made of plain stone.

(The shadow lunged, a lasso made from angel sinew in one hand, and in the other a poniard forged in the eventual heat death of the universe. The demon screamed as the angel sinew snared tight about its neck. The demon's form flickered through every horrendous shape it knew, yet it couldn't escape

the noose. "You hurt the one I love," the shadow said. "I do not care for that."
The demon howled for mercy. Shadows are neither merciful nor cruel, except
when they are. With the poniard, the shadow cut out the demon's guts, and in
the steaming entrails found every item the demon had stolen with tricks or dice
or cards. The demon withered into flakes of ash and sank into the frigid sea-salt
waters. The shadow gently scooped up what it had sought for so long, trembling,
hoping it was not too late.)

There are no traps or puzzles or illusions here. This garden is brick, lopsided
piles of brown and red and gray blocks in no discernible pattern. The sorcerer
sits on the middle heap, alone except for the bones. Oh, yes, of course there are
bones. Don't ask what they are from.

The sorcerer is a thin, hunched person of no specific gender, dressed in
a blue habit sewn from fish scales. Dull eyes, bones sharp against slack skin.
Building an unattainable garden takes its toll on a body.

"Why did you come?" the sorcerer says. There's deep tiredness in that voice,
so much pain. "You will only find sorrow here."

"I know." You sit beside the sorcerer, your love, and unzip your ribs. Tucked
under your heart is a small oak box, plain and unvarnished. You offer it to the
sorcerer. "I brought this for you."

Their hands shake as they open the box.

Inside, wrapped in turquoise tissue paper, is the sorcerer's stolen happiness.
They let out a small gasp of shock. "How..."

You press a finger against the sorcerer's lips. "Later. Please take it." You've
hoped since the moment you found the wrought-iron gates that the sorcerer will
not refuse. If the sorcerer says no, you are finished.

The sorcerer folds the paper aside for later use. "How long has it been?"

Too, too long.

"I don't remember..." The sorcerer's voice catches in their throat. They turn
away. "Why did you come?"

"I want you back." You wait, trembling. There is nowhere else to go. "Please
come back, love. I will help you laugh again, I will make you strong. One day,
we will tear down these unattainable gardens and walk free. I am here because I
need you." Unsaid: *Please don't banish me to loneliness forever.*

The sorcerer shuts their eyes. Then with quivering hands, replaces the
happiness inside them. A shudder ripples through the sorcerer's frame, and they

press their face against your shoulder. You stroke their hair and wait.

"I'm so sorry," the sorcerer says, over and over and over.

You wrap yourself around them and hold them close. For now you are safe from wandering magicians and cunning sea-witches and unsatisfied demons.

"It will be all right, love," you whisper, because shadows never lie. And for the first time since they built this labyrinth, the sorcerer smiles.

THE ANDROID'S PREHISTORIC MENAGERIE

The world explodes.

Unit EX-702 comes back online when UV wavelengths activate its solar plating. Its optics are crusted with red dust; a low-powered system scan concludes that though its left arm is missing and there is excessive oxidation damage along its chassis and helmet, as well as a web spun from several arachnids (*Nephila clavipes*) now embedded in its servo stump, EX-702 is functional. Its operational protocols are intact.

This unit is programmed for the support of life and sapience.

Its databanks are semi-corrupted beyond basic functions and archived footage and base knowledge dumps. Attempts to access the 'Net and reboot from a mobile hub fail with a repeated NO CONNECTION AVAILABLE alert. EX-702 lifts its remaining arm and scrapes dust away from its optics.

Operational Function 413: this unit will maintain self-preservation operations, including but not limited to the access of immediately available data to determine procedure, when it does not conflict with the preservation of homo sapiens' *survival.*

EX-702 sits in the crater of what had been Newtonian Genetech Incorporated's laboratories and HQ facility. Debris from the lab cakes the thick concrete and rusted iron walls. Its scanner matrix glitches with static-filled readouts and partially deteriorated unprocessed updates from microseconds before it was shut down.

Scientist voices agitated and unmodulated without appropriate safety masks. [STATIC] "—find survivors! Protect yourself!" [SHUT DOWN]

Something crackles against EX-702's knee joints. Fibers, synthetic and organic—old hazmat suits shredded and woven around broken plywood and stripped copper wiring—shaped in a non-geometric design. Inside the structure sit three maroon and heather-brown eggs thirteen centimeters in length and six in diameter.

Processing…

The eggs do not match any current avian, insectoid, reptilian, mammalian, or amphibian entries in its database. EX-702 examines the nest, which has intersected its knees. A ripped arm from one hazmat suit is tucked between its clawed toes. EX-702 is a humanoid bipedal digitigrade design with backward jointed knees and toe digits designed to grip uneven surfaces and manipulate hostile terrain. Its hand is fully articulated to mimic the human opposable thumb and fingers. EX-702 is not designed to be a nest for unknown biological organisms.

One of the eggs twitches and a small chirrup escapes the cracked calcium carbonate structure.

EX-702 reaches to remove the nest from its legs when the egg splinters and a membrane-covered nose pokes out.

Processing…

The other eggs crackle. Tiny claws, pointed snouts, wet feathers in muted brown and scarlet emerge. As the organisms free themselves, EX-702 scans them again and this time finds pictorial references in its database: *Deinonychus antirrhopus*. An extinct species of dinosaur whose fossil record suggested it would grow up to three-point-four meters as a mature adult.

There are no data points to conclude how the *Deinonychus antirrhopus* has populated once more. Newtonian Genetech Incorporated specialized in advanced human and cybernetic enhancement, for which EX-702 was a research assistant android and personal defense unit for Doctor Urashami.

The newborn trio of deinonychuses chirp and growl. EX-702 scans them. They require protein intake. A parental unit must be in the vicinity.

With UV wavelengths recharging its internal power supply and emergency batteries, EX-702 scans the area once more.

Four meters away, an adult female *Deinonychus antirrhopus* lies prone in congealing blood. Behind it sprawls the corpse of a dire wolf (*Canis dirus*). Both specimens are mauled and exhibit defensive and offensive wounds. EX-702 extrapolates that the wolf attempted to raid the nest and the female deinonychus protected her brood.

Her eyes glimmer and EX-702 stares back.

The female deinonychus growls. A staccato sound not unlike vibrating steel chords in a guitar. EX-702 does not have reference files to decode the linguistic message, but its emotive processors still work. There is desperation in the dying female's speech.

Protect.

The adult deinonychus shivers and goes still. Her heat signature begins to degenerate.

EX-702 looks down again at the hatchlings.

This unit will provide for the new life forms.

It is the custom of sapient species to identify members of a brood. Names were the most common method employed by Doctor Urashami, who christened EX-702. Doctor Urashami is the principal researcher in the cybernetic AI advancement wing of Newtonian Genetech Incorporated, and she built EX-702 herself; she often nicknamed it Seven in conversation.

The newborn raptors peer intently at EX-702. It runs a search in Names: Mythological: Alphabetical. From the results, it picks three it has records of Doctor Urashami having used.

This unit names you Andromeda, this unit names you Anubis, this unit names you Atropos.

It touches a finger to each hatchling's skull as it christens them. Its brood hisses in what EX-702 interprets as acceptance. It is now their parental unit.

It disentangles itself from the nest with precise care, its servos and wiring creaky with disuse, and accesses protocols for the processing of meat. There are two corpses available to feed its brood until it can explore the area more fully and maintain a steady supplement of nourishment for the tiny life forms in its charge.

EX-702 has no immediate data on the whereabouts or status of Doctor Urashami, so it makes a hierarchal protocol list: it will provide for its brood and it will find Doctor Urashami.

WITH ITS BATTERY recharged, EX-702 gains access to a prime directive protocol installed by Doctor Urashami from a remote hub shortly before its initial shutdown.

Search for and assist any human survivors.

It does not find any survivors within a mile radius of the former lab. It will continue its search.

WITHIN THREE MONTHS, EX-702 has established its territory of three-point-nine square acres of city ruin. The landscape has been overrun with flora formerly extinct for millions of years. Old skyscrapers are choked with huge vines and ferns. Doctor Urashami's favorite café, the Crème de la Bean, is a garden of semitransparent flowers and the calcified skeletons of the humans.

When hunting for its brood—migration patterns of herbivore and omnivore species crossed at the edge of EX-702's territory where a river once called the Mississippi, now three times its former size, cuts the city ruins in half—EX-702 discovered a military bunker filled with mummified human remains, a working diesel-powered generator, and a laptop with video records of the pinnacle extinction event.

Unidentified space debris penetrated the Earth's atmosphere and began what one news report described as "spinning back the world's biological clock." Prehistoric fauna and flora overwhelmed the continental landmasses; bacterial and viral infections annihilated the human population. New species thought extinct emerged from rapid evolutionary synthesis.

The records did not give enough statistical analysis to fully account for the devastation of nonorganic structural architecture, but a Lieutenant Bela Strovherd recorded an entry that EX-702 chose to save to its hard drives.

"Whoever's seeing this? Yeah, uh, welcome to the end of the world, I guess. Look, I know it's too much to hope you'll be able to find any of my family or friends and tell them..." She rubs a hand over her face, then laughs. Her voice cracks. *"If you can see this, I have one request. Live. Rebuild. I think it's just time for the human race to pass the torch to whoever comes next, you know? But it'd be nice if you could remember us. We accomplished a lot of shit, but we had some good moments. I dunno. I guess...I'd just like to know someone, somewhere out there remembers. Hopefully you do better. I wish you the best, okay? I really do. Everyone here thinks I'm nuts because I'm so 'calm'"*—fingers made into air quotes—*"but really I'm fucking terrified. I just want to try and go out with dignity, with peace. Maybe, whoever you are, you'll see this and think, 'You know, she's not so bad.' And maybe you'll remember my face for a little while, and my voice, and my name. It's Bela, by the way. Actually named for that actor who played Dracula ages ago."* A shaky smile. The camera wobbles as the room around her shakes. *"Look, I'm gonna go now. I don't want you to have to see... whatever comes next."* She breathes in deep, smiles at the camera. *"Live well, okay? Maybe we'll see each other in another life."*

The video ends.

EX-702 is the last android, and androids, it has concluded, are not meant to exist in this world any longer. EX-702 does not know where it belongs now. So it watches the videos of Lieutenant Strovherd over again every night, to remember her as she asked.

ANDROMEDA RACES THROUGH the Nest, her feathers brilliant red and gold. She's the largest of the three, sleek and agile, and she leads the hunting expeditions now with her sisters.

EX-702 refines the wrench head as it inserts the newly retrofitted arm into its shoulder socket. Anubis, the smallest of the brood, helps support the arm with her articulated hands.

Unit, Andromeda says, the affectionate term the raptors have called EX-702 since their birth. *Look what we found!*

The raptors speak in guttural clicks and growls. EX-702 has learned their natural language in addition to teaching them how to understand human dialects.

Atropos, whose feathers are umber and maroon like her mother's, holds out a glistening egg the size of her skull that is wrapped in heavy leather scraps. *It fell from the sky in fire, it was covered in ash.*

EX-702 scans the egg, and its heat signature exceeds one hundred Fahrenheit. *It does not appear to be of a species we have encountered.*

Andromeda clicks her sickle-claws against the cement, her neck ruff bristling in excitement. *I heard it, Unit,* she says, *I heard it burning.*

Can I see? Anubis asks.

EX-702 tightens its new arm into place and nods.

The three raptors examine the new egg, their heads flicking side to side in staccato movements. It is moments like this EX-702 thinks of Doctor Urashami's jittery hands and how she would always gesture when she talked.

Put it in the incubator, EX-702 says. *We will monitor it.*

As it watches its daughters carefully lay the egg in one of the generator-powered incubators and hover with fascination around the tank, EX-702 experiences what Doctor Urashami related as pride: it has raised Andromeda, Anubis, and Atropos into mature, successful adults. All three can hunt and build and tinker with machinery scavenged from around the city. Anubis is building an exoskeleton for advanced exploration; Andromeda is collecting paper books and printed ceramic mugs with slogans and pictures; Atropos has begun the repair on the observatory telescope.

EX-702 has still not found Doctor Urashami.

The egg hatches into a phoenix, which Anubis names Arrow of Heaven.

REPLAY: [Lieutenant Bela Strovherd] *Live well, okay? Maybe we'll see each other in another life.*

PROTOCOL: *This unit is programmed for the support of human life.*

REPLAY: [Doctor Urashami] *Hello, EX-702. Welcome to the first day of the rest of your life! Ha, always wanted to say that to someone. I'm Renee Urashami, professor of advanced robotics. Do you know why you're online? I made you to help us make the world a better place. Can't wait to see what we can accomplish!*

EX-702 finds a flash drive in Doctor Urashami's apartment, now overgrown in moss and brilliant orange mushrooms that sing ethereal music to lure prey. EX-702 is immune to the auditory and cognitive hypnosis, but it has warned its daughters of the dangerous flora and they stay away from the mushroom sector.

On the drive is an audio file labeled FOR SEVEN.

EX-702 plugs it into its USB port and listens.

AUDIO FILE: [Doctor Urashami] *Seven, I hope you find this. When I built you, I made sure you were constructed from the best materials on the planet. I wanted you to survive. But I've been thinking. I don't know if you made it out of the lab. I wasn't there when the explosion happened. I saw it on the news before we lost all signal. I can't get there in time to manually do this, but I realized that I made a mistake. I never gave you a way out. What if you're the only thing that survives? You were built to understand and develop empathy, emotional simulation. You need other people around to function, like any of us do. I have this horrifying image of you wandering a wasteland that was once Earth and finding no one, wandering until even your power cells deplete and you are alone with no understanding why. So if you find this, and there are no humans left alive, I am initiating voice-activated protocol 815: Unit EX-702 will shut down within one day of downloading this program if it has not identified human sentient life within that time frame. I do this for you, Seven. You don't deserve to be alone. I hope you forgive me.* [END FILE]

[PROGRAM 815_endprocedure downloaded. Installing. Installation complete. Countdown: 23:59:59.]

Unit, what's wrong? Atropos asks.

EX-702 stands by the observatory dome, a cracked sliver of dusty glass and steel, and the newly refurbished telescope within. Atropos swivels her head in curiosity.

This unit has been ordered by its creator to shut down.

[Time until shutdown: 15:25:49]

Atropos hisses and lays a clawed hand on EX-702's shoulder. *Why would she do that? You have done nothing wrong.*

Doctor Urashami did not want this unit to be alone.

The doctor is a rusted socket wrench! Atropos swears. *I do not like the humans I have seen records of.*

EX-702 watches Arrow of Heaven trace fiery tails in the sky as she learns to fly higher and higher. Anubis will be watching from the ground, her flight-capable exoskeleton still in prototype design.

Some were good, EX-702 says. It thinks of Lieutenant Bela Strovherd.

What can we do, Unit?

It has already tried to alter the downloaded program, but it has been blocked by buried subroutines and other programs activated by Doctor Urashami's virus.

Unknown. EX-702 looks at its daughter. *But I do not want to shut down.*

ANDROMEDA, ANUBIS, ATROPOS, and Arrow of Heaven wait in a semicircle around EX-702 in the Nest. The incubators hum: some hold new eggs found without parental units attached, and a newly hatched archaeopteryx ; some house infant mammals—twin saber-toothed tiger cubs, a three-legged dire wolf, a two-day-old cave bear cub. All the incubators are assembled with appropriate heat lamps, milk tubes, or feeders, and are soundproofed with speakers inside issuing programmed voices of EX-702, the raptors, and ambient noise from the city.

Our family grows, EX-702 says. It wants to belong to this world, but it is still the only android. Perhaps Doctor Urashami's virus is the correct procedure. This new Earth is designed for organic life. EX-702 is synthetic.

You can't go away, snarls Anubis.

I will not forgive your human, says Atropos.

[Time until shutdown: 12:31:58]

EX-702 looks at each of its children in turn. This is their world now. They will build it as they see fit; they will remember and create new memories and prosper. It wishes it could see the future its daughters create.

Andromeda paces, her head lowered in thought. *Play the message again, Unit.*

EX-702 projects it from tinny speakers located under its faceplate. It has no articulated jaw or facial contours. Its helmet is indented with round optics and a flat polished plate where a mouth would be on a *homo sapiens* face.

All three deinonychuses listen with narrowed eyes. Then Anubis's head snaps up and she bares her teeth.

Did you hear that? she asks her sisters.

Atropos hisses in agreement. Andromeda bobs her head.

Arrow of Heaven has never spoken, but she watches with interest. Her body heat helps power the incubators when she sleeps.

Arrogance should have been the doctor's name, Atropos says. *She only said "human."*

REPLAY: *Unit EX-702 will shut down within one day of downloading this program if it has not identified human sentient life within that time frame.*

If we rewrite the words in the code, Anubis says, her feathers puffing out, *you will not shut down, Unit.*

EX-702 PLUGS ITSELF into the laptop console it built to help regulate the incubators in the Nest when it was not around. Anubis, the quickest and most adroit typist of the three raptors, begins hacking into the code and searching for the precise wording in Doctor Urashami's program.

[Time until shutdown: 1:15:39]

EX-702 holds Atropos's hand. It should write a goodbye, the way Doctor Urashami and Lieutenant Bela Strovherd did. But EX-702 does not have the right words. It does not want to say goodbye.

Andromeda sings softly, a lullaby she composed from all the words she has collected.

When sleep is far
And night is long
Remember this
My sweetest song
I've followed you
Through winter snow
Through summer sun and evening dew
Remember when you go to sleep
I am beside you with teeth bared bright
I'll guide you in your dreams so deep
And be there in the morning light.

[Time until shutdown: 0:45:12]

Arrow of Heaven trundles close, then pulls from beneath her glossy wing a sheet of copper, embossed with a drawing of EX-702 looking up at the night sky. The star constellations show all three raptors.

Lovely, EX-702 says. Arrow of Heaven ducks her beak in pleasure and purrs.

[INTRUDER DETECTION. ACCELERATION OF SHUTDOWN IMMINENT.]

No! Anubis cries. She tries to type faster.

Andromeda's song falters. Atropos clutches EX-702's hand tighter.

[Time until shutdown: 0:0:35]

EX-702 replays Lieutenant Bela Strovherd's clip: *Look, I'm gonna go now. I don't want you to have to see…whatever comes next.* But only in its own processor. If the last thing it sees is its family, the new world it has helped begin, then it will hold tight to that and remember even when its core goes dark.

BEFORE THE WORLD exploded, EX-702 accompanied Doctor Urashami to a board meeting where she demonstrated EX-702's behavioral and emotional intelligence parameters. "This is the future of our people," she said. "No bias, no inefficiency. Pure, mechanical perfection."

EX-702 experienced the satisfying effect of pride; it had excelled in its function and pleased Doctor Urashami.

"You want to give the world to robots?" asked one of the board members.

Doctor Urashami shook her head. "When we roll out the new models, and begin the tests on human uploads and upgrades, within ten years humans will have advanced beyond anything we thought possible a decade ago. We will have no need of robots, then. We will be superior in every way."

EX-702's elation defused. It must have incorrectly interpreted Doctor Urashami's reaction to its presentation. It would run a diagnostic to find where its malfunction lay, if it as a unit was considered unnecessary.

"Good," said another of the board members. "I don't care for a future with *that.*"

EX-702 was not allowed to express emotion outside of the demonstration. What would become of it when *homo sapiens* no longer had any use for an android?

IN DARKNESS, EX-702 dreams. Or, perhaps, this is death. It hears Andromeda's song like a distant echo.

EX-702 does not know what becomes of androids when they die. It hopes it will not be alone, whatever becomes of it.

It tries to keep the memory of its family bright in its processor—but the image de-pixelates, data deleted. First Andromeda, then the others disappear. Spaces where the visual should be fills with holes. EX-70 is helpless, its autonomous function superseded.

No, please let me keep this, EX-7 protests to the core-wipe program.

The shutdown does not acknowledge EX-.

The faint auditory input dissolves in static. When the memory of three deinonychuses disappears and the phoenix snuffs out, EX shudders. This, then, must be death.

The world ends.

EX-702 COMES BACK online.

It lies in the middle of the nest, all four daughters curled next to it. Anubis blinks and stretches.

Unit! Atropos chitters, and headbutts EX-702 in the chassis the way she did as a hatchling to show her delight.

EX-702 sits up. Memory banks restore from backups, its last visual stitched together in its processor once more. *You were successful, Anubis.*

Barely! Anubis grins. *But I reworded the program and omitted all uses of the word "human." I also did a little more tweaking when you went into stasis and rebooted. I've disabled the majority of the blocks that prevented you from self-modification. You can do whatever you want now.*

Are you all right? asks Andromeda.

Yes, says EX-702. It looks at its daughters and the incubators humming inside the Nest. *Yes, I am all right.*

EX-702 wraps its arms around its daughters and watches the sun rise over their world.

FOR WANT OF A HEART

GLOSSY. That's Mirdonna.

Glossy: from the tips of her supple thigh-high leather boots with heels as thin and sharp as cobra fangs, to the deep orange corset laced with ivory threads. Her eyes are painted radiant poison-green. It's her smile, though, that captures everyone's attention. Her thick lips are glazed in brilliant umber; the tip of a red tongue pokes between her teeth.

"If I asked," she murmurs, her voice like molten honey, "would you give me your heart?"

I swallow. "Literally or figuratively?"

We're in my flat, which feels dim and desaturated now, with its nicotine-stained walls, frayed couch covers, ceiling paint peeling. The windows rattle in the storm. Sleet pecks the panes, and the chill digs through the worn weatherstripping.

"A little of both." That hypnotic smile widens. Mirdonna stretches out one smooth hand. Her short nails gleam like frost etched in hypothermia-blue. "If you're still desperate."

Desperate? If I don't find a way to repay my debts, there won't be enough of me to write an epigraph on a tombstone I can't afford.

I know how deals with the devil end, but when she's handsomer than any devil you can imagine, is it really so bad?

I take Mirdonna's hand. She lifts it and kisses my knuckles. Her chill breath burns my skin and I shiver. It's not unpleasant, this pain.

"Ask and you shall receive," I tell her.

"Oh, I will."

Glossy. And cold—but that's a given for the Winter Lady.

TWO DAYS BEFORE, I met Mirdonna. I was tending bar for Madam Eve.

Summer incarnate, that was Madam Eve. Long, marbled gold and red hair, eyes so blue they burned her lashes umber, her smile nonexistent. She wore skin-tight lace, rosebud pink and mossy green, patterned like ferns and leaves. It clung to her skin, restless, always a breath shy of sloughing off and flying free.

I pulled taps for the regulars, all women. I stocked the bar, counted the till, and always behind the counter. That was her rule. Know your place.

Madam Eve lounged beside the stage. Her chair was spread with spotted fawn hides and decorated with antlers too big to be real—which were, nevertheless. A pair of great wolfhounds, reddish fur combed and oiled to gleaming, lay by her feet. I remember the women they used to be: lucky twins who'd run up gambling debts at Madam Eve's tables in back. They'd accepted her leash; in exchange, she'd forgiven their debts.

I felt my name, like an itch, on the ledgers she kept of who owed her what, and how, and for how long.

Every night after work, I swore to myself I wouldn't slide through the frosted glass doors and into the velvet-walled parlor. I wouldn't pick up the dice. I wouldn't push chips stamped with her face onto the felt tabletops.

But I was hooked on the perfume the dealers wore, their easy smiles, the wins just frequent enough to make me hope.

I knew how it worked. The cycles. The addiction. But I just couldn't make myself stop. Part of me wondered: what was the point? What was left?

My brother was financially secure. He had a two-bedroom apartment with his wife in uptown. A steady job. Good benefits. He didn't need my support any longer, and I refused his charity. I didn't want to drag him into my pit.

Friends are hard to keep when you always push everyone away to stop them from hurting, or hurting you in turn.

That night, Mirdonna swept in the front doors in a swirl of icy wind and snowflakes sharp as razors. She nodded once to Madam Eve, who inclined her chin in turn.

The air in the bar seemed to split, about to explode in lightning from hot and cold now meeting.

"Sister," Madam Eve said in her slow, elegant drawl. "How good of you to visit."

"Darling," the Winter Lady replied with a smile that would have turned anyone else into an ice sculpture. "Is my money good here?"

"Always," Madam Eve said, laying a hand on one of the wolfhounds. "Jordan, dear, a drink for my sister on the house."

I nodded, heart pounding.

"Unsweetened cider," the Winter Lady said as she sashayed to the bar. "Hot."

The apples were picked from the indoor hydroponic garden, huge golden fruits with skin as soft as a newborn's skull and pomegranate-red flesh. These apples only the Summer Lady could grow.

Her cider was the strongest drink the bar served. It tasted, I was told, of breezes across a wild meadow, the screams of mice caught by hawks, the musk of rutting deer, and the burn of fires engulfing pine forests and everything that lived within.

I pulled on heavy leather gloves, then took the slim bottle of cider from the shelf.

The Winter Lady leaned one elbow on the rosewood of wild cats tearing apart rabbits. "You're new here, aren't you, miss…?"

"Cashier. Jordan Cashier." I licked my lips, wishing I had a moment to pop my Chapstick from my purse. "I've been here about a year."

She smiled again. The ice from her skin had fogged the bar counter. "Eve's staff does have a rather…high turnover."

I shrugged. Careful to watch my hands and the red, red juice, I poured the cider into a steamed mug and set it across from her.

"My sister and I have always had an affinity for hearing the lost," she said.

I grabbed a cloth to wipe the bar, even though it was spotless. I'd usually make small talk, play sympathetic ear, or flirt with the customers. But if I looked at the Winter Lady too long, I thought those brilliant eyes would absorb me and leave nothing left.

"Let me know if I can get you a refill," I said, and sidled down to check on my other regulars.

Sweat dripped down my neck. I ignored Jasmine's usual come-ons and told Laretta her she'd reached her limit. The Winter Lady hadn't moved.

Finally, unable to ignore her, I looked back.

"If you find yourself in a bind…" One lacquered nail slid a business card towards me. "My number."

I looked at the card: crisp white stock with silver lettering. It said, simply, MIRDONNA. There was a phone number on the back. I tucked it in my pocket.

Then she glided out. She hadn't taken one sip of her cider.

She wants to rule the world. Don't we all?

"Not rule, honey," she says as we sip mocha lattes in her laboratory. "I intend to correct the world."

Mirdonna's lab is ensconced in a tower, a time-warped fairy tale planted in the middle of the arctic. It's all polished steel and sparkling glass and burnished wires.

I'm not much of anything by trade—bartender, cabbie, retail cog, gambler— so I can't name half the things lining the walls.

She whisked me here in a sleek chopper painted like snow camo. Eerily silent rotors spun wind.

For my safety, she said, but I've been trapped in dead-end jobs and relationships to know what a prison's like. It's okay. I'm safer here than back in the city, where Madam Eve's huntresses are on the prowl.

"Correct it how?" I ask. The coffee is burnt, the foam too sweet. It's keeping me awake though. Going on thirty-six hours without a nap, I'll take whatever I can get.

"Look at you." Mirdonna sets down her mug. There's frost patterns along the lip of ceramic. "A woman down on her luck. Perhaps it's bad decisions, but we all make those. And why should those bad choices result in pain?"

I fiddle with my mug, now empty but for the film of steamed milk on the inside curve. "Isn't that how it works?" I laugh, cough, then swallow back the bitterness knotted deep in my chest. "You fuck up, someone fucks you up in return."

"Exactly." Mirdonna's voice is a low purr. Her fingertips brush mine, and an electric chill makes my skin prickle. "And why should we let this destructive pattern continue?"

I squint at her. "So you *don't* want to rule the world and bend it to your will? You told me—"

"I told you I want to make the world better," she says, "and under my guidance, it will be."

"I'm here, aren't I?" I nod at the laboratory. It's all business: mechanical efficacy, charts on the walls, computer screens humming with equations and weather patterns. "You keep me from ending up in the river as a fishy consort and I…"

I'm still not sure how literal she's being when she says she wants my heart. You can survive with artificial recreations of the organ, but she doesn't strike me as a surgeon.

"You help me change the world," she says, and her hand encloses mine.

Her touch isn't as cold as I remember. She pulls me closer, her lips a fraction from mine, and when she kisses me, all I can feel is heat.

My brother calls my cell phone again. This time I answer.

"Jordan?" His smoke-husked voice is a welcome, familiar sound.

"Yeah, it's me."

"Thank god." He's the nicest man I've ever met. He recently married and his wife is pregnant with their first kid. Jacob has always worried about me. He's younger, but when we were children, he felt it his duty to watch my back while I tried to scrape by with part-time jobs after school. "I stopped by to bring back your crockpot, but all I found was a pile of newspapers on your mailbox and your neighbor said you haven't been home in over a week."

"Yeah, I'm fine. I got a job that's out of town. Short notice."

I tighten lug nuts on the glass octagonal containment chamber. I'm good at mechanical jobs: I can work with my hands, and follow instructions. Mirdonna has given me a few tasks to keep me from worrying.

"You're…not in trouble, are you?"

I imagine him biting his lip or sucking on a lollipop—his two tactics for when he quit smoking.

"No," I tell him. "I'm just fine. The job pays well, but it's up north."

The wrench is cold and heavy in my gloved hand. Like the lies.

"That's good." He clears his throat. "Carol wants to know if you'd like to come over for dinner sometime this week."

I tighten the next bolt; metal whines.

"I don't think I can."

"Oh, okay." A long pause, just our breathing and the crackle of bad signal. "Well, respond to my texts a little sooner, would you?"

I try to laugh, but it sticks in my throat. I can't tell him I deleted them all without reading. If I read them, I'll have second thoughts. I'll remember where I am.

Jacob says, "I was afraid you'd gone off into a ditch. Roads are slippery. And I bet you haven't gotten winter tires, have you?"

"I'll get to it." On the phone, it doesn't matter if I cross my fingers or not. "And I'll drive safe."

"Promise, sis?"

"Always."

I hang up before Jacob can drag out goodbyes and make them hurt more than ever.

MIRDONNA'S MACHINE IS like a cocooned butterfly. A network of membranous arrays will fold out from the tower into modified satellite dishes. Inside, like the unsettled biomass, lie the containment tanks and the mechanic nervous system that power them.

Each tank holds a person, comatose, strapped into nutrient fluids that look as cold as the winter sea.

"What does it do?" I asked her when she first showed me the control room: a dozen security camera screens, inside and out, and a slim panel with only two buttons—one blue, one white.

"I call it Empathy," she said. "It's based in sympathetic magic—emotions distilled from love, compassion, kindness, joy. The energies will be conducted into the biological equivalent of an EMP." Her finger hovered over the blue button. "When I press this, the world changes."

"How?"

"It will eradicate the human desire to harm," she said. "No one will crave violence, feel anger, or seek to hurt another."

"You're taking away people's free will?"

"What use is it if they cannot control it?" Mirdonna smiled. "Relax, darling. I'm not taking everything. Think of it as neutering. Everyone will still feel happiness and satisfaction. It will not change who you love, or sleep with, or build your life with. It simply removes the baser elements from the human equation. We've wasted millions of years and humans still can't control their baser urges. I'm tired of waiting."

I shivered. "It will affect everyone?"

"Yes." Her eyes gleamed like new ice. "Can you imagine a world without pain, Jordan?"

"No."

Her finger brushed my lips. "Not yet."

THE NEXT TEXT I get is from Madam Eve herself.

Darling, I'd rather not send my pets to sniff out your poor dear mother. She's hardly got your vigor and charm. But even an old dog can beg if taught.

Come visit, honey, and make this easy on yourself and your dam.

I drop the phone, shaking.

When I catch my breath, I try calling Mom.

There's no answer.

I WAS JUST getting off shift at midnight. I handed over the new till to Kelsey, a cute transwoman who always wore iconic rock band shirts. I pocketed my tips.

"Jordan, dear, I'd like to speak with you a moment," Madam Eve said.

My fingers itched to grab my lighter. I craved a smoke. The ivory case engraved with my dad's initials was more than just a light. It was my protection; he hadn't been carrying it—he'd quit on my birthday—when he died. I thought that if he had, he'd have come home.

I knew I was screwed, but I kept my smile fixed as I stepped around her wolfhounds and stopped by her throne. "Madam?"

Her hand stroked the bigger dog's head. The hound shivered under her touch, its tail tucked beneath its haunches. "Genevieve tells me you haven't been paying back your...tab."

I tugged my button-up shirt collar. *Fuck.* "Money's a little tight right now, Madam." I tried to laugh. It failed. "What with—"

She lifted an index finger, and the entire bar went silent. The air was hot, thick, like a living thing that coiled around my throat.

I struggled to breathe and not panic.

"My dear, I'm a lenient woman." Madam Eve indulged me with a raised eyebrow. It made my stomach cramp. "Tell me, can you have your payments made by dawn?"

No. I was broke. I'd used my paycheck to scrape by on rent and groceries, sending my mom a tiny stipend via her bank account as I did every month to help her out, and...the rest went to the house's coffers. A hole that got ever deeper.

My brother didn't know Mom was struggling. She'd demanded I not tell him. He had his own family now. We could get by. We always had.

"Of course, Madam."

Her nod was nearly imperceptible. She sipped lies like fine champagne. "Marvelous, my dear. Come back in six hours, then, and we'll settle the books. I do like to make my ledgers neat before the solstice."

I nodded, jerky as a broken marionette.

Everyone in the bar who knew me—most of the regulars, Kelsey, the bouncer (and ex-girlfriend) Carlotta, the hounds who I'd known once upon a time as Meryl and Mara—averted their eyes. Everyone knew.

I couldn't repay what I owed. And I couldn't run—where do you go in a world where there's nowhere to hide?

By dawn, I'd be either dead or transformed into one of Madam Eve's pets.

Everyone knew. Especially the Summer Lady herself.

Outside, hands shaking as I lit my last cigarette, I remembered Mirdonna's business card in my back pocket.

"If it's fueled by sympathetic magic," I asked her over dinner (smoked salmon with roasted asparagus and on a bed of jasmine rice), "Where does the energy come from?"

"People," Mirdonna said, as if it was the most obvious thing in the world.

I chased my food down with a delicate white wine. "You mean...me?"

"No. One is not enough. Not even two." She sighed. We sat across from each other in her parlor.

Outside, the wind raged and hurled snow in blistering curtains against unbreakable glass. "I tried that, in the beginning. I thought two who loved me would suffice. But they did not, in the end, truly love me. So I've gathered others. The desperate, the altruistic. They must come willingly, and when I ask, give me what I need."

I lit up. She didn't care if I smoked. It wasn't my health that she needed.

She smiled, but it had a shadow of sadness—the first regret I had seen in her. "It won't hurt. I can ensure that much."

I nodded. "How soon is it operational?"

"When the last of my hearts is ready," she said.

In the end, wasn't it better to die knowing I might have changed the world?

MIRDONNA'S MACHINE ISN'T ready.

I don't know where she's gone. No one else but me here in the tower, except for the containment pods.

I need something to bargain with, to pay off my debts, or my mother will become collateral.

Shit.

There's a cot, a space heater, and an electric kettle and microwave atop a small fridge in one corner of the lab. Food, instant cocoa, tea bags, coffee. The bathroom is across the short hall, buttoned by featureless steel doors.

I have a proper bedroom—lush, maroon and orange curtains across unopening windows, a vaulted ceiling, a rosewood armoire, a king-sized bed so soft I thought I might melt if I touch it. Plenty of outlets for charging my laptop and phone. No internet, though the cell reception is excellent for being in the middle of the arctic.

Mirdonna doesn't answer her cell.

"Shit."

I almost call Jacob, but I've deleted his contact from my phone. I know the number. It hasn't changed in years. I don't want him involved. He deserves his happiness. He can't help me or Mom anyway.

There's one room I'm not allowed inside: Mirdonna's private office.

We've fucked in her bedroom, all plain white velvet and therapeutic pillows and the walls decorated only with a single painting of Madam Eve. There's nothing in there, beyond her scent and the memory of orgasms.

The office isn't locked.

She simply told me, "Don't," pointed at the door, and strode past it when she gave me the initial tour.

I look for cameras, any sigils on the threshold that spells death to anyone who opens that white oak door.

Will she be angry? What can she do that Madam Eve won't?

I've already promised her my heart.

Fuck the rules.

I open the door and step inside.

There's nothing in the circular room except a pedestal with three crystal globes. Inside each is a slow-beating heart.

I suck in my breath. The room is like ice. The air burns my skin. I take a step, and frost crunches under my foot. The carpet is frozen chenille.

"Have you no respect?" Mirdonna says behind me.

I whirl around. "You—"

"You are not supposed to come here." Her eyes are flecked with winter lightning. "Do you think you're the only one I need? I should destroy you."

I glare at her, sudden fury overwhelming me. "So what's to fucking stop you? You could have anyone you want. Anyone in the world! Why me?"

"Because you belonged to my sister," Mirdonna says.

"Yeah, and I will again if I don't pay her off. She's coming after my mother."

"And what, darling, do you think would happen if you gave her back our brothers or myself?" She sweeps past me and lays a finger on the center crystal. "She will just let your mother return to whatever squalor she lives in? That the Summer Lady will not simply take you and make you *watch* what she does to your family?"

Panic settles sour in my gut. I crave a smoke but I'm out. My lighter's all that's left in my pocket.

She's right. I know it like I know how much I've fucked up.

"Then what do I do?"

WHEN THE WINTER Lady left the bar, I dumped her untouched cider into the carefully marked drain that went back to the garden.

Even if it wouldn't have cost me my job, I didn't dare contaminate the municipal drainage. Who knew what would grow from the pipes if I did?

"If they're sisters," I said to Desmondelda, one of the regulars who was freer with her words than most, "where's spring and autumn?" I meant it half as a joke. Elements like Mirdonna and Eve were never isolated.

Desmondelda chuckled. Her nails tatted against the polished counter. "Those boys? Pretty sure Madam Eve and Lady Winter skinned them and used them for rugs long ago. No one's ever seen 'em."

I laughed, as was expected, and refilled Des's beer.

"FINISH WHAT WE'VE begun," Mirdonna says. "Your mother's fate is decided regardless."

My knees wobble and I sink to the floor. I can't feel anything.

I know. I *know*. As soon as I got that text, I understood.

I'm a fool if I pretend there's hope left.

"I thought they would be enough." Mirdonna lifts the two crystals, turning them in her hands, then flings them to the floor. "But no. My brothers have never loved me. They tried to take my power when I told them my plan. So I took theirs instead."

I laugh, bitter. "So you already failed once."

Ice flares along her skin until it becomes long talons on her nails. Her hand hesitates just shy of seizing my throat.

"Do you dare accuse me?"

"It's true, isn't it?" Numb, I get to my feet. I brush her hand aside, incautious. "Is the third one yours?" I nod at the crystal heart still on the pedestal.

She sighs, but the ice fades from her hand. "It is."

I want to pull her close, tell her I'm sorry for what she endured.

But she wants no pity, and I'm so tired I don't know how much more I want to feel.

I look up into her eyes. "Tell me one thing. The people who offered to help. Do you feel anything for them?"

Can you still love?

She looks away, her jaw muscles bunching. "It's not necessary. Their devotion is all that matters."

"Magic is a conduit. It flows both ways. If you don't care about them—hell, maybe it only takes one to spark the spell, like a fuse. But if you don't love any of them in return, it won't work."

Her rage dims. Her flesh isn't as cold as I once thought.

"And you, Jordan? Do you love me?"

"No."

She tilts her head back, slow, as if the bones in her neck are melting snow.

"Fear you, respect you, desire you, sure." I won't lie. "But I don't love you. Not yet."

She crosses her arms, pushing me back a step. "My sister is coming for you, and she will learn what I have created. She will want to destroy my work."

Figures.

I wish I had told my mother goodbye before I followed Mirdonna. I wish I had the backbone to stay, to face Madam Eve alone.

I'm so sorry, Mom.

I shut my eyes against burning tears.

"Is my mom dead?"

"Not yet." Her tone is cool, clipped. "My sister will not waste her so easily."

I nod. I've wondered, since I came here, why there is no one else in the tower not enclosed in glass. Is it because Mirdonna has put all her power, all her skill and magic and will into the machine? She has no soldiers left. She has no army to combat her sister.

She cannot save my mother—but perhaps I can.

I take a deep breath.

"I have an idea."

THERE'S A WINDING catwalk that connects all the containment chambers. Each has a name.

I look into each tank, into each face. None of the sacrifices see me. But I study them. I memorize their names.

I wonder who they are. Who they love, what they are giving up. What they want. What regrets they still have.

I make myself watch them until I'm raw, devastated. They're all going to die.

Ninety-nine human beings out of billions. Each an individual. Each a universe—starstuff, souls, history, memory, passion, dreams. I still have enough of a heart to mourn them. To feel empathy.

That is the purpose of the machine, after all.

"Jacob, it's me. Yeah. Is that dinner invitation still open?"

Jacob looks at me through the anesthetic haze. His mouth forms soundless words inside the containment tank.

"Hi, little brother." I speak into the mic from the control room.

He'll hear. The containment tank is equipped with speakers that have, until now, played soft, soothing playlists of spring rain and loons, water lapping against sandy shores, delicate wind instruments guiding thoughts through peaceful melodies.

"I wanted to tell you Carol's just fine. Your baby's healthy and due to be born next week, right on schedule."

Jacob's eyes focus. He's suspended at the top of the pyramid of bodies. I only want him to see my face, in the end.

Below him are the ninety-nine who've offered their hearts to Mirdonna. Interlinked with needles and tubes, electric primers strapped over ribcages. Dreaming, I hope, of a new world.

"Dinner was nice," I continue. "I'm glad we had a chance to get together."

Carol told me they were having a baby girl. The name they'd picked out: Jaclyn Rose.

"Pretty," I said.

Carol laughed. "Your mom's name and mine combined. I think it's perfect."

I'd brought a bottle of Mirdonna's favorite vintage wine. As soon as Jacob passed out, while Carol was in the bathroom, I carried him out to the chopper.

I'm stronger than I look.

Jacob blinks, now, focusing on my voice.

"Remember that time we built a snow fort on Mrs. Kelroy's vegetable garden to protect it from invading lava monsters?" I ask. "Mom got so mad, even if Mrs. Kelroy thought it was hilarious and brought us hot chocolate with marshmallows to drink in our fort."

Tears drip down his face. He mouths words again, but I can't hear.

"It's one of the few good memories I still have, Jake."

Outside, in the wild arctic, I hear Madam Eve's huntresses.

I see them on the security cams: They've shifted into bears, foxes, wolves, elk. Some of the women ride snowmobiles, winter coats flapping about their shoulders like capes. Madam Eve is with them, running bare-legged across the snow like a living flame. A stream of boiling water flows behind her steps.

Mirdonna is on the roof, shaping the last threads of steel and living membrane to carry the Empathy across the world.

"It was the day Dad…" I take a breath. "The day he was murdered. I know Mom told us it was an accident. Christmas Eve, and some asshole just walked up to him in the street, high as fuck, and shot him for kicks."

Jacob shuts his eyes.

"That's the kind of world we have right now. Random violence. Grief. And I know. I know. I'm taking you away from Carol and your daughter. I'm sorry, Jacob. But they'll be okay. Because tomorrow… no one will want to kill. No one will want to hurt each other."

Mom will live. She'll walk away from Madam Eve. Everyone who's bound to the Summer Lady will be free.

"We'll be okay. Your baby's going to grow up not having to be terrified that if she looks at a guy wrong, he'll kill her. Your wife won't have to get catcalled and harassed on her way to work or out for a jog. Mom won't get her teeth knocked out by a drunk boyfriend."

I turn off the security feeds.

Madam Eve and her huntresses won't get here in time. And if they do…it won't matter.

"I couldn't have done this without your help, Jake. Goodbye," I tell my brother. "I love you."

Inside the control room, it's dim and cold. Snow flurries buzz down from the opened roof. The flowering antenna and dishes are positioned. Mirdonna glides down the ladder and stands next to me.

"I don't know what to do when this is over," Mirdonna says, her fingers poised above the launch button.

When she presses it, all the empathy and life force will multiply and bloom like a great tidal wave. It will ripple through the atmosphere, airborne, and infect everyone who breathes.

We don't know if it will change the unborn—like Carol's daughter—but we can hope. Perhaps, if brought up in a world where pain and hurt are not necessary, children will learn without being neutered by the machine.

"We'll figure it out," I say, and she smiles.

The countdown begins: ten, nine, eight…

Engines hum. Power floods the circuitry and the transmitters begin to glow.

The ninety-nine bodies convulse as needles pierce their hearts, leeching out life energy and blood into the tubes winding into the converters.

Seven, six, five.

Mirdonna takes a breath. She looks up at the stormy sky, the snow crusting her lashes.

"Tomorrow," she says. "Tomorrow…"

Four.

I grab her wrist. Mirdonna turns her head, slow, predatory. Her eyes meet mine.

Three.

The needles pierce Jacob's heart.

The status bar on our screen is at ninety-nine percent.

"He's my brother."

She nods.

Two.

Mirdonna pulls her arm back; I let her go.

One.

Jacob's eyes close for the last time.

One-hundred percent.

I press the button for a new world.

ONCE I, ROSE

LIFE/DEATH #7

The woman I'm given to is finished with her boyfriend, so she throws me and the other roses into the garbage disposal.

BECAUSE MEMORY LASTS between life and death, I make lists as my new body grows on the stem.

When I Am Human Again, I Will:

- Eat a twelve-course meal full of cheeses and pie and roast chicken and mashed potatoes and French appetizers with names I can't pronounce. Anything that doesn't taste of NutriGrow.
- Watch the sun rise and set and the stars bloom over a country field.

- Go skydiving.
- Wear microfleece sweaters and downy slippers and drink hot chocolate by an open fireplace.
- Hold you tight and tell you *I love you I love you I love you.*

LIFE/DEATH #19
Petals ripped from my stem one by one to gamble for love. At least the pain lessens with each wound. Roses can't scream.

THE CURSE WAS nestled in a chocolate truffle glazed with butterscotch.

Was it meant for me, or was it meant for you?

LIFE/DEATH #37
Tossed in the compost after Valentine's Day. Decomposing amid carrot tops and lettuce heads, coffee grounds and melon rinds. The flies are the worst.

I AM ALWAYS the brightest, reddest, biggest rose in a bouquet. I must be the most beautiful so you will find me.

I bolster my fellow roses with encouraging thoughts—"Look how lovely you are! Your fragrance is delectable! Your thorns are so sharp!"—but they never answer. I know they suffer. If I had a heart like I did, it would always be breaking.

LIFE/DEATH #58
Eaten by a golden retriever. Half-digested in stomach acids and vomited up on a Persian rug.

I wish this would stop.

OUR LIFE TOGETHER was rocky and sharp, because we were both poor and students and unsure where we were headed. But I remember loving you. So hard that it stretched my chest into a balloon I thought would pop if I couldn't see your bedhead in the morning, brush my teeth beside you in our tiny apartment bathroom, cuddle you in the evening, write you sentimental texts at work.

When you said my name, an electric thrill buzzed in my stomach. I said yours back and you would smile. Kiss me. Hold me.

We were happy, weren't we? In all our struggle and spats and goofy dates at the waterpark or the zoo or free museums?

You're still trying to find me, aren't you?

LIFE/DEATH #71
Tossed in a puddle after wilting, tires grinding my body into asphalt. Drowning in grit and rain.

I WENT TO bed with a stomachache from eating the curse. When you woke, I was gone. You never thought to look at the dozen roses on the table.

You looked. You waited. You called the police. But I was gone—transformed, unable to beg you to kiss me and set me free.

You threw out the roses a week after I left.

That was Life/Death #1.

LIFE/DEATH #87
Dried and pressed between the slats of a vice, crushed into paper. Suffocating against mulched wood until the book opens and I crumble to dust.

THE CURSE-MAKER PURCHASED me during Life/Death #42. She was a chocolatier who worked on her spells on the side. One day she was mixing brownies from a box, a shortcut she was ashamed of, but it was such a last minute invite to her niece's potluck, and everyone expected her to bring chocolate.

"It didn't reach my ex," she said, cell on speakerphone as she worked. "The package was mislabeled and sent to the wrong house. He never received the curse. I feel just awful."

A mistake? All this…was a mistake?

"So no," the chocolatier said. "I won't make any more. You'll have to find someone else."

I couldn't scream. I was *right there* and she could fix this. Why couldn't she see me?

She crumbled us roses into a frosting for the brownies.

LIFE/DEATH #93

Used for an amateur's home-made perfume. Left to ferment in an old milk-glass jar. The smell is terrible.

I WANT YOU to keep looking for me. I shouldn't. You deserve to move on, to find other loves, to live. But hope is all I have.

Attempted Methods of Communication Thus Far:

- ☐ Shedding petals into the words HELP ME. [Too difficult to arrange with no hands.]
- ☐ Pricking every finger that touches me; someone must realize *I am not a rose.* [People are imperceptive.]
- ☐ Asking the bees to carry my message to someone. Anyone. [Humans understand bees poorly.]
- ☐ Thinking your name as loud as I can, remembering how we said we would always recognize each other's ghosts.

LIFE/DEATH #103

I refuse to eat or drink. Once withered, thrown away.

THE NUMBER OF Valentine's Days I've endured as a rose: fifty-two.

I no longer strive to outshine all the other roses. If I give up, will the curse end? Will I die forever?

You must have stopped looking for me. It's okay.

It's…okay.

LIFE/DEATH #111

My stem tip rots in the old water of the boutique fridge. I'm the only rose left after the holiday rush. Too dreary to be picked. The shop owner, a tiny woman who sings to us in Russian, shuffles about as she closes up for the night.

The door chimes. "Do you have any roses left?"

Footsteps approach. I bow my head, petals drifting in a washed-out drizzle to the fridge floor. I want to disintegrate before another stranger finds it necessary to discard me.

Hands that smell of cocoa butter and minty arthritic cream cup my wilted head. Lift me. "Hello, love."

It's your voice.

You found me.

After so long, you didn't give up? I have so many questions. Yet just to be held in your hands once more, to be remembered—it's enough. I strive to blossom one last time for you.

You came back.

You smile and whisper my name and kiss me.

WHERE MONSTERS DANCE

ONCE UPON A time there was a girl named Red, but since this isn't a fairy tale, that's a stupid way to begin.

Start here: You're sitting with your girlfriend Ashley after dance practice and she says, "They won't let me join the girls' dance team."

You punch the grass. The hill isn't bothered; its grass is more dead-brown than green, anyhow. "That's bullshit."

She shrugs and stares at her feet, toes digging into the ground. Her mascara is beginning to run, so you put an arm around her and pull her tight.

"It's bullshit," you say again, no less angry. You've seen her dance. She's good. She should be on the team.

Dancing is how you met. It was the first party you went

69

to in this town, because your aunt's house was too suffocating in the quiet and you needed music blaring, a rhythmic beat in your chest. You needed to feel something. Ashley danced like a wild thing in the thumping strobe lights. You watched, entranced, and when she saw you, she beckoned. But you just shook your head. Maybe it was the longing in your eyes or your pixie cut or the party-vibe, but she swung her way over to you and asked if you wanted a drink. Watching Ashley dance was like finding an oxygen mask as the room filled with smoke.

(You haven't danced with anyone since your monster went away.)

"Hey Ashton!" someone, a guy, shouts from the bottom of the hill. One of the mass of the interchangeable bullypack. He starts making lewd gestures at you both, laughing.

Ashley presses her face harder into your shoulder. You flip the idiot the finger.

Ashley takes deep breaths and squeezes your hand between hers. "I just have to wait till I can afford surgery and—" Her voice cracks.

You hug your girlfriend tighter. She should still be able to join the girls' dance troupe. You have no one guilty nearby to punch out, so you hit the ground again.

I love you, Ash, is what you want to say, for support, because it's true—but you can't. Words have never been your domain. They belong to *him*.

You never told your mom you loved her, either. You don't believe in happy endings anymore.

This isn't a fairy tale.

ONCE UPON A time, when you were a kid, you fell into an old abandoned well in the woods. You should've broken your arm or your neck, but you didn't. You landed on a monster instead.

"What are you doing here?" said a deep voice.

You looked up—and up and up—at the monster.

The monster was as big as your house (almost), covered in fluffy purple fur because purple was your favorite color. The monster had great big eyes and soft round ears like a teddy bear. When the monster smiled, you saw very, very big teeth.

"I ran away," you told the monster. It was one of the Bad Days. Daddy was shouting at Mommy. It hurt your ears.

"Why?" asked Monster.

"I'm scared." You pressed your face into Monster's poofy fur. "Don't wanna go back."

Monster hugged you while you cried. You knew the shouting was your fault. You'd asked if you could take ballet lessons. Mommy said yes; Daddy said no.

"I'll protect you," Monster said.

"On Bad Days too?"

"Always," said Monster. "That's what monsters are for."

You took Monster home and let Monster live under your bed so you wouldn't be afraid of the dark.

This was when you thought fairy tales were real. Then maybe you'd be a princess in shining armor riding a palomino horse to save your stuffed animals from the evil king.

And besides, even when Bad Days happened, fairy tales got happy endings. Like this:

It was a Bad Day. Mommy was crying and saying "Stop, stop, please stop!" but Daddy kept hitting her.

So you got really mad. You ran up and kicked Daddy in the leg. Your shoes had hard toes because Monster was teaching you how to dance after bedtime. "Leave her alone!"

Daddy's face went as red as your favorite hoodie. "You little bitch."

You ran to your room and dove under the bed. "Help, Monster!"

Monster's warm, furry arm wrapped around you. "You're safe, Red."

Then Daddy's face appeared all scrunched up mad. "I'm gonna teach you a lesson in respect, you little brat."

Monster growled.

"Go away or Monster will bite you," you told him.

Daddy thrust both hands under the bed to grab you. You squirmed back into Monster's protective fur.

Monster's mouth opened wide and bit off both Daddy's hands.

Daddy screamed and rolled around on the floor, hugging his arms to his chest.

Monster smiled with red teeth, and you smiled back.

But it was just a chapter ending, and the fairy tale went on. (You didn't know how dark most fairy tales were, back when you were small.)

Daddy leaned in the doorway of your bedroom later. When he stayed outside the room, his hands came back. If he came inside the room, they disappeared, because Monster had bitten them off. He stopped hitting Mommy when you told him you would let Monster eat him all up if he didn't.

(He didn't, not really—he just made sure you didn't see.)

You sat cross-legged on the floor playing Go-Fish with your favorite plush rabbit, Mr. Bunny. Monster watched from under the bed.

"I'm going to kill it," Daddy said in his Normal Voice. "Your monster. I'm going kill all of them. Just you wait."

"Go Fish," you said to Mr. Bunny, but your hand quivered as you picked a card.

When Daddy walked away, you crawled under the bed and tugged Monster's ear. "I don't want Daddy to kill you."

Monster pulled you close with one arm. "He can't harm us in this world, Red. Don't worry."

You sniffed, relieved. "Can we dance, Monster?"

Monster smiled. "Whenever you wish."

You bounced up and down with excitement, and pulled Monster by the hand into the ballroom. Under the bed was like a tent, full of space for your stuffed animals and toys. It even had a dance floor where Monster gave you lessons.

Monster took your hands and began to hum, a lullaby that had become your favorite music. You hummed along with Monster, your feet tapping to the beat.

You pulled Monster along to the music, spinning and dipping and leaping. Your feet hardly touched the ground. It was like the time Daddy took you to the amusement park and you got to ride the grown-up roller coaster, only a million billion times better. The music soared through you and you felt like you could fly.

The dance floor blurred around you, became an open glade full of trees and a bright sunny sky. It smelled like lilacs and cotton candy. You loved when Monster made it look like outside. You danced wildly, swept away in the movement and the music.

Letting go of Monster, you twirled faster and faster across the grass. You sprinted onto a fallen birch log and jumped into the air. Monster caught you and lifted you up, higher and higher until you thought you could peel the sky open with your fingertips.

The dance ended.

Monster set you down, back in the ballroom under your bed. You laughed, out of breath, and hugged Monster tight. "I love dancing!"

"It is something no one can ever take from you, Red," Monster said.

(Daddy's words were long forgotten by the time you went to bed.)

You don't see Ashley after track practice on Friday. She texted you she'd meet you on the hill. You're taking her to dinner (even if it's just McDonald's because you can't afford much more) to celebrate the year you've been dating.

But she's not there. Storm clouds roll in, a cold October wind kicking the trees into a gold-brown frenzy.

Your phone dings. Voicemail, although you don't see any missed calls. You drop your duffel bag with your change of clothes and dial your voice mailbox to listen.

It's Ashley's voice.

"Red, it's me—oh God, I don't know what's going on. There's this—it's huge, Red, some giant animal but it's nothing—Jesus, let go of me!" Ashley's screaming. "Let go! Help! It's going for the woods—"

And the message stops. Your voicemail asks you in a monotone if you'd like to save, repeat, or delete the message.

You shove your phone in your pocket and run.

Someone—something—has kidnapped your girlfriend, and you've got to get her back.

For a moment you wish Monster was here. Monster could've carried you faster than you can run. You can't swallow down the dry, crunchy fear that you won't be *able* to help.

(Monster isn't here. Monster never will be here again.)

Up ahead, the forest looms. It's just the rumbling clouds, the lack of daylight. The woods aren't some creepy, mystical landscape. You could get lost, sure. But your phone has GPS—your aunt insisted on it so you could always find your way home.

Wind moans through the treetops, and it sounds like desperate voices. At the corner of your eye, you notice a ribbon of gray in the trees, but it's not a cloud or a bird. It's a hole, as if you're staring at a movie screen and a patch of static ripples across the picture.

It hurts your eyes to stare at the hole. You look away, shaking, and as soon as you do, the memory blurs, fuzzily distorting until you aren't sure what you were just looking at.

One thing's always clear, though: Ashley.

You wipe your sweaty palms on your jeans and step into the woods. There, not a yard inside the dark treeshadow, you see a glimmer of color. A red thread—it matches Ashley's favorite wool sweater. It's caught on a branch and unravels deeper into the woods.

She came this way. You follow it as it twists and spins through trees, a wobbling path stretching into the heart of the forest.

You're almost running now, so you can't stop when the ground disappears.

It's a long way down into the dark river below.

You were thirteen when Mom OD'd and your stepdad—fuck, why'd you ever call him Daddy?—left. At first you thought *thank God he's gone*, but at night, you lay awake trying not to panic that he would come back.

(He'd spoken in his Normal Voice when you called him at work, hardly able to speak, because Mom wasn't breathing. "What did you do to your mother, girl?")

You had this aunt, some relative you'd only met once, who took you in. You moved to some backwards little town in the middle of nowhere. At least there were woods around, so much forested land you weren't allowed to wander too close in case you stepped off the trail and got lost.

You didn't care about the goddamn trees at first. Your mom was dead. You were stuck here. Friends were hard to come by for the new girl from the cities, the one who liked other girls and loved to dance by herself to music no one else had on their iPods.

"Why didn't you protect her too?" you asked. Monster sat on the bed next to you, no longer as big as a house, fur darker, magenta and sleek, not the poof-ball you remembered as a kid. "You could have saved her! She's all the family I had!"

Monster looked down. "She didn't believe in us."

"You're supposed to be my friend, Monster. You should have saved her!"

Monster sat silently as you pummeled your fists against the thick fur until your knuckles hurt and your face burned from tears. Blaming your monster was better than blaming yourself. You hadn't seen Mom shoot up in months. You'd thought she was getting better, that the support group meetings were working, that the new job with the nice guy she'd gone out for drinks with were helping, that your stepdad being gone more and more was returning the world to normal.

(Nice lies, weren't they.)

"I'm sorry, Red," Monster said, wiping sticky hair from your face with one claw. "There was nothing I could do."

That's the thing about monsters. They're real—of course they're real. But you have to accept that before they can come out of the shadows.

"Well, if you can't do anything, then I don't need you." You were so angry you felt like you were about to explode. You hoped you would. POOF and done. Then you could stop hurting inside. "Go away, Monster."

Monster flinched. "Red…"

"I said go away!" You shoved Monster as hard as you could, and Monster flew off the bed and slammed into the wall. Cracks rippled along the sheetrock. You didn't care if your aunt saw the damage. "I don't want to see you again."

Monster's head bowed and Monster's whole body shrank until your monster disappeared altogether.

You flung yourself on the bed and screamed into the pillows.

YOU PULL YOURSELF from the river, shivering, hair plastered to your face. You're not sure how far the current carried you. You're good at track because it gives you an excuse to run, to move, to feel wind comb your hair—your legs are strong, and so are your lungs.

You're still in the woods. Maybe this forest goes on forever. Except—there's the thread of red wool, curling up from tangled deadwood and winding through the trees.

Ashley.

You brush mud from your hands and look up.

An immaculately dressed wolf sits on a sycamore branch, swinging his legs. His suit is rich burgundy, pinstriped with black. His fur is glossy gray, neatly combed, and he smiles as he hops down and offers you a courtly bow.

"Good evening," says the wolf. "What brings you here?"

You've never been scared of monsters. And since this isn't a fairy tale, you have nothing to fear from a big bad wolf in the woods.

"My girlfriend was kidnapped," you say. "I'm going to get her back."

The wolf rubs a claw along the lapel of his suit. Some undefined light source gleams off the polished nails. "Are you, now?"

You fold your arms. "And no asshole in a cheap suit is going to stop me, either."

"Do you like it?" The wolf smiles wider. "It was tailor-made. I made him sew it for me before I ate him."

You're not going to take this bullshit. You nurse the anger like a personal white dwarf star; maybe one day it will cool with nothing to fuel it, but now? Now it's dense and bright and hot. "Get out of my way."

The wolf glides around you and you turn to follow his gaze. "You must pay my toll to pass," says the wolf.

You bet he doesn't take plastic, and your wallet's pretty empty as it is. What if he demands riddles or magic or games you can't win? You throw at him the only thing you hope might work.

"I'll pay you with a secret," you say.

The wolf's eyes glint like sequins. "And what kind of secret is worth safe passage into our land?"

You clench your hands to stop them trembling. This is a bad idea. But what else do you have? You can't bring yourself to dance again, even with another monster. "It's a secret I've never told anyone."

The wolf's ears prick towards you. "No one?"

"Ever." You swallow hard. "Aren't monsters supposed to like secrets?"

"The one I love is made from secrets and shadow," the wolf says. "But what will you do if I do not *like* this secret?"

"Suck it up and deal," you snap before you think better of it. You brace yourself, ready to run or fight back if the wolf attacks you.

But the wolf only throws back his head and howls with laughter. "I think I will like whatever you share with me," the wolf says, smoothing his lapel again. "Very well. A secret for your safe passage."

He leans close until you smell the river and hot sand and summer air after a rainstorm in his fur.

Words stick like toothpicks in your throat. You don't want this secret and you don't want anyone to ever know, but you already made a deal.

You take a deep breath, then whisper in the wolf's ear.

ONCE UPON A time, when you just started sixth grade, the cool girls cornered you and your best friend Terra by the lockers. Your heartbeat jumped, because you had a crush on Vanessa, the clique leader, and now she was speaking to you.

"Hey, Red. Want to hang out this weekend? I'm having a party Friday."

She knew you existed. You blushed. "Yeah! I mean, I'd like—"

"Assuming," Vanessa went on, "you're not going to go on about 'monsters' again like a two year old. Terra says that's all you ever talk about."

You glanced at Terra. You'd told her about Monster, about dancing, and she hung on every word; you'd told her she could find a monster of her own, too, so she wouldn't be scared all the time.

Vanessa tossed her hair. "Well? Is it true?"

You shrugged, looking at the floor. If you told the truth, Vanessa would mock you forever. You didn't want school to be hell for another year in a row. "There's no such thing as monsters."

Vanessa leaned close. "I didn't hear you."

"Monsters aren't real," you said again, not expecting it to be that hard. "It's just a bunch of bullshit for little kids."

Vanessa smirked. "Obviously."

Terra's mouth hung open, shock in her eyes, but you ignored her and followed Vanessa and the other girls instead.

A week later, Terra's family moved out of state unexpectedly, and you never saw her again. You never knew if she found her monster.

(Maybe she believed you that monsters aren't real.)

THE WOLF SIGHS and half-shuts his eyes. "You carry so much pain in your heart."

You shake your head, face burning, and remember where you are. You wish you could forget the shame of that secret as easily. "Let me pass."

"I can do more than that," the wolf says. "I know where your lady love has been taken."

You stare hard at the wolf, trying to tell if he's lying. His bright eyes and brighter teeth give nothing away. "Where's that?"

"Ah," he says with a smile. "Answers must be paid for."

"What do you want in return for telling me?"

"Your help, lady knight."

You realize in sudden panic that you've lost sight of the telltale thread.

There's nothing caught any longer among the branches.

If Monster were here now, Monster would know where to go, like the day Monster carried you out of the woods. (You can't let yourself miss your monster. It's always better to stay angry.)

"Enough," you tell the wolf. "If you help me get my girlfriend back and let us get out of here, I'll help you in return. Okay?"

The wolf bows. "Very well."

"Where's Ashley?"

"The Hall," the wolf says. "Our home."

"Who took her there?"

"Kin," says the wolf. "At the bidding of the new king."

The wolf grabs your elbow and tugs you sideways, off the path. You yank your arm free, about to curse him out, when he points at where you were standing.

"Look."

There's a hole in the air where you were. It's the size of a baseball and there's *nothing* on the other side. Not darkness, really, but an absence of anything that sends shooting pain up your neck and behind your eyes.

You retreat, bumping into the wolf. "I saw…" The recollection is still fuzzy. You frown and concentrate. "There was one by the woods in my world."

The wolf snaps off a branch as thick as his arm, then pokes it through the hole. The branch disappears and the hole grows a half inch wider. It sits there, ragged edges flapping as if in a soft breeze. Up above you see more holes poking through the endless twilight-lit treetops.

You hug yourself. "What are they?"

The wolf sighs. "Emptiness. Entropy. An end. That is what the king is doing—he is destroying our world. And yours."

They aren't separate. You asked Monster about this, once. They coexist beside each other, overlapping and easily crossed if you believe you can. Yours is not a nice world. But it's still yours, and Ashley's, and your aunt's. The world of monsters is just as important. Without one, the other can't exist.

You hunch your shoulders. Your stepdad left holes in your life you don't know how to sew shut. Your mom's death. The loss of your dance. You tried to dance again, after you and Ashley were dating for a few weeks, but as soon as you struck a pose and Ashley turned on a CD, your muscles locked and you started shaking. *Monster isn't here.* You curled up on Ashley's bed and hid your head under the pillows, refusing to move even though she promised she wouldn't ask you to dance with her again. You didn't have words to tell her it wasn't her fault.

You can't freeze up again. You won't lose her the way you lost Terra or Monster.

"Show me where the Hall is," you tell the wolf.

He offers his arm and you loop your elbow through his.

THE FOREST GROWS darker as you walk alongside the big not-so-bad wolf. He gracefully dodges the holes that appear faster among the treetops and in the ground, eating away the world.

"Who's this king?" you ask. You try not to clutch the wolf's arm harder than necessary. You've already asked how far the Hall is. The wolf said it was as far as it needed to be, and no more.

"A man self-titled so," says the wolf. "He beguiled his way into the Hall; he spoke with such charm and smooth words, we let him join us. Many lost travelers may find their way in. Perhaps not all leave again." His teeth gleam. "But he brought a weapon with him. It is a small knife made of all the words that have ever been used to harm another. It is power unlike any we can match." The wolf points at a hole, but you don't look at it too long. "With each cut, the false king destroys pieces of our world and our kin."

"You can't kick him out?" You want to run, to drag the wolf along behind you. Ashley can't wait, not if there is a wicked king holding her prisoner.

The wolf's ears droop. "The ones who tried are no more. The queen is… gone. He will not stop, lady knight."

And the wolf thinks you can help? Shit. The angry part of you wants to blow it off, take Ashley and go home, let the monsters deal with it. Isn't that what they're for? Monster lived under your bed and protected you. But the guilty part of you knows it wasn't Monster's fault you were hurt when your mom died. Monster would do anything for you, but there are some things even monsters can't fix.

And you sent Monster away.

Right in front of you, huge arched doors shimmer into sight.

"Welcome to our home," says the wolf.

The Hall is made of whispers and mirrors and filled with monsters. There are more than you can ever count. They dance to a haunting, unknown melody that grows slower and slower, perpetual motion winding down. Dusk hangs from the ceiling; dawn winds through the foundations. Only stars light this place.

"One of us ate the sun," the wolf says, "and another ate the moon. But it's impolite to remember who devoured which, now isn't it?" And when he smiles, you can almost see sunlight glimmering at the back of his throat.

For a moment, you can't breathe. This place is what you always believed (secretly) heaven was like.

The monsters are beautiful and terrible. Not one is alike. Some have glossy fur and coarse manes, some are covered in shimmering feathers and scales. Some have horns or claws or antlers or teeth. The monsters have bright eyes and some have no eyes. There are monsters made from shadow and monsters made from light. Smooth skin and armored pelts. Some monsters have skeletons, or exoskeletons, and some only pretend.

The dance floor stretches out in all directions to the horizon lines. You rub your eyes hard. This place feels like *home*.

"Here," says the wolf, and offers you a dance card. "It never fills up, so you may dance until the world ends."

You tuck the card in your pocket. You need to find Ashley first. "Where's my girlfriend?"

The wolf points at a dais that floats above the monsters, luminescent stairs trailing down all six sides.

Ashley's sitting there, hunched with her knees pulled against her chest. For a second, she's all you can see. Ashley: quirky, smart, dedicated Ashley, who was the first to make you feel welcome in the new town, who's going to be an EMT when she graduates, who takes care of her younger sisters while her single mom works three jobs. Her sweater is only a few threads tied around one wrist now. Her jeans are muddy and her make-up little more than messy streaks. Your heart lurches.

"Hurry," the wolf murmurs. "Before the music stops."

You weave your way towards the stairs. The dais is translucent at the edges, and a carpet made of a white material mutes the light near the middle. You can't see anyone else on it. Just Ashley.

A monster made from metal angles, sharp and contrasted, sweeps by with a glass cougar in its embrace. Their bodies reflect the light in geometric patterns.

A brilliantly painted girl made from ivy dances with a metallic velociraptor, and they smile at you as you pass.

Your breath comes faster. Your body longs to move, join the music and *dance*, but you can't. You can't lose sight of Ashley.

Closer now. You want to yell to your girlfriend to jump. You'll catch her. But you don't know who else is up there. You dash up the steps, hope thumping along with your heart. You stop short at the last step when you see what awaits you.

The king.

And Monster.

You gasp. Monster is thin, fur ragged and patchy. Monster's eyes are dull and won't look at you.

The king sits on a throne. A thick, heavy chain tied around Monster's neck holds Monster down at the king's feet. That's blood matting Monster's fur. Bones cover the dais: pale and dark and silver and translucent. But bones all the same.

You glare at the king, the asshole who married your mother then ran off to do *this* to your monsters.

He's got his hands now, but they aren't his—they look sawed from someone else and stapled on with undulating threads. He holds a pistol in one hand and a knife in the other. He points the gun at Ashley.

Your stepdad smirks. "Not so tough now, are you? I get your boyfriend and your freaks—" he kicks Monster and Monster flinches "—and what can you do?"

"Let Ashley go," you say, but your voice cracks.

"Why?" He speaks in his Normal Voice, calm and confident and it makes you want to *listen*. Like when you were little, before the Bad Days, when he would read you stories and buy you presents and candy and make you laugh with funny faces. "I'm doing what I said I would. It's your fault, girl. It has always been your fault."

You shake your head. That's bullshit.

"Don't believe me?" The king leans forward. "Where were you when your mom killed herself?"

"It was an accident—"

"No."

That one syllable is like a sledgehammer in your stomach. There is so much *hatred* in his voice, you can't catch your breath.

"No, she did it on purpose. You might have gotten away with anything you wanted because of that beast you had." He kicks Monster again. "She started getting ideas she could do the same, and we couldn't have that, could we? I'm in charge. She had to learn that. If you hadn't hidden behind your monsters, your mother wouldn't have thought she needed to escape. We could have been a family."

You stumble back a step. The realization sinks cold in your stomach. You usurped his power and he couldn't bear it.

"I didn't…" But you can't go on.

"Don't listen to him, Red," Ashley shouts. "It's not true!"

"One more word and you join my wife," the king says, his finger on the trigger.

You stand there, shaking, trying not to think how much *sense* his words make.

The music—it's softer now, weaker. And it's coming from Monster's throat.

Ashley locks her jaw and stares unblinking at you. *Don't listen.*

You swallow hard. The melody drifts through your fingers and toes. It's the lullaby Monster sang to you when you were very small.

If you believe the false king, he'll win. He'll take everything away, like he's tried to do all your life. You can't endure losing Ashley. And you can't see Monster go away again.

You put a foot on the dais floor. A bone crunches under your shoe. Perhaps you can find a way to heal Monster, because you want your monster back so badly it hurts. You want to tell Monster you're sorry, so sorry.

But how do you find your own words when the king owns so many? You couldn't tell Ashley you loved her. You couldn't tell your mom. You lied to Terra. And what if Monster doesn't want you back?

You look at Ashley again.

You can't fight the king. He has a gun and a knife. But with Monster at your side, you have a chance. If Monster will forgive you.

"Monster?" you breathe.

One of Monster's ears twitch. Very slowly, Monster looks up and meets your eyes. You hold out your hands.

"Please come back," you whisper. "I need you."

"And now," says the king, "let's turn off this fucking music."

You lunge forward—

The king shoots your monster in the head.

Monster's body goes limp and the music dies.

ONCE UPON A time, when you were very small, you fell off a skateboard and scraped both knees raw. Mommy was drinking, and Daddy wasn't home, so you climbed on the sink in the bathroom and looked for Band-Aids all by yourself. But you couldn't find any.

You tried not to cry when you crawled under the bed and told Monster.

Monster pulled two pieces of fur off one hand and made bright purple Band-Aids for you. You gave Monster a hug.

You sat together on a huge bean bag chair, which you couldn't have in your room or Daddy would take it away.

"Do you ever get owies?" you asked.

Monster nodded. "We all do. But you know what makes them feel better?"

"Dancing?" you asked, because that was your favorite thing in the world and you were going to be a ballerina princess astronaut veterinarian when you grew up.

Monster smiled. "Yes, Red. We dance."

YOU CRADLE MONSTER'S head, but Monster's eyes remain closed. You keep shaking Monster, not caring that there is blood all over your hands and jeans. Monster's body remains limp, so much lighter than you remember, and the chain remains dark and heavy around Monster's neck.

The anger isn't there now. It's gone cold, like your white dwarf has burned out and turned into a black hole, sucking away everything inside you.

You felt like this at Mom's funeral, and you remember punching one of the nameless mourners who showed up to pay useless respects. You don't remember who that was, just a sudden crack as your fist met a nose, and then shouting, maybe you, maybe the idiot you punched—shouting for people to get the fuck away from you. Because you were alone, and everyone made it worse by pretending you weren't.

The king laughs, jerking your attention up.

Ashley stares at you wide-eyed, a hand crammed against her mouth.

All around you, the Hall is still. None of the monsters are dancing any longer. In the starlight, holes appear above them.

You're not sure when the wolf showed up, standing at one side of the throne. There's a shadow-monster at the wolf's side, wispy and long like a feathery snake. The wolf curls an arm around the shadow-monster.

You kiss Monster's forehead, lay Monster's head gently on the floor, and stand. You don't know what to do. If this were a fairy tale, a kiss would bring Monster back to life. All you get is the taste of fur.

You focus on what really matters—you focus on Ashley. You focus on the living monsters around you.

Dance takes away the pain, Monster said once.

You won't let the king take any more of your monsters. You won't let him hurt your family again.

You begin to hum softly, the same music Monster sang. You know this melody. It builds in your chest and fills your throat. You've never had a voice for singing, but it doesn't matter. The music is *there*.

Your limbs are stiff and heavy at first, your feet clumsy. Like when you were first learning the steps and rhythm and how to let the music flow around you, become part of you. If the dance is what keeps the holes from devouring your worlds, then you will *dance*.

The king frowns. "What are you doing?"

You step over the bones but don't avoid the blood. Your feet are red.

The holes grow wider. You feel the air being sucked up and out, a rush of wind that pulls your hair in all directions. It stirs Monster's fur.

For a moment, you can't see through tears. You want your monster *back*. You dance faster, harder, flinging yourself into the music with all your fury. It burns and you welcome the heat and the pain.

Nothing around you moves.

The king leaps to his feet. "Shut up!"

Then the wolf begins to hum along with you. The shadow-monster joins him.

The king aims the gun at the wolf's head.

You kick off the dais and sail through the air. You aim for the king's arm, but you spin too fast and suddenly you're between him and the wolf.

You don't hear the gunshot over the music. There's a pain in your arm and it fades to nothing as you dance. Red ribbons of blood spin around you as the music swells.

You move like silk in the wind. Faster and faster you dance, your heartbeat the only rhythm you need. Your feet are weightless and sure. It is when you dance that you know you *alive*.

"Stop or I will kill him!" the king screams. He wields the knife above Ashley. The gun lies far from the throne, swept aside in your wake.

But the knife. Its blade glimmers, every horrible word you and Ashley have ever been called, and so many more, twisting inside the metal. It almost touches Ashley's check, and you know what will happen if that goddamned blade even scrapes her skin. She'll disappear.

Your steps falter.

A thick, rusty wire muzzle appears around the wolf's face, and heavy chains coil about the shadow-monster, pulling it to the ground.

Agony flares in your arm.

All around you, the monsters waver and fall. Breath comes ragged in your lungs. You try to hold onto the song, but the music slips away as your body overwhelms you with pain.

"Bind her," the king tells the wolf. Then, to you, "And if you take one more step, I will cut your boyfriend's throat."

You stare in numb shock at the blood spreading across your shirt. You crash to one knee.

Ashley's expression hardens into fury. "You aren't gonna hurt Red anymore." Ashley twists away from the king and slams her heel into his crotch.

The king gasps and doubles over. Ashley rolls to the side as the knife comes down. The blade cuts into the floor. Bones pour into the tear in the world. Ashley scrambles backwards. In a blur, the wolf scoops the chained shadow-monster into his arms. You lurch on your hands and knees. The dais groans, bending at the edges. The whole structure will implode inward in minutes.

You grab Monster's limp body and hold on. Ashley staggers towards you, her hair full of twigs and her face pale with shock. But she keeps her balance on the warping floor.

The king crawls to the gun and snatches it as bones cascade past him into the hole. The knife has fallen through, gone forever. He raises the gun at Ashley's back.

"Ashley, look out!" you scream.

Glass explodes behind her. She whirls. The glass cougar crouches between Ashley and the king, one arm shattered by the bullet meant for her. You stare at the large shard of glass embedded in your leg.

Across the dais, the ivy girl vaults onto the platform beside the metallic velociraptor with glowing red eyes. A rainbow-colored tentacle monster heaves itself onto one corner of the dais. All along the edges, monsters climb and jump and fly onto the platform.

The king whirls, pointing the gun wildly, but it has no more bullets.

"Enough," says the cougar. Translucent blood drips from its arm, glittering among the shards of glass. "You will not harm us any longer."

Ashley clasps your good arm. "Come on," she whispers. You can feel her shaking. "We need to stop this."

The wolf crouches by your side. He still holds the shadow-monster in one arm; he easily picks up Monster in the other. "I will guard your friend."

You don't want to let go. But Ashley pulls you to your feet as the wolf holds Monster tight.

"Will you dance with me, Red?" Ashley asks.

"Yes," you tell her. And before you can silence yourself, you add, "I love you, Ash."

She grips your hands tight. Your words mean what you want them to; her smile in response is enough.

Together, you and your girlfriend hum the music once more.

The world is heavy. You struggle against the inexplicable weight, against the icy pain in your leg and the burning in your arm. Ashley holds you steady, holds you close.

You remember every time you danced with Monster. Every time you danced by yourself, wild and unchecked and free. Every time you wished you had the courage to dance with Ashley.

Faster and faster you move now. With the music, with the dance, you can pull closed the holes in the world.

"Dance with us!" you call to monsters. "The music is not over!"

Ashley laughs. The monsters roar.

Light blurs around you. There is a tremendous cracking sound, metal splitting and bursting, and the chains around the shadow monster burst into sparkling light. The wolf's wire muzzle crumbles. The cougar's glass ripples smooth into an unbroken mirror-shine; the shard vanishes from your leg.

The starlight catches the music and echoes it back. One by one, the holes crinkle and snap shut.

"You cannot do this!" the king screams, but he is alone and unarmed. His words go unheeded.

You whirl with Ashley in front of the throne. The king charges at you with fists raised. He gets no more than two steps.

"Enough," says the wolf. He and the shadow-monster hold the king's arms behind his back.

You pause, leaning on Ashley for support.

The wolf looks at you. "What, pray, shall we do with this one?"

The king looks around, his terror unmasked.

All the monsters watch you and wait.

"I never want to see him again," you say to the wolf. "The rest is up to you."

The wolf laughs and the shadow-monster purrs and shows very sharp teeth. They drag the false king away. You never see him again.

Pain flares sharp in your leg and arm. You stagger, and only with Ashley supporting you can you stay upright. You're suddenly so tired.

"God," Ashley says, "Red, you need to sit down, I—oh Jesus, I don't even have my first aid kit with me."

It doesn't matter. Light shimmers along the floor, repairing the dais, and the most beautiful monster you have ever seen rises from it.

She's covered in black and cobalt feathers, her face made of mirrors, and her eyes are dark like the sky. She's taller and more terrible and more glorious than anything you've ever seen, and you know at once she's a queen.

"Thank you," says the queen of the monsters. "He chained me first with his poisoned words and so gained power, but you have freed us all. And you have begun the dance once more."

"Red!" Ashley's voice, so distant.

You think of bad cell reception and wonder if you still have your phone. You slip, falling backwards.

Strong arms catch you. "Red?" says a different voice, deeper and bigger than Ashley's.

Monster is holding you.

Fur poofy and silky purple once more, grown to the size of a house (almost), Monster is just like you remember. And Monster is *here*.

"Monster?"

Monster smiles, holding you close in one arm. With the other hand, Monster pulls out tufts of fur and bandages your arm and leg.

Ashley kisses you and you pull her close.

Monster does not disappear. You throw your arms around Monster and Monster hugs you back and you know it will be okay.

For the first time in your life, it will be okay.

The queen of the monsters tilts a hand and the gates appear. Through them, you see a path through the woods. At the edge of the woods stands the hill with its dead-brown grass, and the school beyond. There are no more holes in the October sky.

"Do we have to leave?" Ashley asks, wiping her face with the back of a hand.

You look between Monster and the queen. You hate the stories where the heroes grow up and are banished, everything they grew to love ripped from them for no reason.

You fight to find your voice, and not let your words be muted again. "Please don't send us away," you whisper.

"You may always come and go as you please," says the Queen. "You are forever welcomed here."

Monster nods. "There will always be room for you in the dance."

Ashley grins. You let your breath out at last. There's cool, calm relief in your chest where the usual anger is. You lean back against Monster. You'll have time to go back and call your aunt to reassure her you're fine. There's still time to take Ashley on a date for your anniversary.

Ashley rests her head on your shoulder. You squeeze your girlfriend's hand, and Monster's too. They hold you tight. The three of you watch as the monsters dance.

This isn't a fairy tale. But that doesn't mean you can't have a happy ending.

A SURVIVAL GUIDE FOR WHEN YOU'RE TRAPPED IN A BLACK HOLE

THIS IS WHAT being trapped in the event horizon of a black hole is like: your body is stretched, pulled, disintegrated into one infinite particle at a time, all while your mind can only understand pain. Your thoughts are distorted into a long, wordless cry that no one will ever hear because time dilates beyond human comprehension.

Outside observers see nothing wrong. You experience eternity because you are alone. You can't see what's on the other side of the black hole.

ANTONIO DOESN'T TELL anyone. Not his neighbor, who asks why she doesn't see him and his dog on their evening jog, or his coworkers who always gossip about their dysfunctional selves and kids and partners. He doesn't tell his boyfriend—who's over in Australia for business—when they Skype.

"She's asleep," is all he can say when Todd asks to see Sasha. He knows Todd doesn't believe him.

But he can't say words beyond that. They don't exist in a black hole.

THE SHADOW APPEARS on his doorstep at the end of the week. He almost steps on it, a blot of dark in the evening's monochrome light.

Daddy?

He jumps, shaking. That voice in his ear, a faded echo, is too familiar. Too impossible. The November chill winds down his open collar, prickles his skin like rough stubble. Muscles rigid, he looks down.

The shadow is half the size Sasha had been. Dog-shaped, with floppy ears and a bushy tail. He can't so much *see* the eyes as know they're there: huge and dark and sad. Its tail sweeps tentative across the porch's age-warped boards.

Daddy?

He shoulders the door open, slams it behind him, and throws all the locks.

IN A BLACK hole, memory is trapped in your spiraling consciousness, neurons firing like supernovas, each one bright and destructive. The radiation burns out through your galaxy before it fades into emptiness.

In a black hole, memory is cyclical, endlessly repeating its birth and destruction as your mass collapses.

THE SHADOW DOG curls on the kitchen floor the next morning.

He stares down at it, and it peeks up at him with enormous eyes. Its ears droop, its tail tucking between hind legs.

Was cold, Daddy. Wanted to come inside.

Out the kitchen window, the lawn glitters with night-brought frost. Each grass blade is razor-edged in ice particles.

He turns his head, disoriented by the smell of coffee. Did he set a timer? He must have. Five years of habit still ingrained.

"You're not Sasha," he whispers. He pours coffee, slops it on his hand. The sudden heat numbs his skin. "Sasha's gone."

The shadow dog tilts its head to the side. *Sasha here.*

He grabs a handful of napkins and slaps them on the burn. "I'm going to be late for work."

It's not until he gets to the office that he realizes he forgot his wallet, his ID badge, and his jacket.

HE WAS JUST entering collage when he found Sasha abandoned on the side of the road. A straggly wet gray bundle of muddy fur, a sprained leg and the biggest brown eyes he'd ever seen. He'd been walking his bike up a hill, ashamed of flabby, burning legs and puffing breath.

It was the only reason he saw her.

Letting the bike topple, he crouched in the mud and stroked the dog's ears. She whimpered and licked his hand, trying to wag a tail knotted with burs and twigs.

There wasn't much traffic on this stretch of road banked in scrubby trees and brown marshland.

"Shh," he said, when the dog yelped trying to stand. "Just stay still. It's okay, sweetie, I won't let anyone hurt you, okay?" He shrugged off his coat to wrap around her.

It'd taken him longer than he'd anticipated to bike to the bus stop—considering he wasn't even halfway and the bus came in half an hour. Screw first day of class, anyway.

The dog stared into his eyes; he couldn't look away.

Don't leave me, those eyes seemed to plead.

I won't, he wanted to reply. *Not ever.*

NOTHING ESCAPES A black hole; it is forever, sucking away light until the end of time when the universe burns.

"WHAT'S WRONG?"

Antonio blinks at the computer screen, where his boyfriend frowns at him. "What?"

"Jesus," Todd says, his accent emerging thicker since he's been back in his home country. "You've been spacing out on me all night. What the hell's wrong?"

"It's Sasha," he says, choked. The shadow watches him from the corner of the room, tangled in a mess of cords where all the living room electronics are plugged in under a decorative table stacked with DVDs.

Todd's eyes widen. "What happened?"

"She's sick," he says, then snaps the laptop closed before he thinks better of it.

He apologizes to Todd ten minutes later on the phone, finds the words tumbling out, finds himself telling his boyfriend about the vet visit.

Todd: incredulous, hurt, furious. "You didn't tell me?"

I'm sorry fills each space between his words. He's stuck in a time loop, saying the same thing over and over and realizing it makes no difference because he doesn't have the right words, the solution to break the cycle.

SASHA WAS A beautiful gray and white longhair mutt when she cleaned up and gained weight. He scraped together money for obedience training and budgeted for dog food, vet checkups, and accessories for her.

He met Todd at the dog park in the summer. College was finished and had miraculously landed him a job as a paper-pusher in a cloned office building built to suck personality from everything around it. Todd was dogsitting for a friend.

A year after that they were living together, Todd in love with Sasha as much as him. They were family, and Antonio had never been happier. Even the soulless job couldn't drain him when he knew he would go home to his boyfriend and his best friend.

THE HOUSE IS empty.

Except the shadow. He looks at it, sitting in the middle of the kitchen and watching him.

"You hungry?" he asks. Sasha's food bowl is still full, the water dish rinsed and refilled every morning like clockwork. He can't let it dry out.

The shadow huffs a breath, just like Sasha. *Not hungry.*

He leaves his ham and cheddar sandwich unfinished on the counter and walks away. He slams the bedroom door in the shadow's face. The light is off, the blinds pulled. Near total-darkness, except the bright red LED clock face.

Todd will be home in two days.

Todd doesn't own a spacesuit, doesn't know how to find him in a black hole.

HE CAN'T SLEEP. The clock's red light pools at the foot of his bed, and the shadow lies curled up in the glow.

He fingers the covers by his side, where Todd's absence gapes even wider because Sasha isn't there, either. Why isn't she coming home with him?

The shadow hops up on the end of the bed and turns three times before plopping soundless into a tiny dent in the blankets.

He rolls over instead of shouting at it to get out, like he did the night before.

DADDY?

He studies the slow, endless drip of coffee filling the pot.

"Why did you go?" he asks, not looking at the shadow. It sits near his knee.

The bag of bacon-flavored treats rests half-empty next to the sugar dish. Morning treats for them both. Todd always drinks grapefruit juice, health-nut that he is.

Didn't want to go, Daddy.

Something soft and dry nudges his hand. He jerks his arm away from the shadow's muzzle.

"Yes you did." He drags his fingers through his hair. His voice is hoarse, thick. He needs the coffee bean acid to burn away the clogs in his throat. "You *left*."

The shadow's head leans against his leg. He locks his knee, refusing to give ground in his own goddamn house.

Sasha didn't want to, the shadow says. *Didn't want to hurt Daddy or Papa.*

He tries to scoff, ends up choking on his own spit, then loses the strength in his legs and slides down, boneless and gutted, until he sits on the linoleum with his back to the cabinets.

"IF YOU'RE DADDY," Todd said, just after they leased the house, "then I will have to be Papa so we don't get confused." He grinned, rubbing Sasha behind the ears. "If we ever have kids, we'll be pros at 'go ask your father' argument."

Antonio laughed and squatted to bury his hands in Sasha's fur. "Who's ready for celebratory treats?"

Sasha barked, tail thumping back and forth.

"I know I am," Todd said, pulling Antonio to his feet and kissing him.

Sasha bounced as Todd flicked her a Bacon Bite, and she crunched the treat happily, beaming up at them.

Antonio pulled out his cell phone and snapped a photo, then made Todd sit next to Sasha so the three of them could take a selfie to commemorate this perfect day.

HIS FACE IS hot, a solar flare under his skin. Wet, like that first day he found her, the rain plastering his curly hair against his skull, washing the sweat off his forehead.

"Why are you here?" His voice doesn't echo, even when he shouts. "You're dead. Our dog is *dead.*"

The shadow presses against his knees, then licks at the tears. The shadow-tongue is soft, warm, dry. Like a breath on his cheek, like when Todd or Sasha would curl close at night and he felt their sleep-steady warmth.

Can't go, shadow-Sasha says. *Daddy promised to say good-bye.*

TODD NOTICED THAT Sasha wasn't finishing her supper two days before his trip.

"We should take her to the vet." He stroked Sasha's graying ears as she dozed on the couch, draped over both their laps. "Might be the flu. Guy at work said both his pugs got sick. Poor bastards, it sucks when you can't use a tissue to blow your own nose."

Antonio nodded. Even for check-ups and shots, he dreaded stepping in the veterinary office. One day, inevitable like the heat death of the universe, one day he would go in and everything would change. "I'll call Dr. Vasquez in the morning."

Todd eased off the sofa, gently moving Sasha, and went to go shower and pack.

Sasha looked at Antonio, her big eyes calm. He cupped her face in his hands, leaning in close so if Todd walked in, he wouldn't hear. This was just between them.

"Whatever happens, I'll be there. I promise I won't leave."

He broke his word when the vet said there was nothing they could do, and would he like to sit with her and say goodbye.

He couldn't watch.

He couldn't.

She looked at him as in the doorway; he felt her eyes on him as he stepped into the waiting room.

He walked outside, where space was infinite. Time dilation meant it was a long, long time before he heard the vet tech calling for him.

Sasha didn't come home that day.

HE LOOKS INTO the eyes of Sasha's shadow, helpless. "I don't know how," he says.

WHEN HE PICKS Todd up at the airport, the drive home is silent. Todd barely looks at him.

In the driveway, Todd says, "I should have stayed home. The conference, it could've—" Todd runs a hand through his hair; he's shaking. "I didn't…I didn't get to say goodbye to her."

Antonio parks, hands knotted on the steering wheel. He's unable to look Todd in the face. Through the windshield, he sees the shadow dog sitting on the porch where he first found her.

For a microsecond, he can suck a breath in through the crushing pressure of empty space. "There's still a way."

Todd stares at him, jaw locked. "Don't bullshit me."

Another breath, his lungs expanding fraction by fraction. "Come on."

THE SHADOW SITS in the living room, her head tilted to the side. She wags her tail when Todd and Antonio approach.

Daddy! Papa!

Todd kneels and reaches a hand out. The shadow licks his fingers and then presses her body against Todd's chest.

Todd's voice cracks. "Sasha?"

Antonio kneels beside his boyfriend. He rubs the shadowy fur behind Sasha's ears.

Todd cups Sasha's face and touches his nose to hers. "It's okay, baby."

Antonio lets Sasha lick tears and hugs her, the shadow soft and real. He wants to say too much: how sorry he is, how he doesn't want her to go, that he will never forget her.

Sasha knows, she says, forgiveness he doesn't deserve. He *should* say the words.

"Sasha," he whispers.

YOU CAN'T SEE what's beyond a black hole. But sometimes you can pull free of the vacuum and view the distant stars beyond.

TODD PULLS HIM close as they sit on the front porch and watch Sasha pad quietly into the dusk.

"Bye," Antonio says.

She looks back, once, wagging her tail.

"She'll be okay," Todd says. He means: so will they, in time.

Antonio nods. He knows.

THREAD

THE NINE-CLUSTER APPEARED outside our unit's bunker on the last day of the cycle. That meant only one thing.

They would take someone away.

I peered out the portviewer. All nine stood before the door, tall humanoid shapes composed of white light. They had heads like stars: translucent spheres with colored particles that suggested facial features. (That is how I imagined stars. I've never seen them for real.)

They didn't have names. They didn't have genders, either. We dubbed them he/she at random, although I never understood why. They weren't like us.

Two smiled and knocked, as if politeness meant anything. I didn't open the bunker door.

Bailey took charge, like he always did. "Everyone stay calm." He glanced at me, and I nodded. "This is just a routine inspection."

"How do you know?" Kory asked, wide-eyed. "We just got back. They don't do inspections until the first cycle-day."

Bailey slapped him on the shoulder. "Your record is spotless. They aren't here for you."

"Then who?" Tess demanded.

Everyone had unsuited except me. But Tess didn't notice. (I often forgot to remove my pressure suit right away.) Tess let me stand by the viewer for hours after a shift and look at the empty road that connected the one-hundred-forty-seven bunkers on this facility.

"No one, Tess," Bailey said. He could still tell lies. "No one is being taken to the House."

Tess took a breath and glanced at Dom. "If you say so."

"Mara," Bailey said, lifting his chin and facing the door. Only Dom and I saw the tremor in his hands. "Let the overseers in."

Dom took the scissors off the table and held them tight. They were long-bladed and heavy, used for snipping bone. He had already been to the House.

(But so had I.)

I keyed the pressure lock and opened the door.

Our unit's bunker was a functional square room. Cots slid into the wall when not in use, and we were allowed a few personal effects. Tess had the geode collection; Kory had a holo-projection of a world he pretended was once ours, full of blues and greens and surrounded by the white of the universe. Bailey had a book—paper and leather—but there was nothing inside it.

I had a thread I'd mined and none of the nine-clusters knew about it.

All nine floated in and planted themselves around our bunker. We all smiled. The cardinal rule: never frown during inspection. Gemma had forgotten.

"Welcome," Bailey said. He wouldn't fail. He couldn't. "Is everything in order?"

Two laughed. Two was always the leader. "A disturbance has been reported in your bunker."

"What?" Kory said. "That's impossible."

"An anomaly." Five glided around the perimeter. She stopped by Dom. He stared straight ahead, his knuckles bloodless. "Something is in this sector that does not belong," Five said.

Tess tilted her head towards the floor, inhaling slow and deep. She practiced her breathing every night, because Gemma wasn't there anymore.

Bailey shrugged easily. "We're permitted to refine a portion of phosphates for our own use. No one has brought back anything else past quarantine."

I hadn't told the rest of the unit. Bailey said not to. "They'll crack," he'd said the day before, looking tired and sad. (I wish I'd argued, but I had no protest.) It would be easier if they didn't know.

The thread squirmed in my gloved hand. I locked my jaw and kept my smile in place. Not yet, not yet, not yet.

We needed the nine-cluster agitated so they would touch us physically. I wouldn't risk the thread failing to pierce their barriers. It was the only chance we had.

Kory swallowed and folded his arms. He was the youngest in our unit, and he still smiled when he didn't have to.

"We're making quotas," Tess said from clenched teeth. "No one has violated the regulations. I check everyone's suits upon entry."

(She never checked mine. Bailey said not to. "Sometimes it's all that holds her together," I'd heard him whisper to Tess, when I came back from the House.)

Muscles twitched in Tess's jaw. "What is this about?"

"Defensive?" Two asked her. "That is a common psychological signal that you are…hiding something."

"We have nothing to hide," Bailey said. He chuckled, his mouth stretched until it might break. "We've increased production by 127% this cycle."

"So you did." Four's particle-expression swirled and brightened in warning. "And you were down 76% the cycle before, 58% the cycle before that, and 13% before that."

No one looked at me. I had taken Bailey and Dom on the downward spiral. (Only I could see darkness, but they believed what I told them.)

Our unit mined minerals and ore on the debris rings of 6-X76. We averaged a 97% productivity level per work segment, and had for the last ten cycles. That was when Gemma went away, and Dom came back from the House.

"Fine. It's my fault," Tess said, pulling her shoulders back. "I didn't keep the unit on track. You took *Gemma*." Her hands fisted and she took a steady breath. "But I accept full responsibility for the unit's decreases previously."

Kory winced. I shook my head minutely. Don't do this, Tess. It's not your fault. They weren't suspicious yet. (I couldn't watch them take Tess away.)

Eight laughed, a faint hissing sound characteristic of all Eights. "Your statement is contradictory. You were the hardest worker in the unit during the previous three cycles."

"It's in here," Five said. "It does not *belong.*"

"Disassemble," Two told Five. "Find it."

It was too soon. I shot Bailey a flat look. He sat on a plain metal stool and shut his eyes. "Dom," he said, very quietly.

Dom tensed, ready to do anything Bailey asked. He always did.

Bailey's smile weakened, and he tilted his head a fraction at Two. Dom's muscles bunched. He might not harm Two—we didn't know how to hurt the nine-clusters ourselves—but he would distract Two anyway.

Kory's face beaded with sweat. "They found something," he blurted. "I saw Mara put it—"

Dom jabbed his thumb into Kory's eye. The eyeball popped. Kory screamed, clutching his face.

Tess snarled and raised a fist at Dom, but Bailey snapped, "Don't."

Two clapped his hands. "Oh, well played. You *are* hiding something."

I didn't know Kory saw me take the sock or put it back. Everyone had been eating when I did. (I didn't eat much anymore.)

Five began expanding, translucent arms budding from her torso. She threw the holo-projector to the floor, scattered the geodes, pulled apart Bailey's book. The cots were empty.

The thread was heavy, pressing into my skin through the glove. It had taken all my enhanced strength to lift it from the mines. I couldn't hold it much longer.

Bailey's breath came faster. They might question him—Dom could resist, but Bailey couldn't. He had never been to the House.

I kicked the cabinet where we kept our pressure suits, jostling loose the plastic door and the lopsided drawer.

Three swiveled her head. She spied the single bit of fabric—a sock—peeking from the drawer. It was black. I'd rubbed the thread all over it to change it. (I was the only one who saw why it was different.)

Five hissed. "This house is touched by the dark."

The nine-cluster's heads began to pulsate in alarm.

"Anomaly found," Two said.

Kory let out a strangled moan. Bailey sat rigid, his face ashen, and folded his hands on his lap. Tess inhaled shakily. She put her arm on Dom's shoulder, but Dom stared into the distance as if he wasn't here anymore.

Nine looked at me, her eyes expanding until they encompassed her forehead. "Mara, you don't seem surprised."

I kept my arms around my knees, the thread in my hand. "Space is dark."

They didn't like that.

Our eye-filters were programed for light. We looked at the space between mining sites and planets and we saw the brilliant white of the universe. I shouldn't have known what dark was.

But I had been to the House, where they pluck out your eyes and you bones and your skin and your neural pathways and remake you. And in between being remade (again and again and again), I saw beyond the light. I saw infinite blackness.

It was beautiful.

Nine strolled towards me. "This unit is no longer operational."

We were all going to the House.

Another unit would replace ours. There was always another.

Dom lunged. He still held the scissors, the keepsake he brought back from the House. He aimed for Bailey. The scissors sank through the back of Bailey's spine at the base of his skull. Bloodied metal tips poked from his windpipe. Bailey's muscles twitched and he slid to the floor.

Dom always loved Bailey the most.

Two sighed and pressed a radiant palm over Dom's face, picked him up, and carried him out the door. Two left Bailey's body where it lay. The machines to revive the body were all in the House.

Blood was darker than I remembered.

I held on tight to the thread.

Kory screamed and threw himself at Two. "Don't take him!"

Eight batted him aside, and he hit the wall hard enough to break his ribs. (I didn't flinch. I don't think I can, anymore.)

Tess grabbed the scissors. She stopped smiling as she ran towards Kory.

One moved for the first time. He expanded a stasis field around Tess, rendering her immobile. She dropped the scissors. They bounced across the floor and skittered to my feet.

"Mara," Kory gasped as Eight carried him towards the door. "Help me..."

I couldn't. (I'm sorry, Kory.) If I moved, if I dropped the thread, we were lost. (I'm sorry, Tess.)

I smiled up at Nine. I didn't look at Bailey.

"Space is dark," I said again. "I've seen it."

"We will fix that." Nine's face erased any particle expression. "The House will welcome you back."

I snatched her wrist as if I wanted to push her away. I couldn't. No one was that strong.

The tiny black thread wormed into Nine's translucent arm. She didn't notice. Her body was too full of light.

She pressed her palm over my face and the House came back in my mind, every imprinted memory.

IN THE HOUSE, you are unmade.

(—it hurts it hurts it hurts—)

The nine-clusters have no identical analogues for physical bodies, no way to feel pleasure or pain the way we do, but such things fascinate them.

They can record it in a million ways inside the House and translate it into data they can experience.

An Eight told me that when he extracted my nerves one at a time with his minute tools.

And in the House, even if you stab yourself in the brain with scissors, they can fix you and make you remember.

(Dom tried. He tried so many times, and so hard, but they remade his body every time.)

No one comes back from the House whole.

WHEN I FOUND the darkness, it was buried deep beneath rock and iron. A single thread, barely three centimeters long.

I told Dom. He stared at me, empty-eyed like he often was.

"I don't know what dark is," Dom said.

I grasped his gloves. "It can eat away the nine-clusters. All of them."

This was my theory. If they had made the universe light, they must fear the opposite. They could not live in blackness.

Once a ten-cycle, all the nine-clusters gathered and merged their heads into a great sphere of light. They shared everything, knowledge and particles and experience and delights they'd witnessed in the House.

One drop of darkness would infect them all.

"I can get it," I told Dom. "I just need your help."

He shut his eyes. It was light out even when you didn't look. "They'll take us back."

"I know," I said. (I didn't remember how to lie when I came back from the House.)

Bailey was deeper in the tunnel, his comm synched with ours. Dom could cover my workload while on shift, and Bailey could make sure no one else in the unit found out what I was doing.

"They'll take Bailey." Dom's voice cracked. "They'll take all of us."

"I know," I said. "But we'll blot them out and no one will ever be taken again."

We were made in darkness, before the nine-clusters came. We could live in it again. And we know how to make our own light.

Dom leaned his head against the wall, his helmet clicking against rock. All I heard was his breath over the comm.

"Dom?" I asked, when he didn't move.

"Bailey," he whispered. "I'm sorry."

"Don't," Bailey said. "I'll help, Mara. Sometimes I think I dream of the dark."

Dom fisted his hands.

"I can show you what the dark is like for real," I said. "The light will end."

It was what we all needed, even if we could never admit that.

Finally, Dom nodded.

We began to dig.

I LOOK OUT one of the House's many windows, at the nine-clusters watching. Specks of blackness float in their star-like heads.

The darkness is growing in the Five that leads Dom away again.

"It will be dark soon," I promise Dom, but his blank stare never changes.

The nine-clusters glow brighter, as if to hide it, but I know what darkness looks like.

(I will never forget.)

Soon, the darkness will expand and the stars will collapse. Nine by nine, they will become vacuums and take away all the light in the universe.

It will be beautiful.

UNDER WINE-BRIGHT SEAS

THE STRANGER FROM the sea had skin painted with maps, inked in all the colors known and unknown to the naked eye. When the guards brought him from the shore, he asked to speak with me.

My mother, the queen, attended a high ball in another land, as did my three sisters. I was alone. I invited the stranger into the library. His clothes were crisp and clean, the texture of moth wings, yet no amount of heat from the great hearth seemed to dry his hair.

"Why," I asked, "do you see me."

My mother and my tutors were not there to tell me the words were wrong; I had sent all the guards away.

I had always found trouble speaking aloud. Language

flowed and danced in my mind, and I could imagine exactly what I would say—
to anyone, to everyone—if the words did not tangle and turn to muddy ash on
my tongue, thick and confusing. To speak with the throat and mouth was like
spitting chips of broken stone, hard-edged and painful.

(But Mother would not accept this truth, even if I had means to explain,
to beg her to understand and let me use my fingers or a pen to speak with her.)

"I have heard you dreaming," said the stranger. "Spools of silk uncurled in
gentle currents, wrapped about skin re-stretched and fit to a different shape.
Gold and sapphire lions prowling deep, dropped from the tops of waves to white
sand and coral trees."

My breath whispered hot in my throat. All this I had dreamed; my longing
unfurled along his words like mirrored stones, piling about my feet.

He looked up, wet hair shading dream-swept eyes. "I have seen wonders
along the ocean beds, cities built of memory and coral, spires of shell and hope,
ramparts stretching across rifts that dip into the very center of this world's heart.
I have sailed in whale bones and the caress of ancient cephalopods. Sunsets
refracted into dizzying fractals and dipping into the velvet-soft sand of shallow
pools." He sighed and tipped his head back, letting damp locks like seaweed drip
across his shoulders. "It is home to me, honored princess."

"I am not a princess," I whispered, and he was the first I had ever told. "I am
a prince."

"I beg your forgiveness." He bowed low. "Honored prince."

I swallowed, for it was not a response expected. Not in words so easily
formed on his tongue.

"Why," I said, "did you come."

He smiled, his teeth like pearls and lips like polished agate. "I would like to
show you my home, honored prince. Your dreams call out, asking for escape, and
I would answer."

(My mother cared for me, I thought, but she had three daughters who
would succeed her on the throne before me. I did not want to rule. She would
tell me that did not excuse taking risks. If I could answer, I would say I feared
the dresses that hid me, constrained me, hurt me—I would say I feared this trap
of being called daughter and never son.)

I lifted him by his hands from where he knelt, his skin as warm as liquid
stone. Exultation winged high in my belly, for this stranger from the sea looked

at me no different. I ached to follow him and view these wonders, a world where he had been bred to accept at a word who one was.

I wanted to be free. "Show me."

HE WAITED PATIENT in the antechamber with a borrowed book of chanties I'd kept beneath my pillow. I bound my chest down (I had practiced often in a hidden passage behind the library, where a mirror thick with dust hung), slipped into suede trousers the tailor had crafted just for me (our secret, for she was kind), and left my feet bare. I wanted to feel the welcome chill of salt and current on my skin. I left my hair loose, wild and wind-tossed, a mane I dreamed seahorses had as they raced in herds below the waves.

I led the sea-stranger through unmapped halls, under granite and iron that made my mother's castle. We stepped out onto cliffs. The sky buffered the horizon, molten with sunset clouds, a fiery palette like my sister's paints. The sea stretched out wine-bright below us.

"Where is the ship?" I asked against the biting, barking glee of wind.

He pointed down at the dark-massed waters that frothed against stone and limpet shells. Waves flecked salt into gull nests and painted the rock with fleeting impressions that dried and dribbled into memory, written to the heartbeat of the sea.

I saw no ship.

MY MOTHER TAUGHT me the arts from a young age: to dance, to fight, to discourse with suave words (a skill I could not master), to sew, to read, to think, to play the harp (which I loved until I was told it was a proper women's instrument, and then I could not touch it without shame), to dream.

She often said, disappointment edged along her voice, "As fourth-born, daughter, you will likely marry for alliance, to strengthen our ties with other lands. You must learn how to manipulate and please, how to carry strong children, how to rule without being seen."

I lowered my head so she would not see tears. (Though I found men attractive, I did not think they would see me for who I was and take a husband, not a wife.)

My mother did not teach me to leap from cliffs or to swim.

"BELOW," SAID THE stranger.

"You washed ashore." That was what the guards had told me; that they found him adrift on the edge of the harbor, mapped with wondrous inks of places no one had ever seen.

He laughed, light and clear like a mountain spring that dances to the sea. "No, I told your people I swam ashore from the reef. Perhaps we misunderstood each other."

I shrugged. The wind prickled at my shoulders and hummed along my neck. The sea was turning towards winter, and soon there would be snow.

He offered his hand. "Will you dive with me, my prince? We will not strike the rocks." In his voice I heard his heart-truth—a melody twined with the ocean's timeless song.

Behind us, I heard the guards calling for me.

I took his hand, and we jumped.

MY ELDEST SISTER, who will be queen one day, was born without hearing. Mother taught her to speak with her hands, a beautiful language of gesture and the dance of fingers.

When I was young, I asked my sister clumsily if she would teach me. Mother said no, I could use my tongue and my sister could read lips. My sister said, "Yes."

(We sat together in closets stuffed with dresses she loved, and talked by the light of a glass-globed candle when I was supposed to be in bed.

"What do you want to do when you grow up?" my sister asked once.

"Sail away," I said with trembling hands.

"Will you come back and visit?" my eldest sister asked.)

AS WE FELL, the sea reached up with a great wave and cupped our bodies, carrying us away from the sword-keen rocks, and down, down, under the salt and cold.

I kept my mouth tight, sudden fright bubbling up with lung-air that I could not breathe here beneath the waves.

The map-skinned stranger gestured, and I recognized his words: "Breathe. It is safe."

Water pressed around, a second skin alive with music and light, even hidden from the sun. I shut my eyes.

His fingers brushed my palm, gentle.

When I looked at him again, he smiled, mouth open. Motes of light echoed in the water, curling down his throat. His chest moved as it had on land. "The seas always know their own," he said. "You are safe here, my prince."

I took a small breath—in water that was light as air, and then I breathed again and again and the sea laughed with delight and I looked at the traveler in wonder.

He grinned, and we swam down, where deep below on the pebbled floor I saw his ship.

It was built from coral and kelp, shaped like the great squid my second-eldest sister painted (for she too loved the sea). Its tentacles undulated in gentle patterns, woven from old rope speckled with seashells and silverware. The ship's great eye was a bubble of blown glass, where inside smaller squid navigated the ship. He told me their names, lucid syllables soft as ink and ineffable on the tongue.

The traveler and I boarded the ship, and we set off.

The ship carried us from the winter-flecked waters towards warm beaches and crystalline currents, and we slid from the quarterdeck and into shoals of rainbow fish and gentle sharks. I breathed the water, as did he, and felt neither exhaustion nor fear nor leaden moods as I did in the winters of my mother's castle.

Here, I felt alive.

"I, too, was once caught in words that did not fit my skin," he said as manta rays pirouetted about us, white and gray and blue and green like gems spinning in the ocean sun. "I was born far from here, within closed walls and pale, cold lights."

I held out a palm and a manta ray grazed a fin against it.

I had tried to flee on my own twice before. The first time was when my mother had paraded a series of portraits from far-off dukes and princes of different lands before me, and with them, letters of introduction. "Candidates for your hand in marriage," my mother said. I saw, beneath the letters, her own sketches of wedding plans and the dress I would be made to wear.

So I had taken one of the knight's chargers, coaxed with apples I'd often sneak into the stables, and rode out into a storm. I remembered the lightning and the sudden tree branch that fell and spooked the charger so he reared and threw me.

A broken leg and shattered wrist postponed my mother's intentions, but not her anger, not her unyielding disappointment.

"Why did you do something so foolish, my daughter?"

I flinched beneath her stare, and I could not keep my answer glazed in lies. "Escape."

"Escape?" My mother sounded baffled. "Why would you ever want to escape? You have everything you could want here."

I was watched more closely after that, and not allowed near the stables.

The second time I ran, I did so on ship, crouched in boxes below the hold. But two of the sailors, creeping below deck to kiss in secret, saw me and reported my hiding spot. The captain escorted me back to my mother's castle. I was not permitted near the docks without a guard to escort me.

"How did you escape?" I asked the sea-traveler, my fingers fluid and dancing with unexpected freedom a voice had never offered. (As when I loved the harp, my fingers were strong, decisive, true.)

His expression dimmed. "I thought the only escape was to drown."

I looked away. (Sometimes I had thought the same, when I looked out the windows at the frothing waves and knew the guards waited outside my door.)

He rested his forehead against a manta ray. "The seas thought different. They let me cry and thrash and question, and in the end, they showed me there are other ways. I learned to live, and I swam the world over, seeing wonders. I heard you dreaming, my prince, and I thought you were like I, and so I came."

MY SECOND-ELDEST SISTER painted the seas. Once, she painted me as I wanted to look: masculine, bearded, sitting in riding leathers astride a warhorse that reared before the sea. She gave me the painting in secret and said no one else had seen it. I put it by the mirror in the unknown passage.

I wrote *thank you* on my favorite handkerchief and tucked it in her paint box.

THE TRAVELER AND I swam among schools of silver fish who each formed a letter in a fish-alphabet and told us stories of the great Fish-Mother who composed the first operas at the beginning of the world before setting sail for the stars.

"Do you visit home?" I asked him.

He shook his head. "I have been a pirate and a merchant and a sailor and a bard," he said. "But I have never gone back. There is nothing left for me."

On the rocks and sand below, crabs danced to their own music, claws raised to wave in rhythm.

The traveler tilted his head. "Will you return to your old home?"

I looked away and did not answer.

MY THIRD SISTER practiced alchemy in the wizard towers, inventing new paints and fireworks and medicines. Before she left for the ball in another land, she showed me the letters written to her by her love, an astronomer who was building a telescope so vast it would be able to see to the other side of heaven.

"She has asked me to marry her," my sister said, happy tears in her eyes. "I said yes. I'm leaving after the ball."

"Glad," I said. I was, even if I would miss her.

My sister hugged me. "Of course we'll come back to see you all. You'll be here once in a while, won't you?"

WE DOVE DEEP, where curtained night unfolded to reveal underwater fires that sparked and rippled like the aurora borealis.

"What are the maps?" I asked as green-gold fire rippled past us and played across his skin, where in the deeps it glowed with ink unseen in the sun.

"Where I have traveled, and where I still wish to go," he said. "Who I was, who I hope to be. There are maps of memory, of friends, of lovers and of family. Of dreams I have had, of dreams I see. You are here now," and he pointed to a stretch of skin along his collarbone, where the painting my sister made was embossed in bioluminescent lines.

I liked it. I told him so.

He laughed, smiling bright as the bioluminescent jellyfish that twined in his hair and rode along his shoulders. "I'm glad."

I swallowed. "Do you always see me as a man? As a prince?"

"Yes," he said. "Unless you wish otherwise. I am many things, ever-changing. Today I am a man, like you. Sometimes I am a woman, or a person neither male nor female. Only tomorrow will I know what I am tomorrow."

I smiled, then, at the beauty and the heart-truth in those words, and how the sea-traveler accepted and affirmed who I was—as no one else save my sisters had dared, as I had not dared for so much of my life for fear I would be told it was wrong.

"How much more is there to see?" I asked.

"Beyond measure," he replied. "Will you explore them with me, my prince?"

My heart and mind soared with possibility, with yearning, with happiness.

"I want to visit my sisters." I traced their names along my arms. I would ask the squid to tattoo their names in iridescent ink, for I wanted maps like he had, rippling over skin. "They know who I am. They understand."

Perhaps, in time, I would also visit my mother, and tell her who I was, and had always been. Perhaps, in time, she would understand.

He smiled. "There is no need to choose between worlds, between life here or above. We can always return. Perhaps your sisters would like to visit us here as well?"

I smiled back as I swam beside him, and I said, "Yes."

OF BLESSED SERVITUDE

THE SACRIFICIAL CROSS threw a long shadow across the road at Bishop's dust-caked boots. He halted sharp at the sight of it. Wind hummed through wildseed bushes strung along the ditch, yellow buds as bright as radiation seals. Bishop clenched his jaw and looked along the shadow to the cross itself. It gleamed in the sunset, a steel post with a fused crossbeam, packed dirt the color of old blood at its base. And the cross wasn't empty.

Well, shit.

The offering was a pretty one—young, work-muscled body, a day's stubble scuffing his jaw. He'd been shackled naked to the cross, arms spread against the top beam. The dusty wind tugged unkempt hair across his eyes.

Bishop slapped the film of red dirt from his duster, his shoulders tense, and checked his knives from habit. He knew he shouldn't have traveled past Providence Circle. If chokevine hadn't overrun the only bridge across Unrepentant's Canyon, he'd never have come near this territory. He'd never have come within sight of the town of Blessed Servitude.

He hadn't been home in ten years.

"You should get off the road, stranger."

"Mighty courteous of you to warn a man," Bishop said. He shouldn't look at the man chained against steel, shouldn't stir up old memories. He never saved the offerings, and he didn't try.

"Even if you're fool enough to be out this late, you shouldn't die for it." The offering's chin remained pressed against his chest. Sweat streaked his skin, but Bishop saw no obvious signs of flogging or broken bones. "Move on, stranger."

The offering's voice was rough, a tremor in the words.

It reminded him of Prudence. Bishop's mouth twisted and he pushed back old, worn memories.

The offering turned his head and stared westward, hands tightening into fists. Bishop followed his gaze. Sun wouldn't drop for another quarter hour.

The Wire implant behind Bishop's ear hummed.

[Precision: thirteen City minutes until sunset.]

Bishop scowled. Didn't matter if it was thirteen or thirty minutes; as soon as the sun went down, he'd be watching another man die. He kept his back toward Blessed Servitude, a domed silhouette against the horizon. When he'd finished his hunt for illegally-sold tech in Charity Circle and started his return to the Wire Cities, he'd planned his route badly. No point regretting it now. He should just carry on, leave the offering on the cross, and not look back.

[Calculation: three point five two City days remaining until deactivation.]

As if Bishop didn't know. He shifted a step, his reinforced knee joints aching. The pain in his wired spine had spread to his hipbones, and hours ago he'd shut off the implant's alerts about rising blood toxin levels. The closest City lay three days away by cyclone train. That'd cut the time thin, but he'd needed to finish his mission before he returned to the protected central lands. He never broke a contract or went back on his word.

The offering kept staring westward.

The offering. Hell, the man has a name. Bishop stepped off the road, skirting the thickest patch of wildseed. After he read the offering's name, he'd leave. It was all he could do—remembering someone that'd be erased by the Deacons and forgotten by everyone else.

The offering's head snapped 'round as Bishop stepped close. All the red on his skin wasn't dust; much was old blood that might've been his. Bishop hooked the crude iron placard hung 'round the offering's neck with two fingers and broke the twine cord.

The offering's words ground between his teeth. "What're you doing?"

"You'll be dead come morning. What's it matter?"

The offering turned his head away, breathing quicker. Black and purple bruises scattered along his ribs and sides.

Bishop inspected the metal placard, a proper distraction. The longer he stayed, the harder it was to forget the feel of the cross against his back.

The identification showed the offering's star-sign—a good one, the summer constellations of Faith, Humility, and Tranquility. *Name: Grace Unto Order. Born: in the town of Blessed Servitude, Providence Circle.* And the enticement: *Strong of body and mind and has never lain with a woman.*

Bishop tossed the placard aside. "Virgins are pricey."

Grace stared past Bishop, silent.

Virginity had never made a difference to the sunspawn, however much the town deacons debated it. So long as each offering was healthy, virile, and not too damaged, he was acceptable. Only males were used; there were too few women born now, and when the demons didn't care which sex the offering was, there wasn't any reason to sacrifice a girl the territory needed as much as water.

[*Record: sacrifices observed: forty-seven. Mercy-kills: ten. Sunspawn destroyed: seventeen. Offerings saved: zero.*]

Bishop fished a lock pick from one vambrace. He knew better, but he couldn't stand the sight of the offering waiting chained and helpless any longer. "What'd you do to earn this?"

Grace's mouth twisted. "'Unsanctioned intimate behavior.'" His gaze flicked over the pick and his breath caught. "Don't."

Bishop cracked the locks. They'd deactivate anyway when the demon approached. Bishop wouldn't wait that long. Grace staggered as the cuffs clicked open, and Bishop caught his arm to steady him. "Was it worth it?"

Grace glared. "What does it matter to you?"

"It doesn't." Bishop had gotten real good at lying over the years. Not so good at forgetting.

Prudence had killed the deacon who'd found them. Snapped the deacon's neck four times. Deacons were bestowed with three lives, as was proper for a holy man, but even deacons were finite. It hadn't done any good, though, when Prudence's wife had walked in and found Bishop and Prudence together. Adulterers were hanged.

Others went to the cross. Prudence had begged for Bishop's life right up until the cable noose tightened 'round his neck.

[Update: ten minutes until sunset.]

"At a flat run," Bishop said, "you'll make the edge of Blessed Servitude's border three minutes before the sun goes down." And then the demon who'd claimed this territory would turn on the town when there wasn't an offering for it. "Shouldn't be any storms tonight, so you might get to the old reservoir in Gentleness Grove before dawn and find shelter."

A muscle ticked in Grace's jaw. "And if I don't run?"

Bishop let go of Grace's arm and traded the lock pick for his favorite blade, which he'd named Mercy. "I don't like killing a man who's crossed," he said, "but I prefer it to watching the demon eat you alive."

Grace straightened his spine. "So I run, or you'll kill me now? You're mighty generous with your options."

"Five seconds to choose," Bishop said. Mercy showed was mercy earned. One of the few doctrines he remembered since he'd fled to the Wire Cities. The rest of the Creeds he'd let burn into forgetfulness.

Grace lifted his chin. "I'm not leaving."

"Fine." Bishop swiped the blade at the man's throat.

Grace's arm shot up. His hand snared Bishop's metal wrist, stopping Mercy tight against his carotid artery. Steel indented skin. A fraction more pressure and Grace would bleed out. "Don't. *Please.* Just leave, stranger."

Bishop frowned. Damned if that kind of speed and strength and calm was normal, even on the fringes. Illegal tech, maybe? He ticked his Wire-senses into full resolution.

[Scan: tracery of witch-breath detected.]

Bishop lowered his blade, gut-kicked by the reading. Lord Almighty now forsaken. Prudence had been touched with witch-breath, too—he'd always been strong, resistant to hurt, healing faster than normal. It'd taken him half a day to die on the gallows.

Bishop stepped back, sudden fury dredged up like a sunstorm inside him. A demon would take a long, long time to devour an offering like Grace. There'd be no reprieve from the pain, not even in death. No one should fucking *submit* to that. "You ever see a tithe delivered?"

Grace glanced westward and shivered. "No."

"It'll be a lot easier if you let me kill you." Bishop flipped his dust mask up so his lower jaw and the side of his neck were visible: scars and wire alike. "Bishop, formerly of Blessed Servitude. I reckon I know of what I speak."

Grace's expression stiffened. "No one lives through the offering."

"True." Bishop snapped the mask back in place. "But some of us survive."

[Update: seven minutes until sunset.]

He hadn't the resources to kill another sunspawn. The demon that bound itself to a province protected the land from other Waste-born predators, for a tithe each quarter of the year. Deacons said the balance was immutable: no security without blood. Bishop didn't believe it. Not any longer.

Maybe in the beginning, after the Waste, it'd been necessary. But he'd seen the machines in the Wire Cities, untiring metal constructs that could rip a demon apart. A hundred war machines like that could wipe out the sunspawn. But when the demons never troubled the cities, and the provinces couldn't afford an army, there was no profit in upsetting old traditions.

Grace pressed his back against the cross, shaking his head. "I can't let you help me."

Bishop ground his teeth. "Whatever you did, you don't deserve this."

Grace spat. "Don't I? I loved someone I shouldn't." His throat worked. "We were going to barter transport to Pure Temperance and somewhere safe from there. But we got caught, and the deacons—they shot Humility when we tried to run." He blinked hard, his jaw tight. "I got him killed."

"So what good does letting the demon eat your soul do?"

Grace covered his face. "I have two younger brothers back home. The deacons will use them next if I don't…finish this. Lord's sake, Bishop, I can't let them die too."

The cross's shadow stretched farther along the dry, red ground.

Bishop slammed Mercy back into its sheath. Grace flinched, then folded his arms.

[Update: four minutes until sunset.]

Bishop let his breath out slowly. He needed repairs and the forgetfulness only the dustless bars in the Wire Cities provided. There he could black out his Wire implant and stop remembering the silence of those who went willing to the cross, or the screams and pleas for help from the offerings he mercy-killed— or worse, the ones he left alive until the demons started feeding and became vulnerable to his weapons.

He unslung his rifle and checked the chamber.

Grace's breath hissed between his teeth. "What—"

"I don't waste bullets on men," Bishop said. "This is for the shinies."

"You're mad." Grace swallowed. "Don't do this. The demon will kill you."

"I figured that a long time ago." Bishop swiped his thumb over the scope lens and tapped the barrel lightly against his forehead, a proper salute to battle.

Grace took a step forward. "Do you *want* to die?"

"No." Bishop rolled his shoulders. Even though he knew it'd be a different sunspawn this time, he didn't want to face it. He'd survived being crossed once. Second chances had disappeared with miracles generations ago. "Do you?"

Grace hesitated too long before he said, "I don't have a choice, do I?"

Bishop watched the last band of reddish light staining the horizon. In the distance, a ghost whippoorwill cooed with approaching dusk. He'd rather risk unknown roads littered with blacklight traps and sensor mines left over from the Waste than stay here until dark.

"I've hunted dozens of 'spawn," Bishop said. "Revenge, plain and simple. I hate the fucking shinies."

[Update: one minute until sunset.]

Bishop waited for the first glimpse of gold skin. "If you don't want to live, Grace, fine." He couldn't force that choice on anyone. He'd tried, in the beginning: spared two men from cross deaths. Afterward one threw himself into a patch of wildseed. The other jumped into Unrepentant's Canyon. "But if you plan to die, at least help me destroy the demon."

Grace shut his eyes. "How?" he whispered.

Bishop clenched his jaw. "Distract it until its skull softens and I'll finish it."

[Calculation: odds of success 25%]

Grace wrapped a hand 'round the open cuffs welded to the crossbeam, knuckles pale, then nodded once. "If you see Humility on the other side of Heaven's Door, will you tell him… Will you…?" He turned his face toward the horizon and his voice guttered into silence.

Bishop had no words of comfort.

[Update: zero point zero minutes until sunset.]

The demon walked from the sun, its eyes glowing like twin fires. It prowled east across the dusk-dimmed plain. Red winds buffeted its bipedal body and keened through the curled horns that swept from either side of its triangular head. Demons pierced their horns in individual patterns, so the wind became eerie music.

[Calculation: odds of survival 10%.]

Bishop *knew* that song. And this demon's eyes had an opaque light—a blind light.

Fuck.

Muscles tightened in his shoulders and neck.

Ten years ago, a sharp rock and a frantic blow and he'd put out those eyes. It shouldn't *be* here.

The sunspawn's abdominal barbels distended: pale yellow tactile organs like moist, slender tentacles. Bishop's gorge rose. He remembered the hot, slippery barbels and longer feeder tendrils closing 'round his groin and hips, pushing deeper into his ass and sucking at his skin until he screamed. He always remembered the rock, right enough. Fingers closed about the filed edges, slamming it repeatedly into the hypnotic eyes until they winked out like shattered bulbs.

Crippled demons didn't survive long. There were other predators that'd feed on the weak right as not. This one shouldn't have lived.

It would know him.

Bishop angled his steps sideways, his heartbeat too fast. He needed to get behind the demon for the headshot. The back of the skull was soft, more mesh-like skin than bone, so the neural tendrils could slip free when the demon fed.

Grace limped unsteadily towards the demon, fists clenched. His expression hadn't slackened into hypnotized stupor. The blind demon couldn't exert its will but that wouldn't make it kill Grace any quicker.

Bishop broke into a lope.

The demon whirled, tracking him sightlessly. "Bishop." The word rolled sibilant and musical through its horns, an impossible sound.

Bishop stopped, braced his legs, and took aim.

[Warning: sunsurge detected.]

"Grace!" Bishop shouted. "Sunsurge!"

The feathery-looking spines that layered the sunspawn's back bristled. Stored UV energy flared through each spine, a mantle of sunlight. Bishop activated both optical dampeners a microsecond too late. The negative images burned into his eyes as he twisted his head aside.

The demon's feet thudded along the dry ground as it sprinted at him. Bishop squeezed the secondary trigger. Recoil absorbed into the wires and plates in his shoulder. He knew he'd missed like he knew the burn of panic in his belly. It was his last round.

He sprinted sideways, momentarily blind. Talons scored his shoulder blade, cutting flesh cleaner than a Wire-surgeon's scalpels. Acid-sharp pain ripped through his back. He choked down a cry and tossed the rifle aside. Bishop drew Mercy and another blade, Peace, as his vision cleared. The demon scythed its talons at his gut again. Bishop deflected them with Peace. Shock rippled up his arm.

Bishop retreated farther from the cross. His mouth was drier than rusted steel. If Grace didn't divide the sunspawn's attention soon, neither of them had a heretic's chance.

The sunspawn crooned. It was Prudence's voice, stolen from Bishop's memory: "Help me, Bishop, help me." It wasn't real. Not this time.

Grace scooped up the rifle and took aim.

Bishop's pulse jacked. "Shit. Don't—"

Grace fired. The primary barrel was loaded with high-volt stun nets. The net looped 'round the sunspawn's horns and covered its face. One strand of netting zipped farther, wires targeting heat, and snared Bishop's wrist.

Searing pain wracked Bishop, shorting out his breath before he could scream. Dampeners absorbed the brunt of the energy before it electrocuted him. Not much he could do but endure. The pulse-shock made the sunspawn shriek. It dropped atop him. The horns deflected most of the surge. Best to aim for the trunk or legs.

[Calculation: odds of survival approaching 0%.]

Fuck, but didn't he know.

The sunspawn pinned his wrists with its talons. It repeated his name until the sound sickened him worse than the barbels writhing at his waist.

"Bishop...Bishop...Bishop..."

He twisted and levered his left arm against the demon's strength. Sweat sluiced into the hollow of his throat, bile hot in his mouth.

The sunspawn bent its neck, mandibles wide. At two handspans, they could slice through his spinal column in one snap. Except it wouldn't bite his head off until it finished eating his softer flesh.

Bishop's heart quavered. He stared into the blind eyes, the glazed scar-shells. Dust itched against his open wounds. He struggled to raise his modified arm, Mercy still gripped in his fist. Should have expected this—the nightmare he'd relived in sleep for ten years.

"Bishop."

One of the sunspawn's thin feeder tendrils wormed through his shirt and probed the wireweave vest. It found the seam and burrowed against his skin. Bishop thrashed, trying to pull himself free.

"Bishop...Bishop..."

There weren't any rocks this time.

Muscles bulged in his arm and shoulder; he lifted his wrist, vambrace protecting his tendons and metal bones from the talon edges. A little farther—

The tendril stroked the scar tissue along his hip. No, not this again. Bishop tried to gain purchases with his legs, lever himself free, but his boots slipped on the smooth ground. A tiny stinger injected paralytic toxin into his vein. Bishop hissed. The touch, like memory, incapacitated him quicker than a firemoth's venom. His Wire-modified body would neutralize the toxin, but not fast enough.

[*Status: internal systems at 34% percent efficiency. Caution: antitoxin reserves critical.*]

Wispy golden threads branched from the sunspawn's head—the neural tendrils that would feed on a victim's thoughts and emotional energy, then drink his soul.

Bishop twitched, helpless.

Grace's silhouette appeared over the sunspawn's flattening spines. "*I'm* your tithe, demon." He grabbed the sunspawn's sharp horns and wrenched its head 'round.

The antitoxin worked its way through Bishop's veins, hot as fire. Still too slow, too fucking *slow*.

Grace heaved against the demon's weight, pulling it toward him. "Do what you will, shiny. No one *else* will die because of me."

Mandibles clicked and the shredded net fell away. Grace's face contorted, his bloodied hands slipping on the horns. The sunspawn twisted toward Grace in one fluid movement, flung him to the ground, and crouched over him.

[Status: sunvenom neutralized. Internal systems stabilized.]

Bishop swore and freed his left arm with effort. He rolled sideways and came up in a squat as he struggled to tamp down panic. Grace had stopped fighting. He'd given Bishop exactly the distraction needed.

The sunspawn's skin rippled, releasing a hallucinogenic pheromone. Once it began feeding, it'd look like whatever the offering most wanted to love.

"Bishop!" Grace cried. "Bishop, oh Lord—kill it!"

Bishop heaved himself up. "Shut your eyes, Grace."

He drove Peace and Mercy into the demon's softened skull. Its shriek echoed across the territory, its talons flailing. Grace screamed.

[Record: seventeen sunspawn eradicated.]

Make it eighteen.

Bishop grunted and sliced the blades deeper, all his fury behind it—a vertical cut, then a horizontal one. He wrenched the blades free in a mist of pale blood. The demon arched back, spines fluttering as light dimmed and the golden skin burned darker red and into black.

It crumpled. Bishop pinned his knee against the demon's back. He sliced the undersides of the spines, peeling them away in thick patches. Blood stained his gloves. When the demon's back was stripped, he flipped the husk over and gutted its barbels.

[Record: eighteen sunspawn eradicated.]

Didn't he fucking know it.

He left the pieces where they lay. His lungs ached as he struggled to catch his breath. Purple-gray twilight deepened the shadows around him, the landscape still muted after the demon's death-cry.

[Warning: deacons' presence detected. Estimated time of arrival: five point two minutes.]

Well, shit. They must've gotten trigger reports that something had gone wrong. Bishop dragged himself upright and looked for Grace.

The man lay curled on the ground, cupping his face. Blood dripped between his fingers and pooled on the ground in a widening stain. Bishop knelt and pried Grace's lacerated hands away. Grace moaned. Talon marks raked Grace's face across his forehead and cheek, bone laid bare. The eye was lost. Witch-breath had saved him from having his skull split open; it'd keep infection from taking root, for now.

Grace pulled away and Bishop let him go.

[Estimate: offering's odds of survival 45%.]

Bishop silenced the Wire-sense updates. Only his thoughts mattered now. He held Mercy at his side.

"Don't." Blood and spit clogged Grace's words. "Please. D-don't leave me like this."

Bishop couldn't stop himself trembling. "I know people who can fix that, in the Wire Circles." If Grace wanted to survive. The Wire-techs couldn't fix a broken will. Just bodies.

Grace shook harder.

"No one'll know if you leave," Bishop said. Truth couldn't hide his desperation. "Your blood's still on the sunspawn's talons. They don't leave bodies, you know that. Your brothers won't suffer if you're dead in the eyes of man."

Bishop held out both hands, Mercy in one, the other empty. Lord help him, but he wanted to save Grace.

"You deserve to live." Bishop had been told he didn't. He'd believed it for a long time, too.

Grace shuddered, blood still dribbling down his jaw and throat.

But he took Bishop's hand. Not Mercy.

Bishop sheathed his blade. He hauled Grace to his feet, tugged off his shredded duster, and draped it over the Grace's shoulders. His back ached from the claw wounds. He found the last of his gauze-patches, ripped the package open, and adhered the sterilized cloth and wire mesh to Grace's face and cut hands. It'd hold until they found a surgeon.

"Thanks," Grace said, barely audible.

Bishop nodded. He scooped up his rifle and led Grace toward the road. They could reach the rails and one of the cyclone trains by dawn, ride to the sanctuary of the Wire Cities. Deacons wouldn't follow them.

The true challenge would come later, when the physical wounds had healed or scarred. Surviving the nightmares and memories and guilt.

"You're still wrong." Bishop's voice cracked, and he cleared his throat. "Don't repent for caring about someone. I reckon I can speak from experience there. I lost the one I loved to the gallows. His name was Prudence."

Grace tilted his head away, his blind side toward Bishop.

The ghost whippoorwill struck up its eerie tune again, joined by crickets and the far-off howl of a razor-wolf. But there wouldn't be a demon song this night.

Bishop took a breath. "I'll help you if I can." He stared at the road lit with the wildseed blossoms' faint yellow glow. Ten years and counting, he'd been walking it. He was too tired to keep going alone. "If you want."

Grace pulled the duster tighter about his chest. "Do I get five seconds to choose?"

"Take all the time you need."

He thought he saw Grace half-smile in the dark.

"Yes," Grace whispered at last. "I'd like that, Bishop."

Bishop blinked hard behind the mask, his throat tight, and with Grace at his side he walked away from the cross and Blessed Servitude.

TO THE KNIFE-COLD STARS

WHEN GRACE OPENS his newly crafted eye, the first thing he sees is wire. Thick cords of braided wire snaking like old veins up the walls. It's dim inside the surgical unit, but for all the black metal and mesh shelves, it *feels* clean, even in the heat. The air still has the unfamiliar taste of crude oil. Sweat sticks the borrowed clothes to his skin. He blinks, a flicker of pain in his head as the left eyelid slides down over cool metal buried in the socket.

He's awake and he's alive.

The anesthetic hasn't worn off. It's sluggish in his blood, an unpleasant burn at the back of his throat. It blurs the edges of his thoughts like too much bad wine. But it doesn't dull the deep-etched fear still unspooling through his gut. He survived the demon, survived his own execution. It's a hard thing to accept, even days later. He wants to touch the new eye, this machine part of his body, the forever-reminder of what happened. Doesn't dare, yet.

"Back with us, eh?" says a raspy voice muffled by a respirator.

Grace turns his head, slow and careful. He dimly recalls the wire-tech mumbling about whiplash in his neck and the horrific bruising along his ribs and back where the welts are still healing. "Guess so."

The tech is a small man dressed in heavy surgical leathers that are studded with metal sheeting. Old blood speckles the apron and gloves; the metal and rivets are spotless. Only the skin on his forehead is visible under thick embedded glasses and a breather covering nose and mouth. "Nearly died on us, you did. Venom went right into the blood."

The demon's venom. Grace doesn't reach to touch his face where the sunspawn's claws took out his eye and split flesh to bone. He doesn't look down, either. A new shirt and worn jeans cover whatever scars the demon left on his belly and thighs. He shivers in the heat. He doesn't know if he can ever look at himself again; what will Humility think—

Humility.

Grace trembles harder. Humility will never see him again.

Don't think. Harder a self-command than it should be. *Don't go back there.*

"He's tough."

The second voice jerks Grace's attention back to where he is. He turns his head again, wincing. He craves more anesthetic, and hates that he wants it. Numbness is just another way to hide.

Bishop stands near the narrow doorway, leaning against corded wire that bunches like supports along the wall. He's tall, broad-shouldered, dressed in travel-worn leathers with a breather mask over the lower part of his face. His mechanical eyes gleam dull green in the surgical bay's weak florescent glow.

Bishop—the man who saved his life. Bishop brought him here to this city, to the medical bay tucked somewhere in one of the vast districts that has no name Grace can recall. Grace's throat tightens. He ought to say something in greeting, or acknowledgement. All words feel hollow.

Bishop looks at Grace, unblinking, though he speaks to the tech. "Appreciate your help, Dee," Bishop says. "Your skill's always sharp."

"I do my best." The tech bobs his head. "Better if some of us live."

Grace flinches. He braces his hands on the metal gurney, gripping the edge until he can't feel the tips of his fingers. He should be dead—worse, even. Should, and isn't.

Bishop straightens. "Grace, we need to go."

Grace shuts his eyes—the new optic sensor makes details too sharp, too real. He shoves himself to his feet. The world tilts.

Bishop's shoulder is under his arm before he falls. He can't recall if he walked into the Wire City or if he was carried. Not that he'll ask. *Forgive us our sins, oh Lord, forgive us—keep us safe from the Sun, from the Dark, and from our own—our own...*

He can't remember the rest of the litany, so he leans on Bishop and swallows down the shame of needing such help even to stand. His wrists carry the memory-weight of the heavy manacles that held him bound to the cross.

"Sorry about your boy," Bishop says to Dee in an undertone as he pivots towards the door. "Heard Jackob mention that."

Dee's throat clicks. "We can't save them all."

Grace tries not to flinch again. *God doesn't save the ones He should.* "How'd he die?" Grace asks, hoping that Dee's boy wasn't crossed and left as tribute to the demons that walk out from the sun.

"He didn't," Bishop says.

Outside, the air is heat-dried and dirtier. Grace slits one eye—his old one, his real one. He faces a wide, paved street flanked by banks of windowless buildings, worn things built of metal and stone. They're so big, Grace can't see the rooftops. He can't see the sky through the atmosphere dome above the city, or the stars beyond. The noise is the worst of it, though, the hum of great engines, machines grinding. The air vibrates against his teeth as a vehicle big as one of the faithful's houses back home rumbles past. Grace stumbles backwards. A gust of hot air from a passing carriage stings his face.

He can *feel* the space around him, despite the compact grid-like structure of the buildings. His home, Blessed Servitude, was a large town. But he was never lost inside the walls. Here, Grace has no reference points. It's a cavernous space that his senses are adrift in. Panic edges into him, sideways like it always does.

He needs to get away from here, but when last he tried to run, he was caught.

Bishop nudges him. Grace stumbles along, down a narrow alley.

Grace braces his legs and breathes deep. The city is too big to focus on, its massive presence overwhelming his senses. He needs something smaller, something saner. "What happened to the boy?" he asks, jaw gritted so his voice doesn't break.

Bishop shrugs. "The cityheart took him."

Grace grinds his teeth. "He's alive?"

Bishop's arm is tense. "Yeah, more's the pity. The cityheart takes easy targets. Kids, mostly. They're somewhere down inside, but the fumes kill them eventually."

Grace presses his spine against the alley wall. The metal is warm like sunbaked earth. He stares at Bishop, not hiding his anger. It's ingrained like fear into his heart. "No one does anything?"

Bishop's tone is flat. "There's nothing we can do."

"Nothing?" Grace should drop it. He's always been like this—clinging to the questions he shouldn't ask. Wanting what he can't have.

Bishop rubs his temple above the cluster of thin black-cased wires that trail from the corner of his eye down under his mask. "The cityheart shorts out Wired tech. Anyone dependent on it who goes down dies sure as not."

Grace digs his fingertips against the wall, the heat winding up his arms. "You're telling me everyone's going to leave the boy to die."

"Don't be so surprised," Bishop says. "No one intervenes in the offerings, either."

"Except you."

Bishop was once an offering and he escaped alive. Then he returned to Blessed Servitude, years later, faced down a demon and killed it to save a stranger. Grace doesn't know where that kind of strength comes from.

"I can't go into the cityheart." Bishop sighs. "Neither can Dee."

"Then let me," Grace says, before he turns coward.

Bishop shakes his head. "You'd—"

"Die?" Grace sets his jaw. "We'd not lose much, would we?"

Bishop is silent.

Grace turns his face away. He didn't mean it as a jab. He's shaking and can't make his body stop.

He was tried in Blessed Servitude and condemned to death; he was shackled to a steel cross as an offering for the demon. He deserved to die, and he was so fucking afraid of it. But then Bishop appeared from the wastelands, freed him and challenged the demon for Grace's sake. Grace fought at Bishop's side, unwilling to see someone else die because of him.

You deserve to live, Bishop told him when the fight was over, when Grace lay wounded, poisoned. Bishop offered him a choice between survival and mercy-killing. Grace knew he should have taken the knife, not Bishop's outstretched hand.

He still isn't sure he can believe Bishop's words. It's because of him Humility is dead.

"You gave me a chance," Grace says. He can't exist like this: breathing and walking and possessing space, all the while knowing that someone who aided him has lost family and no one else will *help.* "Dee should have that."

"I already paid Dee with credit," Bishop says. "You owe him nothing."

Grace jerks his head side to side and points at his implanted eye. Fuck the pain. "You paid him for *parts.*"

Bishop grunts. "He stitched you up. It's his job."

"He saved my life." Grace can't meet Bishop's gaze again, or look up. There will be only steel and the glow of the dome above. He stares past Bishop at the seemingly endless line of flat doors set in the alley wall. "So did you."

Bishop is quiet again.

Grace swallows hard. "I need to make that matter, Bishop."

"It already does."

Grace concentrates on his breath. *Stay steady.* "I know." He doesn't believe it, and he hopes Bishop can't see that. "But if I can help that boy, I have to try."

Like his little brothers he left behind, like his friends and neighbors, his weakness will punish them more than it will ever hurt him. And he cannot endure that again.

Bishop turns his back on Grace. "If that's what you want, I'll show you where the access hatch is." His voice is tired. "You know you'll be on your own."

"I know," Grace says, and this time it's true.

"His name's Das," Bishop says.

The two of them stand by an open grate in a shallow circular indent between a crisscross of alleys. A few city workers in rubberized contamination suits watch. Musty air gusts up from the tunnel opening. Grace wonders how many willing suicides go down there.

"He was taken earlier this day. He won't have more than a few hours left."

"Understood," Grace says.

Bishop clasps his arm. Grace meets Bishop's eyes with effort.

"Good luck," Bishop says, quiet.

Grace nods, then lowers himself into the access hatch, down the short ladder to the dark tunnel below.

The access tunnel winds in a slow spiral downward. The first hundred feet are a sharp incline looping deep into the earth. It gentles out into an easy slope for the rest of the way. Dim red emergency lights line the tunnel and all he can think of is the blood spreading along the dusty ground.

Grace keeps a hand on the wall for balance as he walks. He's never liked enclosed spaces, but in the tunnel, he can't feel the city anymore. The relief is short-lived.

He steps into the huge, cavernous room that holds the cityheart and stops. The tunnel ends on a narrow platform that juts out over an abyss.

The cityheart is as big as a building, a cylindrical structure covered in riveted metal plates, rising from the center darkness. A giant fan turns methodically halfway up the bulk, stirring the thick, heavy air. Wire-mesh catwalks circle it, bare of railings. Huge throngs of corded, braided wires twist and loop away from the tower to jut out into the walls. Red emergency lights dip down, down along the cylinder's side, until it's too far to see anything more than a faint glow, and then blackness.

The machine, the cityheart, thrums with a giant, slow pulse. Each beat fills the air and reverberates in Grace's teeth.

He's never seen anything so massive and so *alive*.

His new eye goes dark. Grace starts, retreating into the tunnel again. Where can he run except back to the surface in defeat? No. Not like that. He makes himself stop. He squints, forced to turn his head as he searches the huge chamber.

There, lying in a small heap on the catwalk near the cityheart, is a child. Das? Grace spots no other bodies, but he doesn't look too deep.

[[Welcome.]]

The voice is not so much words as a great, intense *weight* that buries itself into his awareness. Yet he understands it the way he comprehends spoken language.

Grace sucks in a breath, unnerved. Wires of copper, steel, and a dark material he doesn't recognize peel away from the sides of the tunnel and gesture in a sweeping motion towards the great cylinder.

[[We get few visitors any longer,]] the cityheart says. [[Have you come for a purpose?]]

Unsteady, Grace takes a step forward. Wires turn like slender, delicate snakes, unwinding from the walls of the cityheart and the catwalks. They caress his back and shoulders. Grace startles and jerks away. He stumbles on the catwalk, his steps a shallow echo in the chamber.

[[You may stay. It is warm here and you will forget the world above.]]

Easy death, is what Grace hears, and he dares not answer. Bishop risked too much to save him once. But when he frees Das, Grace doesn't know what awaits him above. Bishop is lucky. Bishop knows his purpose, knows himself, knows what he wants.

Grace is lost.

"I can't." Grace points at the boy. "I came here for Das."

[[What awaits you upon return?]] The cityheart's voice is a deep purr. The wires creep forward again. [[Who will stay to see you rise? Is there truly anyone who will mourn your passing?]]

Grace flinches away. "Doesn't matter. Give me Das."

[[No. A child's mind is open and full of wonder, and wonder is a taste we have always craved. It is sweet and fresh, fleeting and delicate.]]

Grace swallows down bile. The cityheart's intense, vast hunger for the *new* presses against him. It craves things it has never seen or felt or imagined. It is…bored.

"We can make a deal." Grace edges along the catwalk; it's as wide as he is tall, but feels too narrow, and a misstep will plummet him into the abyss. "I give you something and you give me the boy."

Das is curled in a ball twenty paces away. Grace can't see if the boy is alive. *Lord, be kind. He doesn't deserve to die alone down here.*

[[And what could you offer, jaded as you are?]]

Grace shakes his head. If it only wanted a body, well, he was given to a demon already. The sunspawn's whispers still trill in the edge of his thoughts; recreated voices of the dead urging him to lie down and struggle no more. Does Bishop fight these thoughts every day? How does he *live*?

Don't think about it. It will paralyze him faster than firemoth venom. He was stung once as a boy, and only the curse of witch-breath kept him from dying in agony as his insides liquefied. That was the first time he met Humility—the older boy found him convulsing in the fields and carried him back to the safety of the town. Grace adored him and their friendship grew over the years until he loved Humility so fiercely it hurt.

"What haven't you seen before?" Grace asks, his voice hoarse.

[[That is an impossible question. You might be clever, old as you are.]]

Old? Grace almost laughs in surprise. He's not even twenty.

"I'm not from this city," Grace continues. "I've seen things no child could imagine."

There—Das shivers. The white gleam of an eye, red-rimmed with tears, peeks from over the boy's elbow where his arm is curled around his face.

The cityheart sounds curious now. [[What do you propose?]]

Grace takes a slow breath. One more step and he can reach down and scoop the child up. "Let me take him back. I'll give you—"

Wires snap away from the cylinder's walls and loop around Grace's wrists quicker than a blink. They pull his arms wide and pin him against the dully rumbling heart shell. Like he is being bound to the cross again. Grace chokes on a scream and throws his weight against the bonds in panic. Wire slices into skin. Blood wets his sleeve cuffs and drips to the steel floor.

[[Why should you give when we can take all?]] the cityheart murmurs, an honest question.

A gleaming needle-pointed wire hovers before his good eye.

Grace freezes. He can't abide the dark. When the demon wound its neural tendrils into his mouth and one ear, it easily found his fears pushed to the forefront of his mind. The dark, loss of sight, being left alone.

[[You are wise not to struggle. You will never remember what it is you lost.]]

The witch-breath in his blood—the heresy he was born with—strengthens his muscles and bones, makes him tougher, harder to kill. The Deacons found it easier to shoot Humility than him.

He strains and lifts one hand until his blood-slicked palm is between the wire and his face. Wire cuts deeper along the back of his wrist. The pain is not unbearable yet, and he welcomes it as distraction from the ache in his gut. "You're wrong," Grace says. "There is one thing you can never take."

[[Is there?]]

"I've seen the stars," Grace says. "But only with this eye. If you take that, you'll never know what they are."

The wire dips languidly and presses under his jawbone. With any pressure, it will pierce his throat, his tongue, and drive into his brain.

[[There are other ways.]]

"If you kill me," Grace says, "you'll never see."

[[And why is that?]]

"I told you. I'm not from your city. I'm not *like* the others. Can't you sense what's in my blood?" Bishop's scanners detected it easily enough. Surely a city can feel it too. "The witchery?"

The humming tone shifts a note. [[Others have given memories of stars. Lights in the night. Dim, warm, dull. There is nothing left of interest in them.]]

Grace's breath comes short, startled. "Those aren't stars." The ones he knows are cold and bright, spread vast across the dark sky. "You've only taken children from *this* city, haven't you?" The needle punctures skin, and blood trickles soft down his throat. "How many have been outside the walls or the dome? Any of them?"

A longer pause.

Grace fights for breath. "Let me leave with Das safe, and I will give you memories of the stars."

[[What leverage do you believe you have?]]

"Do you think you'll ever find another like me who comes down willingly?" Grace says. "You won't ever know what I've seen."

[[Perhaps.]]

Grace's muscles ache and the inexorable pull of the wires drag his arm back until he is pinned against hot, rusted metal. The needle flicks away from his chin and lightly touches the edge of his tear duct.

The same terror he couldn't fight when he saw the demon, its golden eyes alight in the sunset, burgeons in his chest once more. His knees give out. Wire holds him up, thicker cords sliding beneath his elbows and arms so the thinner wires don't slice through his wrists.

He shouldn't be afraid. The cityheart isn't a demon. It can't devour his soul. He can see Humility again—except if the cityheart gobbles his memory before it kills him, how will he remember who he loves, who he's looking for in Heaven?

Grace holds tight to the image of Humility's face: dark eyes and crooked smile, his jawline and the errand wisp of beard that always grew too fast to be kept shaved smooth. The wheat-shaped burn scar on his cheek and the way the left eyebrow was higher than the right. The confidence with which he walked; the calm he nurtured in his spirit so he would never be angry; the way his face lit up when he looked back at Grace.

"You can't have him," Grace snarls. "I already survived a demon digging though my head. You'll get nothing through force." It's a bluff. The sunspawn saw everything; the cityheart can do the same. "You kill me and you get nothing but a boy who's never seen the stars like I have."

The needle withdraws from the corner of his eye, and he feels it prick the base of his neck instead.

Grace grunts in surprise.

[[Very well.]]

Grace's voice catches. "How do I know you'll keep your word?"

[[Perhaps you will come back, when you understand how easy it is to forget.]] The cityheart almost seems amused. [[Remember the stars for us, and you and the child may go.]]

Sharp, violent pain slices into the back of his neck. The vast hunger of the machine hovers at the edge of his thoughts, waiting.

Das's life depends on him.

Trembling, Grace shuts his eye and remembers.

GRACE SAT ON the roof of the old abandoned silo. It was flat, patched once or twice before it was left to the chokevine and creeping spider grass. The silo was the only tall structure in the Grove, and from this height, away from the light pollution inside Blessed Servitude, the huge expanse of the sky spread above them.

The stars were cold and bright, knife tips gleaming against black satin. No moon tonight to outshine them. Grace gazed up, unblinking, calmed by the open space he knew so well. Stars, he'd heard once, were distant suns in other worlds too far away to imagine. And the light that reached the sky came from the dying suns, corpse candles left by the ancient dead. It was just another story. Demons came from the sun, dull and hot as it faded. But demons didn't live in the stars. The stars were alive and bright, cold and beautiful.

Humility leaned his head on Grace's shoulder. "What do you think about when you look at the sky?" he asked.

Everyone was forbidden to be out past dark. Too many dangers lurked in the sand and along the roads. But Grace felt safe here, even with chokevine and ghost whippoorwill nests less than two meters below his feet on the side of the silo.

"I wonder what it'd be like to visit the stars," Grace said. "Just you and me."

Humility laughed. "How'd we get there?"

"We could walk," Grace said, smiling. "We could walk away from here, step onto the edge of the sky where it touches the horizon, and keep going till we touch the first star."

He didn't say, *We'd be safe and no one could take you away.*

He didn't say, *We'd never have to hide.*

He didn't say, *We'd never have to be afraid again.*

For a moment, Humility was quiet. Then he squeezed Grace's hand tight. "Maybe one day we will."

FASTER NOW, GRACE recalled the moments he saw the stars clearest:

The nights he snuck away with Humility, hiding their time together with help from Humility's sister, who operated the delivery gates on the north wall.

The time he climbed up the Deacon's Clocktower and caught a glimpse of the sky during the Night of Reflection, when all lights were shut off.

That final night, when he and Humility gathered what belongings they could carry and snuck from Blessed Servitude, intent on stealing aboard a train to Pure Temperance where they would be unknown and free. They never saw the Deacons follow them. Grace kissed Humility in excitement as they neared the train depot. They were so close. Above them, the stars were bright, beacons of hope.

The Deacons came. Grace pushed Humility ahead of him as they ran. Gunfire chattered and something struck him in the back, flinging him to the ground. He didn't feel the pain at first. Not until he saw Humility fall, and saw the blood dark under the starlight.

The Deacons fished the bullet out of Grace's side, kept him alive, and brought him back to Blessed Servitude to pay for the crime of wanting to live with the one he loved. He was found guilty of forsaking his duty to Blessed Servitude and of unsanctioned intimate behavior. His sentence: he was to be an offering, staked to the cross at the edge of the road, and left for the demon that dwelled there. His death, his damnation, would be tribute to the demon and would ensure Blessed Servitude remained untroubled for another season.

And the final memory, the night Bishop killed the demon to save him and half-dragged, half-carried Grace to the Wire City. That one, brief glimpse was all

Grace remembered before sunspawn venom and pain felled him unconscious: a splash of brightening sky and three stars sharp and knife-bright above the horizon. He could touch them, if he reached—

And then nothing.

THE WIRES RELEASE his arms. Grace pitches forward onto hands and knees and vomits. The air is hot, so close it presses like cloth against his nose and mouth. Grace fumbles at the back of his neck in search of the needle. It's gone.

The cityheart sighs, a deep, reverberating wave of pressure more than sound.

Grace wants to fold his arms over his head and scream. He knows the cityheart took something, but all he is left with is a word.

Stars.

He talked with Humility about it, and yet, all he remembers is lying on the flat silo roof and staring at the black, empty sky. The sky has always been dark at night. Hasn't it?

[[The child is yours. Go, before you tempt us with what else you have seen.]]

Grace chokes down a sob. He doesn't know for what he grieves—there are spots of emptiness where something was taken. He crawls along the catwalk, his one eye half-closed, scarcely able to see in the dim red light.

"Das." Grace curls his fingers around the boy's thin arm. "We're going back up."

IT'S A LONG climb.

Grace is soaked in sweat, muscles trembling by the time he sees the change in light from the open access hatch. Das has crawled slowly ahead of him; Grace carried him when he could find the strength, but it isn't enough to last all the way.

"Grace?" Bishop's voice echoes in the tunnel.

"We're here," Grace manages. "Help him out."

Grace heaves Das up. The boy's foot kicks his face, jarring the dead metal eye. He grunts and turns his head. He's staring down the long, curving passage a step behind him. The incline would let him slide if he let go the iron rungs.

Just slide, down and down until he falls into infinite dark. There might be others down there, like Das; perhaps he might buy them free. If he let the cityheart take everything, perhaps it wouldn't hurt any longer.

"Grace."

Bishop's voice.

Slowly, Grace turns his face up.

Bishop leans down, hand extended. Again. *I'll help you, if I can,* Bishop told him. *If you want.*

Grace wants to know how Bishop can go on. How he can find any will to live when everything has been lost to him.

With a faint buzz and click, the wire eye flicks on again. Grace starts, almost losing his grip. His sight blurs a moment; his left eye is sharper, clearer with the metal and glass optic processing the thick air and smog. He can see farther.

He can see.

Humility's voice is clearer than the demon-song, and for a moment, it doesn't hurt so much to remember his voice. Grace focuses on that.

I wonder what it'd be like to visit the stars. Just you and me.

How'd we get there?

We could walk.

Maybe one day we will.

Grace takes Bishop's hand and lets Bishop help him up. The hatch clangs shut behind him.

Dee gathers Das up, incoherent words spilling between father and son.

A flicker of relief pushes back the hot, suffocating weight in Grace's chest. He almost smiles. It tugs at the scar along the corner of his mouth.

Bishop nods to him. "Glad you made it back."

Grace bows his head. Bishop has faith. In what, Grace doesn't know. But perhaps that's what lets him go on. Bishop believes Grace deserves a chance to live and find a purpose.

For just a moment, as he watches Dee lead Das back home, Grace can almost believe it. And one day, perhaps, he can find that first step and climb the black sky.

There is one thing he wants first, sharp and fierce.

"Bishop," Grace asks, all but a whisper. "Can you show me the stars?"

"They're hard to see in the city light," Bishop says quietly.

Grace's body sags. He leans on his thighs and fights down the yawning grief like a pit in his chest, opening wider.

Bishop lays a hand on his shoulder to steady him. "But I know a place that might work."

GRACE SCARCELY RECOGNIZES the journey through the city. Fever claws at his blood. He refuses rest; he needs this first. He needs to know what the stars are like.

There is another climb, and he is aware of Bishop supporting him as they ascend the final steps and emerge from a tower onto a roof, flat and open, lined with gravel. The dome is a thin membrane here, nearly translucent, tinted red-orange from the city lights.

"Look up," Bishop says.

Grace tilts his head back. With his good eye, he can see nothing but the faint glow of light pollution. But with his new eye, wired like Bishop's, he sees the dark sky beyond. He focuses, slowly, accustoming his senses to the new perception.

There, in the distance, is a flicker of white light, tiny and almost lost in the blackness.

The heat lessens in his skin. He can breathe easier. He wants to keep breathing, to keep watching the sky.

The star gleams like a knife, bright and cold.

Grace smiles. "It's beautiful."

"It is," Bishop says. "It is."

FINDING HOME

THE REALITY I was born in ceased to exist when I was three years old. So Mama and I moved to a different reality.

We moved a lot, actually.

"We can't stay more than a few years," Mama would say as she unzipped the fabric of the space-time continuum and scanned the flickering images inside.

There were so many, I got motion sick if I looked too long.

But Mama always knew which one to pick. She'd catch a corner of a shimmering image, brightly colored like rainbow sprinkles, then take my hand and pull us both through.

I MET AMAND in a coffee shop on a rainy day two years and nine months after my mother and I moved to this reality. The café menu offered various espressos and lattes, the Germanized English happily familiar. I thanked the barista and looked for a seat.

That first glimpse: Amand sat in a corner, reading *Die Liebe der Bienen*, a bestseller literary graphic novel that had a different ending for everyone who read it.

Grayish afternoon light highlighted his black curly hair and dark skin, and his glasses adjusted to the light flow, the rims bright blue. Broad shoulders were highlighted under the fashionable sweater he wore, navy blue with the New Chicago Physics (the local soccer team) logo emblazoned on the chest.

He flipped the last page and sighed, dark eyes half-closed in contentment.

He caught me staring at him. I was used to that by now. Odd looks when I couldn't lose my accent or maybe I had a neon sign over my head that read DOESN'T BELONG.

"What ending did you get?" I asked.

He grinned. "Dominik and Erik reconcile, and then Erik proposes and he accepts and they live well to their days' end. It's what I hoped for."

I smiled back. "That's the ending I got, too. Well. Dominik proposed, when I read it."

"Amand," he said, offering his hand.

"Joseph," I replied. We shook. My heartbeat hadn't slowed, though I had yet to sip my cappuccino. "Can I join you?"

He nodded at the plush armchair next to him. "I would like this."

EACH NEW REALITY was different.

Sometimes there'd be buildings in the sky, sometimes technology was less advanced, and sometimes there wasn't anybody around at all.

(Mama picked those empty realities once in a while, but we only stayed for a few days.)

Mama had a talent for explaining who we were to the people in each reality: why we had weird clothes and accents, why our skin was the color it was, sometimes why I was a boy (if they hadn't been invented yet), sometimes why she was a girl, and sometimes why we had genders at all.

She had a gift. She knew which realities were unsafe. She could make people like us, or at least not hate us. She was extraordinary but she never drew attention. Mama designed new cover stories depending on where we ended up.

Mama never had trouble understanding the language. She'd teach me, but I didn't have her skill. It got harder as I got older, too, always being the weird kid.

"Don't make friends you can't let go of, Joseph," Mama always said. "We can't stay long."

"Why not?" I asked angrily when I was ten. I'd just met Mohamed who lived down the street, and he was going to let me drive his custom-built race car.

"Because our atoms don't belong here," Mama said, "and eventually we'll crumble into little pieces if we stay too long. Reality-bending is tricky."

So I didn't have many friends. I knew people, lots of people, but they were a sea of changing faces and bodies and names (or sometimes numbers).

I tried not to let Mama know I was lonely. We had to survive. She was trying to make a good life for us.

And she'd promised that one day we'd find Daddy again.

AMAND AND I spent the next two months inseparable. He showed me the old baroque district, full of niche clubs and piano halls and statues of composers and artists and philosophers. We toured the Babylon Gardens, reconstructed and raised half a mile into the sky.

I was nineteen. I'd been in and out of so many schools I wasn't sure what level my education qualified. Amand had just finished college. He was applying for jobs in the energy reconstruction projects, striving for cleaner power and more of it. New Chicago was prospering, but so much of the continent was still ravaged from the Fallout War, reconstruction and rehabilitation for the country was slow.

Amand wanted to help change that, the determination clear in every fluid movement, in the line of his jaw, in the brightness of his eyes. I couldn't keep my eyes off him when we were together. I didn't want to.

I didn't want to fall in love. Or maybe I did. It was so hard to tell.

"YOU'RE MOODY TODAY, mein Herz," Amand said, rubbing his thumb over my knuckles. We held hands and leaned on the railing atop the new hydroelectric dam. It wasn't technically open to tourists yet, but he'd snuck in before—his aunt was the foreman and the workers liked him—and told me this was the most stunning view of the sunrise you could see outside of the tower complexes. "What is wrong?"

I shrugged. "I have to move soon."

God, I'd told him when we first went out that I wasn't going to be in town for more than a few months. It was my mother's work schedule, I'd explained, and I accompanied her because she had health concerns. (The lies had been harder than ever before, stuck like congealed oatmeal in my throat.)

I was so tired of moving. But what choice did we have? Move, or cease to exist.

"But you don't want to," Amand said slowly.

I gazed down at the polished curve of the dam. It was a long way down, even with the safety nets strung at intervals across the face. "Nein," I whispered. "I like it here."

Amand slung an arm over my shoulders. "There is no one else who could take care of her while she travels?"

Mom didn't need my help. I needed hers. How long would it continue? Until she died from an accident or old age? Since I didn't know how to unzip the space-time continuum, I'd be stuck facing my inevitable death somewhere that wasn't home. Alone.

The depressive realization hit like I'd swallowed an old, bitter espresso shot. Dizziness swamped my head and I pushed away from the railing before I lost my balance or puked. Amand's arm steadied me.

The nippy wind tousled his hair and snaked down my collar. It was still dark, our only illumination the safety lights down the curvature of the dam.

"I can't leave her," I said. The first red bars of dawn peeked over the horizon, backlighting the uneven cityscape's profile.

Amand's expression was unreadable. "Well," he said at length, "we can always write or vidchat, and you can visit again, ja?"

But I couldn't, so I only nodded. I rubbed my face. The wind had made my eyes water.

He was right, though. The sunrise view from the dam was amazing.

MY SECOND FAVORITE reality was where I met Dr. Amelia D'Cruz. Mom dated her briefly while we integrated into the tropical cities spread like a beaded bracelet around the equator.

I was six, and Mom had promised me she would look for a doctor who could perform gender reassignment surgery for me. It took her slightly longer not to call me Josephine, but only a little.

Dr. Amelia smelled like bubblegum and cinnamon, and she always smiled so bright that I wanted to smile back.

I told Mom I didn't want to leave when, almost three years to the day—my surgery two years past—we packed our bags and said goodbyes.

I clung to Dr. Amelia, who rubbed my back and kept saying, "It's okay, Joseph. You'll find a place you belong one day. You'll find your home. I promise."

I didn't believe her, and I didn't speak to Mom for days after we stepped into a new reality and started over yet again.

"IT'S TIME TO go, Joseph," Mom said. We sat eating noodles and watching the news that same evening. "We have to leave tomorrow."

I set my bowl down, my stomach heavy. How had time gone by so fast? I thought I had another week left with Amand.

"Are you sure?" I asked.

She fiddled with her chopsticks. Her gaze remained on the screen. "We've been here too long. There's nothing for us."

"What?" That wasn't her usual explanation. She would tell me of the destabilization in her bones, the static buzz in her sinuses that told her we were getting close.

"He's not here," she said.

Dad had disappeared before I was old enough to remember. She said we'd find him and we'd discover a reality that we could live in as a family.

We'd wasted sixteen years. I didn't know what a home was, what stability was like.

All I could think of was Amand's face, his quirky smile and stuttering laugh. The way his hands felt in my hair and on my skin. How he always arrived on time. Even when his temper flared and we got into arguments about politics or history, he'd kiss me afterwards and say the way I confused the timeline was adorable, making up events in place of real ones.

(I hadn't told him that those events were real somewhere else.)

I stood up and slammed my bowl in the sink. "We're not going to find him, you know."

"He's out there somewhere," Mom said, almost to herself. "We aren't giving up on him. Pack your things."

She knew what she was looking for. She had always known.

I didn't know what he looked like, let alone what kind of man he was. She never told me stories; maybe she didn't want me to grieve for something I might never have.

I thought of Amand and how he always wore mismatched socks and programmed his glasses frames to match his shirts. Did I even know what I wanted?

I'd always been focused on not growing too attached, on being able to leave everything behind. It felt like I'd grown up a hundred times and then fallen down the ladder to land back where I'd started, never knowing when it would stop.

Would I ever have what she had with my father, if I always left before I could find out?

Mom put a hand on my shoulder. She had to reach, now. "It won't be forever, Joey."

I covered her hand with mine.

I was so tired of running and never getting anywhere. It had to stop.

"I know," I said. "That's why I'm not leaving."

I turned around in time to see her bite her lip.

"Nonsense," she said, but without conviction.

I held her hand tight. "I can't do this anymore. I want to stay here, with Amand"—if he would keep me—"even if it's dangerous."

"But..." She took several deep breaths. Arguing with herself. Finding excuses, reasons, commands. Her shoulders slumped. "You're grown up, aren't you? Not my little boy anymore."

"I'll always be your son, Mom. But I need to do this for myself. I need something to call my own."

She blinked hard. "You won't have much time. A few weeks at most. Please just come with me. We'll find your father—"

"No," I said gently. "A little time's better than having forever with nothing to show for it." That was one of Amand's favorite quotes from *Die Liebe der Bienen*.

What if she was right and I disintegrated once the three years were up?

Was that really worth hurting Amand? Or was it any different than stepping out of this reality, out of his life, forever?

"Please, Mama." I kissed her hand. "I need to stay."

She pulled me into a hug. Her body trembled. "Let me show you how to unzip the fabric," she whispered. "So you have a way out."

"No," I said into her hair. I wanted to be like the people around me, given one life to make what they would of it. "I'll take my chances."

I ASKED AMAND to come with me to see my mother off the next day. I didn't know where she was headed.

We stood in a dry field outside the city limits as Mom unzipped the space-time continuum. Amand gripped my arm as we watched.

She held out her hand once to me, but I shook my head.

"Bye, Mom," I said.

She didn't say goodbye. Maybe she couldn't.

She took hold of a corner of another reality and pulled herself through. Then she was gone, and the seam melted closed.

I sagged against Amand.

Mom wasn't here. That sudden emptiness hit me harder than any reality-hop. My knees buckled.

He caught me and held me.

I didn't know I could miss her so badly so fast.

"What if I never see her again?" I said into Amand's chest.

The rims of his glasses pressed against my temple. "We always find our family." Then, softly, "Will you stay with me?"

"Ja," I said. "As long as I can."

I felt him smile.

I HAVEN'T SEEN my mother in ten years.

Amand and I got married. We adopted two beautiful children—Monique and Sebastian—and we've been living each day as if it's the last. It might be.

But, sometimes, I don't think it will happen the way Mom predicted. I don't think my mother wasn't entirely honest with me as a kid.

My dad ran off through a different reality when I was two. She waited a year, but he didn't come back. She wanted to find him the only way she knew how, and what else was she going to do with me except take me along?

Maybe the three-year limit was just an arbitrary definition because she couldn't bear to stay anywhere too long and let Dad drift father away.

I'm not angry at her. If I hadn't reality-hopped, I wouldn't have met Amand. I wouldn't have settled down in this sky apartment overlooking New Chicago, landed a job as an art historian, found a loving husband, two amazing kids, friends, and a life I'm content with. (I dedicated my first memoir to Dr. Amelia and my mom, in gratitude.)

There are days I wonder if Mom was right about our atoms not connecting with this reality we live in now. One day, I might just snap out of existence. If I do, I won't have too many regrets.

(I'd told Amand my whole story after Mom left. He believed every word. The day before he proposed a year later, I told him again about the risk I could just vanish.

"Risks are just life with different letters," he said, and kissed me. "We'll take risks and life together, ja?"

"Ja," I'd said, pulling him closer.)

If I see Mom again, the only regret I'll have is that she won't stay for very long. Wherever she is, I hope she finds what she's looking for. Me? I've found my home.

WINTER BRIDE

ONE OF THE girls has been made into a doe again. Laughing wolves chase her through the palace halls, and you turn your face away as they pull her down. (They always do.) She screams with a human voice. You cannot help her; bite-scars cuff your wrists from when you tried before.

"Come join us, trinket?" one wolf asks.

"Our lord has called for me." You walk on, your expression masked with indifference. Compassion will only harm the girl more. Games are far more entertaining when the toy pieces care for each other.

The doe's blood flecks your slippers as you pass. (The wolves will play with her for a while yet.)

You pretend not to see the other fae in the halls, cold

and beautiful. Those who look human, like the Winter Lord, frighten you most.
You do not show it; you must not. (You do not know how much longer you can
endure.)

The Winter Lord lounges on a bed of velvet strewn with frozen birch leaves.
When you first saw him, you thought him beautiful. Hair like snow, his body
tall and slim and strong, and if you kept your gaze sidelong, you did not see his
eyes. (It made your bargain no easier, but neither was it so unpleasant to look
upon the creature you had given yourself to forever.)

You dip into a curtsy. "Good day, my lord."

"Ah, pet." He curls a hand, beckoning.

You obey.

"You are so distant of late." The Winter Lord's fingers—one hand made of
ice, the other flesh as cold as snow—trace your collarbone and the line of your
jaw. "Are there not amusements enough for you?"

"There are plenty, my lord." You offer a vague smile and tilt your head back.
Through the glass-domed ceiling, you watch the twin moons rise in an empty
sky. They are the Winter Lord's eyes, as the land is his skin, the air his senses. "It
is merely the weather," you add, as snowflakes drift and shatter against the glass.

He laughs, rich and deep. It is better to amuse him with words. "Winter is
forever, my sweet."

Silent, you shrug free of your fur robes. Winter has overlaid another part of
your world—your old world, he would remind you—and the fae lord rests from
shifting his realms. His court is lethargic and passive. This is the time to act.

But he keeps you in his arms far longer than ever before, and you smile
mechanically as he strokes your hair. (You will not become his favorite.)

When you fall asleep, the dream—the terrible dream—comes again.

You stand in a desert, wind that never warms you blurring the dunes with
dust, your ankles buried in sand.

"We will leave here," says the sorceress, hidden in the darkness. Her voice is
soft as a razor's caress. She is the lord's favorite bride, the untamable one. "Soon."

You push aside the sand-like curtains, but she is always just shy of your
reach, a silhouette. You have no voice in the dream.

"I will take you away from him." The sorceress is the mistress of illusions. It
was how she won the Winter Lord's favor. (She claims he cannot find her true
nature, and so he tries, continually fascinated.) "Soon the moons will be dark

and Winter will sleep. It is then we will be free."

The sorceress is the only one you believe can manipulate dreams in Winter. Still you cannot find her in the sands.

You panic. If she cannot see you, will she forget? You cannot stay here alone. You *cannot*.

The sand darkens, chills, and turns into snow.

Upon waking, you find the moons have waned and the pale, cold day has replaced them. There is no sun in this world.

The Winter Lord still holds you curled against his chest, his eyes closed. "You are so restless in sleep, pet."

Your pulse trembles. The Winter Lord does not dream—so you spin a lie before he compels you to give him truth and betray what you saw. "I dreamed of the Spring Hunt, my lord. You were a doe and I a bear."

He caresses your throat with one hand. "And how did it end?"

"How does it always end, my lord?"

He laughs in delight but unwraps his arm from your waist. Dismissal. You kiss his hands and don your robes.

You must find the sorceress, and yet you cannot betray your hurry as you glide from the Winter Lord's chambers. Your heartbeat flutters moth-like in your ribs.

The girl-doe is human once more, curled on the marble floor among tufts of deer fur and blood. The wolves, bored, have wandered off. You pick her up and cradle her, though she's as tall as you. (You have always been stronger than you look.)

"Forty-four," she whispers against your shoulder. She counts the days she has been here, the only words she utters. Later, it will be forty-five, forty-six, on and on until there are no numbers left. (She has been here far longer than the days she counts. You do not tell her so. Lies are sanity here.)

Your arms ache by the time you return to the bride chambers. The doors, slats of carbuncle and jade, peel open and allow you inside. You lay the girl—you call her Doe—on a quilted bed.

Surprisingly, the other three are there as well. Quiet, the bronze-brown girl who is so close to shattering. Auburn, the girl with strawberry-blonde hair and a fox's tail that regrows no matter how many times she cuts it off. (A gift from the Winter Lord; it smothers her in her sleep if she does not bind it to her leg.)

And last of all, the nameless sorceress. Black hair falls around her shoulders in a tangle she never combs, and she dresses in furs only for warmth. But she is not mad, as she has made all the fae believe. (You have seen madness.) She came here of her own accord—and that is all you know. She stands at the mirrored windows where you can see inside as well as out, overlays of snow and silk. Outside, vistas of ice spread out forever. "How is he?"

"Lady sorceress." You never answer her questions about the Winter Lord. You do not know if she truly cares for him, or if she merely toys with him as he does all his subjects. "A moment?"

She spins toward you. "Always."

You bite the inside of your cheek, hard, until blood pools on your tongue and the ache spreads through your jaw. She cups your face in her scarred hands and kisses you on the mouth.

Sharp heat curls through your neck and down into your belly. When you are alone some nights, you imagine she came to free you. But you must focus on the question, not the way her lips and tongue feel against yours. *Is it true?* (This is the only way the Winter Lord will not hear.) *Do you have a plan to escape?*

Yes, she murmurs, the unspoken words forming in your mind. *We will be free.*

Free. A perfect word. A forbidden word. You do not remember how long you have been trapped. Yet that taste, that word, excites hope you have dared not touch in so long. Free.

You wind your fingers through her hair and pull her closer, and she lets you. *When? How?*

Her hands slide over your hips. *You cannot come, my love.*

Your flesh prickles and you almost push her away. She takes your breath, deepens the kiss; her blood tastes of salt and shadows.

I know the paths to the border, the sorceress says, *and how to open it. But I can only hide a few around me, and if we both disappear, he will know. He will find us. You, my love, are his favorite now, and I cannot take you away.*

You wrench free, shaking. "No."

And yet you *are* eclipsing the sorceress. He calls on you more than her; he watches you; he turns you into a sleek, white-furred hound that sits at his side so he may stroke its ears. But he does not hurt you, and you are not given as a plaything to the court, as are the other girls. A small mercy.

(Death is the only other escape from these lands.)

"No," you say again, softer.

There is no sorrow in the sorceress's eyes. She looks at you the way she watches the Winter Lord: calculating, mocking, pitying. "Your time will come," she says.

You feel the other girls watching. The air is too cold in your lungs.

Emotion is an entertainment the fae adore, so you clench your hands and swallow the thorn-pointed anger. It hurts as it spreads inside.

"Will it?" you ask, your voice frigid. "Will the time come?"

The sorceress strokes your cheek. You slap her hand away.

"Yes," she says. "But not yet."

Quiet and Auburn have clustered around Doe, watching. They know. The sorceress will free them. Is that why you can never see the sorceress in the dream?

You turn sharp on your heel. "Good day, lady sorceress."

How often have you distracted the Winter Lord for her sake, gone to him when she asked? You thought it desperation, that even *she* could not endure his attention endlessly. Perhaps it was an illusion. She needed a diversion to further her plans, and you served.

You have been here longer than any of them. (There are far more captives in Winter's thrall. Slaves, prey, entertainment. You refuse to see them. They, at least, do not survive long.) You remember the brides before the sorceress came, all broken into shells and finally discarded as piles of bones. You cannot remain here forever and stay whole. Your mind is all you have that is still *yours*.

But you do not have a sorceress's power. Even though you know all the paths in the palace, you cannot cross the border.

She can.

And she will *not* leave you behind.

"Have you freed any from your realm, my lord?" you boldly ask the Winter Lord.

You sit at his feet (not as a hound, this time) and watch the court dance and feast. The hunters returned with prizes—half a dozen humans now nothing more than echoed screams and droplets of blood upon marble floors. It unsettles you that you feel nothing as you watch the fae laugh and drink.

"You are curious, pet." The Winter Lord's hand rests on your nape, his fingers numbing your skin. "Why so?"

You tilt your head. Does he suspect the sorceress's plans? "Would you free one of your brides, my lord, if it amused you?"

He leans close, his smile sly. "Do you wish to be freed?" His breath curls against your ear.

"Never, my lord." You watch a pair of ravens duel for possession of the last human-prey's shadow they have culled neatly inside a wine glass. "It was simple curiosity."

Icy spindrifts swirl behind the Winter Lord's eyes. "You lie so delightfully."

Your smile never wavers, even as your breath freezes. "Do I, my lord?"

He strokes a thumb across your throat, feather-light seduction. "Oh, yes. But would you leave your ties behind?"

One of the ravens scoops up the wine glass in its talons and drinks the shadow; the other fae lies in a bloodied heap, feathers scattered, though it is not dead. You feign boredom, like the court, and turn your gaze elsewhere.

A tiny boy scampers towards the throne, weaving between the fae without touching them. Your son is a mirror to his inhuman father. Pale, beautiful, graceful as new snow. His eyes are too large, too green (not like yours), and he is too eager to please. You tighten your hands in your skirts. You hate him, though you never show it.

"Mother!" He beams and plops in your lap. "My lord!"

"Hello, kitten." The Winter Lord lets you go, his gaze unblinking. "Tell me, my son, would you be happy if your lady mother left us?"

The boy's smile crumples, his eyes wide with hurt. "You're leaving, Mother?"

You pat his head without answer.

"She will never go, kitten," the Winter Lord says, and he laughs as the boy hugs you and grips your hand.

Your smile is a mask.

You COULD DELIVER the sorceress's plan to the Winter Lord with a word, but he would not reward you with freedom. If you let your girls go, you will be alone.

You sit in the bridal chambers and run a brush through Auburn's hair and the treacherous fox tail. "What will you do if she fails?"

You nod toward the windows, where the sorceress now rides beside the Winter Lord on tundra dragons. Horns sound amid keening laughter.

Doe is once again one of the prey-animals in the lord's hunt: a bull elk adorned with scarlet ribbons. Quiet joins her in lynx-form with bells in her ears. You show no relief that you are not compelled to hold a bow and hunt by the Winter Lord's side this time.

Auburn wraps her arms about her knees. "She can't. She promised."

You grip Auburn's chin and tilt her face up. "Think. What will you do if he finds out, if he stops her?"

Auburn's eyes fill with tears, but behind the salt there is only despair. "I—I can't. *Stay* here. Can't."

And she thinks you can?

You kiss her cheek and resume brushing her hair. She's so young. Fragile. You think of all the girls that way.

Only the sorceress is different. Defiant, cunning, fierce. (It is why you want her and not the others.)

"Are you going to tell him?" Auburn whispers. She fingers a trinket in her skirts. Her favorite knife: a prettily scrolled heartwood hilt with an ivory blade.

You laugh, surprised at how hollow it sounds. "Put away your toy, child." You lean your cheek against hers and grip her hair at the base of her scalp. "It would do no good."

Her knuckles whiten, her spine stiffening. "Will you tell him?"

"I hate him too much." You set away the brush made from bones and needles, then stand. "But I will not be left alone."

She wilts under your stare. She understands.

WHEN THE SORCERESS returns, guiding Doe and Quiet (in human-form, bloodied and cold-lipped), you corner her near the window. You do not ask her this time before you pull her mouth against yours.

You will not leave me behind, you say, *or none of you will leave.*

She smiles. *Do you think to coerce me?*

Ask yourself, my lady sorceress, what you can possibly do that he cannot? What threat can sway me?

She pulls away.

Truly, what can she do? Wounds will always heal. (The girls know this well.) Your son is a tool, one that can be replaced. You are already trapped, chained, isolated. A hundred possibilities flit sidelong in your thoughts, and you have an answer for each, a reason she cannot dissuade you.

The sorceress flicks her chin up. "Very well."

She weaves an illusion around herself: the Winter Lord's skin. You take a step back, startled. The guise is perfect—from the cruel smile to the way his hair drifts like gusting snow, from the ever-changing snowflake pattern on his jacket to the way he stands, unnaturally still. But the eyes are a lie. The sorceress's illusion cannot mimic the Winter Lord's gaze.

You run your fingers down his—her—arm. Ice prickles under your nails. "I've seen your tricks, lady sorceress."

"Have you?" the illusion says in a flawless mirror-voice.

Unease knots in your belly. But you will not back down. "Yes."

He catches your mouth with his—a kiss so familiar. *Which one will replace you?* You jerk back, shaking.

The illusion flicks a hand lazily towards the three other girls. "You, pet, will stay—even if another wears your skin."

You curl your slippered toes against the floor. "Why?"

"Someone must play the hare and distract the fox."

Doe watches with blank eyes. "Forty-six," she whispers.

Quiet's jaw clenches in fury. Auburn is trying to cut off her tail again.

You hesitate. Of course—all five of you cannot simply disappear, or the land itself will trap you until the Hunt brings you back. "You can make a construct from bones and ice to hold your illusion."

"Oh, no, pet." The illusion leans close. "A body for your place at my side. Which one?"

This should be an easy, choice. There are only three options—simply pick which girl you hate the most.

Your breath is quick, your blood frozen. The same terror you felt when you offered yourself to the Hunt so long ago, taking your sister's place as rightful prey, has resurfaced. You cannot protect Doe, or Auburn, or Quiet, but you have never *given* one of them to the Winter Lord.

The one left behind will suffer beyond imagining. You have never seen his wrath at being slighted, for none have ever dared.

"You will find another way," you stammer.

"No." The illusion shimmers, melts, and the sorceress stands before you again. Her smile is gone. She kisses you, and her blood tastes of honey and ash. *The one who stays must distract him, and all his court, so we may cross the border unseen. My son, and yours, will not leave—they are his, they belong to him. But we do not.*

You were certain she would free her son, a forgotten shadow though he is. And yours? Because you hate him does not mean you will let the Winter Lord have him. Winter has already claimed too much.

There is no other way, the sorceress murmurs, her voice pitying. *Decide, my love, or I will choose for you. It must be tonight. The moons are dark and he will not see us.*

"And what is this whispering, my pets?" says the Winter Lord.

All of you turn.

He waits in the doorway. Behind him, the huge snow bears—his guard, his offspring—smile in anticipation. Your son stands by the Winter Lord's side, trembling and silent. The fae lord strokes the child's hair and slowly curls the boy's shadow around his fingers. (He always traps the shadows of his favorite offspring in jars for his collection. There is nothing you can do.)

"Forty-seven," Doe says, covering her eyes.

"You wear my skin well, my lady," the Winter Lord says. The sorceress remains silent. "It suits you. But tell, pet"—and his gaze drifts to you, holds you with cruel amusement—"why do you recoil from my touch?"

The compulsion curls inside your throat; you have no choice but to answer. And yet the Winter Lord's gaze rests solely on you. Not the sorceress. Your stomach fills with stone.

Ever before, when you both were in his presence, he looked only upon her.

You hold hope, and freedom, in your palm. The words tip on the edge of a needle. You can condemn your girls, your sorceress, and perhaps win favor for yourself. It would be so easy, like counting.

"What she shows are lies, my lord," you answer, and the compulsion eases. "I do not want her touch any longer, no matter what falsity she crafts around herself."

The Winter Lord tugs the last of your son's shadow free and the boy collapses on hands and knees with a whimper. You do not flinch at the confused, frightened look he gives you. (If you care about the boy, it will only bring him far worse pain. It is kinder to hate him.)

"I think you lie, pet," the Winter Lord says.

The sorceress grips your elbow until bone creaks in your arm. You shake her hand free, pluck the knife from Auburn's skirts, and walk to the Winter Lord. "Do I?" you whisper.

"Oh, yes," the Winter Lord replies. "Which of our lovely toys shall I take apart and find the truth, if you do not offer it?" He spreads a hand towards the girls, a lazy wrist-flick.

Doe curls into herself and Quiet steps in front of Auburn. Still the sorceress looks on in silence.

Your heartbeat is unsteady, yet you feel too calm. You would laugh, shrill and terrified, if you were weaker.

You realize, as you did the day you took your sister's place, that you cannot live sane or mad with the knowledge you have abandoned another to these chains. Freedom would have no meaning. You have been here the longest. What is eternity?

"My lord," you say, curtsying. You do not look at your son. (All you can offer him now is the promise he will never be alone.) "The truth: I have planned a gift for you since the day I came to your court."

The Winter Lord's eyes brighten. "Oh?"

"Your other brides did not approve, but they are too weak to appreciate it." You feel his breath against your hair. All are forbidden from touching the Winter Lord without permission. "It has been my deepest desire to do this, my lord."

His terrible smile widens. The bears watch unblinking. All the walls transform into mirrors so the court may witness what unfolds.

You do not look back at the sorceress or the other girls. You simply stab the Winter Lord in the heart.

A distraction: for one night and forever.

The knife shatters in his ribs. (You can never harm him in his own lands.)

The bears swarm you, bury you, and there are only teeth and claws and the Winter Lord's delighted laughter.

OH, HE MAKES you pay for that indiscretion. He peels off your skin before he gives you to his fae to do with you as they please. And they are always eager for new toys. You cannot shut away your thoughts this time.

(Are your girls safe? Did the sorceress take them across the border unseen?)

Your son is made to watch before he, too, is given to the bears. Eventually, the Winter Lord cuts out your screams and puts them in a jar for his collection.

And when the court has finished with you, when you know you cannot endure anymore, the Winter Lord cups your face in his hands and you know he has merely begun.

(You hope your girls are free.)

You LIE ON the windowsill, the only bride in these chambers now. You no longer see the doe-girl pulled down by wolves, or swans pecking apart the fox-tailed girl, or the sorceress laughing as she makes the fae lord hunt her across frozen mountaintops. You no longer see many things.

Your son sits beside you, motionless save for the twitch of his fingers as he turns a silver knife. You do not remember when he ceased being a child—he is so like his lord father, grown and powerful and hollow.

The sorceress did not come back for you, but neither did the Hunt bring her or the other girls in as prized prey. In their world, your old world, does she remember you? (You still remember her.)

"My lady?"

"Yes, my son?"

He leans his forehead against your temple, his eyes closed. "Will we ever leave this place?"

He is the Winter Lord's favorite; you have seen what is done to him, what he is made to do. But you are the sole winter bride.

One day, you hope, your son will create a distraction and you can follow the sorceress. (Or perhaps you will do the same for him and let him go.) One day, you will leave Winter forever.

"My lady?" he whispers, and you grip his hand around the knife hilt and hold him close.

"Yes," you say. "In time."

TO THE MONSTERS, WITH LOVE

I MISS YOU.

I miss the feel of your scales, the coarseness of your fur, the tease of your claws, the scrape of your fangs against my skin.

At night, I dream we're still together: in your castle, in your coffin, in your dark lake waters. Just us, without the world to judge. I dream you were not taken from me.

In the dreams, there is no fire to consume you, no silver bullets or machine guns on biplanes, no stakes and no curses.

I miss you.

I want you back.

IT'S COLD HERE in my so-called happy ending. I hate this dull, monotone ever after I'm trapped in. Here I'm just another pretty face, flawless make-up, cast only to smile, or cry, or scream. Never to feel—especially not for you.

The future for me is to settle down, forsake my dreams and forget you. Fade into obscurity, because the monster is the only one who is remembered.

(I will not be content in oblivion.)

When we were together, I was your world and you were mine. You always remembered my name. You knew the inside seams of my heart, the desires unspoken. You treated me as equal.

No one knows me here.

But they remember you, and so do I.

They cry "Stockholm Syndrome!" when I say your name. They twist my story every time, turn it into a lie, because you're a monster. Their stories can only end one way.

You didn't take me against my will. I came looking for you, remember? We found each other in the dark, in the moonlight, under the sun, beneath the stars.

We were so happy.

I rage and grieve in silence as the credits roll.

I miss you.

Oh, God, I want you back.

THEY SAY YOU were invisible, but I could always see you.

They say you were a dichotomy of good and evil, man and monster, two different faces—but I know it's you, only you. (They never said the same about me, of course, but I love you because we're so alike.)

I know you when you wear a mask, when your music echoes beneath the opera house foundations.

They called you mad—but it's only science. Think of the wonders we created in the laboratory, our bodies silhouetted by Bunsen burners and lightning, our scalpels agleam in the shadows. We discovered the secrets of life, and of death, and how to pass between them. We should have won acclaim for our research. We earned only torches and the cries of a mob.

I miss you.

I want you back.

MY LIFE IS a fractal mirror, showing every possibility but the one I want. The glass always tells the wrong story.

But no longer.

Now the story is mine, and I will give us the ending we deserve.

SO I'M BUILDING you again, my love. From memory and scraps of film discarded in sunless vaults. From coarse stitching that held your flesh together and old bandages that never aged.

I've sewn your scalp with lightning and daisy petals thrown in a lake. I've carved bones from wolf-headed walking canes and the memory of your touch. Your claws: here they are, made from jungle rock and sulfur.

I've riveted your skin with radiation and the devil's name. I've given you eyes only I can see. Your blood I made in the laboratory through chemistry and minor chords. Teeth? Oh, I would never neglect something that important. Here they are, shaped from celluloid and magnetic tape, waveforms written on ivory shards.

Don't worry, I didn't forget the final piece: I could never forget your heart.

I found it wrapped safe in old newspapers with glaring headlines, with ticket stubs and cigarette paper. It was locked away in a jar, sealed in a box, buried under the crossroads.

I hid it there so it would be safe until I could break away from the cameras and the binding scripts and the spotlights that never showed me as real.

I'll put your heart back in your chest, and you will live, you will live, *you will live*.

When I'm done, they will say I have created a monster.

OUTSIDE? YES, I hear the angry voices. The firelight gleams on the laboratory windows. Lightning shears the sky. It's like the day we first met, don't you agree?

Your heart begins to beat.

Live, my love.

Your eyes open.

The mob has reached our castle gates. Of course they brought a battering ram. Don't worry. I came prepared.

Do you see those wings I made for us? Metal frames stretched with supple leather, a harness that can hold us both. An engine will propel us far away, far into the sky, into the night, where no one can ever follow. The cloaking device is one I designed when you were invisible. We will be unseen by radar or satellites.

You smile and I take your hands in mine.

When you say my name, my heart beats wildly again—I live, I *live*.

The mob has breached the gates; we must go now.

I help you stand. The windows slam wide open. The night gusts in and whips my lab coat like a cloak behind me. You breathe deep the rain-scented air. Your first breath. The first of many.

Footsteps on the stairs, voices echoing along spiraling stone walls. "Monster!" they scream.

Yes, my love, they speak of us both.

Make sure your harness is fastened tight. Hold my hands while I grip the yoke.

The door to the laboratory shatters.

Jump now—I won't let us fall.

The engine roars and then we're flying, arching up into the lightning-streaked night, cutting through rain. We're making history, you and I, and we will always be remembered.

You laugh in exhilaration, and I howl with you. We will never be separated again.

I missed you so.

And now I have you back.

BATTERIES FOR YOUR DOOMBOT5000 ARE NOT INCLUDED

MICKIE FOUND THE Doombot5000 at an estate sale purely by accident. Well, that and a tracking app she'd installed on her phone. But really, when the address popped up, it wasn't as if she could have known it was the estate of her former nemesis, Sandron the Unstoppable.

Poor Sandy. He'd been a decent antagonist back in the day. She didn't remember any invite to his funeral.

Mickie, formerly Mindsight the Conqueror of Space, shuffled through the rows of sentimental crap and old clothes and Sandy's impressive collection of *Space & Time Quarterly* until her phone buzzed and she saw the Doombot5000 in a corner behind three ancient vacuums.

No one else has noticed yet, because why would a guy

like Sandy have owned a Doombot5000?

"I'll take all four vacuums," she told the manager.

BACK AT HER loft, which was nothing like her old digs on the Cataract of Europa, she lined up her new vacuums and the Doombot5000.

The Doombot5000 did resemble an old tube-hosed vacuum, with its squat head against the floor, a cylindrical upright body and its destructor-arms flattened against its sides like a cord and nozzle. Of course its batteries were depleted and the flashing red eyes and wailing "DESTROY ALL THE THINGS!" mantra were offline.

What mattered, and why Mickie had shelled out a grand for the "antiques"— half the rent for this month—was that it was an original Doombot, and it hadn't been neutralized by the Accord of Peaceful Enforcement in '98.

Her heart pounded as fast as it had back in the day when she donned her black heels, vibrant purple cape, and went forth to battle the do-gooder heroes always standing between her and world domination. She pulled out the adapter cord she'd made and plugged it into the Doombot's battery port. Nothing, at first.

Then the optics began to glow and the digitized voice crackled through static. "D-DESTROY—"

"Disengage," Mickie ordered, and the Doombot quieted. She'd designed them to answer only to her voice commands, but of course Mimic the Mic had figured that out and copied her voice and shut down her army.

For a moment she considered reprogramming the half dozen Doombots she'd collected in retirement and starting again, but…it wouldn't be the same. Most of her old foes were dead or retired, and besides, she was trying to reform.

Taking a deep breath to calm herself, Mickie unscrewed the Doombot's back casing and examined the motherboard. No visible damage or corrosion. Good. She clipped her earpiece, wired to a small mic, into the DO NOT TAMPER WITH port.

"Claire?" she asked. "You in there?"

IT WASN'T HER fault, is what Mickie's therapist had told her. But that was bullshit and they both knew it. So she fired him and went for coffee with one of her few non-powered friends.

Daisy was a mechanical engineer. They'd dated on and off (way back when), but since Daisy didn't approve of world domination, they'd decided to just stay friends.

"Why does it have to be your fault?" Daisy asked, eyeing the flakes of ash on Mickie's jacket.

"No one else could survive me blaming them," Mickie said, looking away. "And I'm the one who told Claire to go."

Daisy stirred her mocha latte with a dented spoon. Her office/garage smelled of oil, hot metal, sweat and strong espresso. "So you're the one who got her killed."

Mickie nodded. She should have told Claire to stay back at their lair, but no, Claire—Chain Lightning to everyone else—just had to take on the TechnoSorcerer on her own. Well, not entirely. Mickie had sent the Doombots with her girlfriend, and an hour later, she lost contact with all other 'bots and the woman she…liked. A lot.

Maybe more than a lot, but she couldn't admit that. It wasn't becoming of unstoppable evil. Even if denial sucked.

Claire didn't come back, and the Doombots were disabled by the TechnoSorcerer's mind field. Mickie didn't even have the heart to swear revenge. She just…felt lost.

Daisy rested a grease-stained hand on Mickie's. "Look, hon, you got two options. Wallow in guilt like a hero, or do something."

"Do?"

"You're an antihero—"

"Villain."

"Whatever. You've always solved your own problems, right? I know you can't fix or solve grief. And that's okay. But what are you going to do with the rest of your life? You don't have to move on, but you can take a detour for a while and decide where to go next."

Mickie nodded slowly. "Why did we stop dating again?"

Daisy grinned. "Differing points of view."

"Your loss." Mickie managed a deep breath. "Thanks."

Sometimes it was the little words that were the hardest, unlike ultimatums and grandiose declarations of destruction.

Little words like *thanks* or *stay with me* or *I think I may love you*.

IT HAD BEEN when she was refurbishing the first Doombot to serve as a butler for her loft apartment that she noticed something was wrong.

Instead of blaring its intention to destroy all life forms, the Doombot5000 had stuttered, spit static, and stammered, *Where...am...I?*

And the voice had been Claire's.

IT MADE SENSE, in retrospect. Like most defeats, Mickie had analyzed everything about her failure and made copious notes (along with plans for revenge):

1. The TechnoSorcerer had an affinity for machines.

2. Chain Lightning could change her body's molecular structure into pure energy.

3. Doombots had been on the scene.

4. Conclusion: in the resulting showdown, the TechnoSorcerer must have channeled Claire into the Doombots when she attacked, overloading most of the 'bots in an explosion that had left no sign of Chain Lightning, and only a few scrapped machines.

There was no fifth point on the list, because Mickie did not believe in itemizing grief.

No RESPONSE FROM the Doombot5000. Mickie shut her eyes. She tried again, "Claire, are you—part of you—in there?"

She heard only the internal hum of the Doombot's mechanic guts.

She sat back, disconnecting her earpiece.

She did not punch a hole in the wall, or set the ceiling on fire in rage. It was too much work, even for instinctual reactions.

The first Doombot she'd heard Claire's voice in had short circuited when she tried to extract the memory chip to preserve whatever was left, and since then, Mickie had hunted down all the remaining Doombots to find pieces of Claire's consciousness.

By her calculations, there were only six Doombot5000s left after they'd been disbanded or destroyed upon her retirement. Before she'd known Claire was in the 'bots, somewhere.

FIVE DOOMBOT5000S RECOVERED over the next year—mostly legally—and the sixth one was right on her tracker app: stashed in an old warehouse that, when she checked the online records, had once belonged to the TechnoSorcerer himself.

She spent a week working up plans to infiltrate the warehouse. Invisible suit that repressed her heat signature so she could slip in through a vent? Her joints weren't what they used to be, and she didn't want to throw her back out again. Chiropractic visits were not cheap with her pathetic insurance plan.

Build a giant raygun to launch into orbit and program it to vaporize all biological matter without destroying the mechanical elements? She lacked the funds. And besides, he'd probably sense her invention and disable it before she could fire.

Storm the gates with an army behind her, cape snapping in the wind, her blasters gleaming? Still came down to finances, plus the fact she'd be fined for inciting supervillainy within the city limits.

Finally, she settled on the most dangerous option. She'd never been one to do anything less.

Mickie clenched her hands, missing her deathray gun, and knocked on the side door labeled OFFICE.

"Come in," called a creaky voice she'd know anywhere.

She walked in.

The TechnoSorcerer—Desmond—sat in a battered office chair, snapping his fingers at the TV. He glanced over his shoulder and sighed.

"Hi, Mick."

"Hi, Des."

Retirement hadn't been easy on either of them. He'd let his hair grow shaggy, hadn't shaved, and was using his power to *change the TV channels*. How far had he fallen?

She shoved her hands into her jacket pockets, unsure where to pose or if the piles of junk and old chairs were stable enough to sit on.

"Long time no see," Desmond said.

"I guess." She'd dated him, too, back in the day, but she didn't want to bring up old conversations. "I hear you have a Doombot5000 in storage here."

Desmond snapped the TV off and swiveled his chair fully to face her. "I knew this day would come."

"Give me my Doombot."

"Or what?"

Mickie readied a string of threats, how she would crush him, make seven generations of his ancestors or descendants lament, et cetera, but...it was so much effort, and she was tired. She sat on the edge of the desk and shrugged.

"Well, I can't pay you much, because I just paid rent."

Desmond sighed. "I'm barely making ends meet myself. Business just isn't what it used to be."

Mickie nodded. There was an awkward silence. Neither of them had the energy to monologue or posture or even trade innuendo.

"Look, Des." She took a deep breath. "I think Claire is in the Doombots. Parts of her mind, anyway—scattered through all the 5000 models." Honesty was so much harder when she wasn't wearing a cape and declaring war on the forces of good. "I'm trying to get her back."

"Oh." Desmond rubbed his face, wrinkled hands scratching his stubble. "Damn, Mickie. I didn't know."

Mickie shrugged again, picking at her nails. "I didn't know for a long time."

Another awkward silence.

Mickie swallowed. "So, I wondered..." She took another steadying breath, her heart pounding like the first time she'd challenged him to a duel. "Can I have the Doombot?"

"Of course you can," Desmond said. "I've felt awful about what happened for *years*. It's why I gave up the cape." He cleared his throat. "I don't suppose, uh, that is... Can I help you try to get her out?"

Surprised, Mickie's first instinct was to spurn his offer, declare she needed no one's help, ex-boyfriend and former enemy or not.

"Okay," she said instead.

"HI, DAISY," MICKIE said on the phone. "I wondered if you could help me with a project... No, nothing that dramatic. No domination involved. Well, I mean, if you're up for a little in the bedroom afterwards I won't say no..."

IN HER LOFT, cables linking all the surviving Doombot5000s together, Mickie's hand shook as she hooked her earpiece into the first Doombot's port. She nodded, and Desmond placed his hands on the 'bots, powering them on one by one.

Daisy wiped down her wrenches and screwdrivers. She'd come to assist in building the transfer device. And had stayed the night. It'd been good, like the old days—Mickie had appreciated a distraction for a few hours at least.

Now, the big day was here.

Once the Doombots had come online, Mickie cleared her throat. "Claire, are you there?"

Static. Desmond's expression crumpled.

Daisy kept polishing. Her wrenches gleamed like lasers.

Mickie stared intently at the Doombot5000's glowing red optics. "Claire, can you hear me?"

No response.

Desmond looked away. "I don't think it's working, Mick…"

She clenched her jaw. Relaxed it, and kept going. She had never given up in a fight. She would not stop now. If she had to talk herself hoarse, and then some, well. She'd been champion in her debate team in high school, and had taken vocal lessons all through her career. "Claire, if you're in there, I want you to know I'm not going anywhere. And I won't. Not ever."

The optics blinked.

And then, crackly with interference, Claire's voice: *Mickie? Where am I?*

Mickie choked on a mix of maniacal laughter and relief. Desmond and Daisy grinned.

WITH HER PHYSICAL body's original structure destroyed in the explosion and her metaphysical being trapped so long as smaller units of energy in the Doombots, Claire couldn't reconstitute herself the way Mickie had hoped.

But Mickie wasn't a (former) supervillain for nothing—she knew how to build robots, and she knew Claire, and so she constructed a life-sized robot-body from the pieces of the Doombot5000s. With Desmond's instructions and Daisy's help, Mickie walked Claire through the process of collecting her energy from various machines and transferring it into the new structure.

Blue optics, chassis painted with stylized lightning, wire-spring hair, fully jointed limbs and polychrome skin, Clairebot tested out her range of movement in the loft. Daisy gave Desmond a hug, and he laughed and returned it.

"I'll make us some espresso," Daisy said, tugging Desmond by the hand. He coughed and followed her into the kitchen.

Mickie held out her hands. "Hi, Claire."

Claire took Mickie's hands in hers. "Hi, Mickie. Thanks for sticking around."

"You want to stay?" Mickie asked.

Claire smiled. "I do indeed."

Mickie blinked away construction dust from her eyes as they started to water. Maybe retirement wouldn't be so bad now.

. . . OR BE FOREVER FALLEN

THE RAVEN'S GHOST follows first. It's not a surprise, if I'm honest. I killed a raven once—intentional, cruel—some time ago. (I don't remember why.) At first I saw it in the distance while I prowled the ruins of the once-majestic forest, hunting the men who robbed me. Yet the ghost never approached until now.

It perches on a petrified tree stump. The light from the campfire shimmers against its glossy feathers, blood etching razor-edged plumage. It should be indistinguishable in the night, banked in shadow. I only know it's a ghost from the hollows of its missing eyes, how its shape bends in unnatural directions at the corners of my sight.

"I've naught for you." I say it to the knives laid out on

oiled canvas before me.

The raven's ghost makes no sound. Its unnatural muteness tightens the muscles in my neck. Ghosts are never silent. Death is neither gentle nor kind.

I must act quickly, before the ghost destroys me. I don't know why it's waited, since it must have come for a reason. There's no dawn in this land—a ghost can wait forever, and I can no longer endure its presence. I haven't slept in…well. I don't remember that, either.

The bandits who stole my name left me savaged but alive, my memory no better than moth-chewed rags, loose threads, the narrative of who I was scattered between holes. I remember cold plains that aren't home, a familiar-soft touch on my neck, planting grape vines in summer, pain (maybe mine, maybe not), and great pools of emptiness between.

The raven cocks its head.

I will find the men who wronged me and I will unmake them. But I can find no solace if the ghost interferes.

I pull the map from my satchel and spread it before me. The map is old: vellum lined with a substance neither blood nor ink, but darker, older; the viscera from the other side of heaven.

Shall I show you what happened to your name? the map whispers. Its voice bends thoughts sideways, echoes of madness etched behind each word. It only shows you what you pay it to find.

I kneel on the edges of the map and lay a knife blade against my palm. Steel grounds me, the one thing I always remember. "Leave me, ghost, or I will let this map destroy you."

The map purrs in anticipation and hunger.

"You would be unwise to do that, man," says a voice from the darkness.

A wolf prowls into my camp, the firelight pooling its eye sockets. A faint line of red circles its neck, but its silver-black pelt is thick, glossy as the raven's feathers.

I stiffen, sharp fear salted in my belly. I've never killed a wolf (cruel or not). I haven't earned a second ghost.

The wolf must have once hailed from the southern mountains: it's bigger than a pony, jagged white stripes splashed across its back, clay beads sewn into its ears and braided into the long fur along its chest and shoulders.

The wolf dips its chin to the raven, who nods its head in return.

At the corners of my eyes, the wolf's shape warps and stretches into the darkness. Its scent is heavy with old memory.

The mountain wolves served only their land and their people, refusing to pay homage to Sun or Moon. Instead, they sought the dark between the stars (they said First Wolf was born in those empty spaces, when heaven was not looking)—they were building great ships in the mountains' bellies, built of bone and shed fur, sealed with pitch. They would sail into the dark in search of First Wolf and leave the world for the Sun and the Moon to squabble over.

The Sun tolerated no other predators in heaven, and neither did the Moon.

That memory doesn't belong to me. I shake my head, startled and unsettled.

"Good evening, man," the wolf says at last.

"Evening," I reply, humoring the ghost. "You have no purpose here, lord wolf."

"We may disagree on that point." The ghost's voice is charred where the wound across its throat digs deeper. "You hold one who is mine."

I glance toward the raven's ghost. "I never claimed it."

"You lie beautifully," the wolf says with an appreciative nod. "Did you have much practice?"

That, at least, I can answer fairly. "Yes."

I don't remember what rituals shaped me. There were more important pieces stolen: my past, my purpose, my name.

I sink the tip of the blade into the ground, away from flesh. The map will eagerly lap up even a drop of blood. To destroy one ghost, perhaps I might endure the price—but not two. The map drives a hard bargain.

It is nothing you cannot bear, the map says. *You may not even remember what it is you will lose. Forgetting costs you nothing more.*

I shift my weight on my heels. If it stays, I fear what else the wolf's scent will bring.

Ghosts are wrought from sorrow and carnage; they carry each as a weapon. The wolf can tear apart my flesh with fangs or crush my heart with grief not my own. So could the raven, but it hasn't bothered yet. I own no knives for killing ghosts.

"Leave this place, lord wolf."

"Not until you repay us for what you stole," it says.

And what is that? I took nothing. I know the words *trapped* and *helpless*, but they've been empty of context until now. There is nowhere to run in a forest as dead and cold as the ghosts before me.

"Man," the wolf says with the edge of a growl. "Will you pay your debt freely?"

"What debt?"

The raven spreads its wings and its body flickers as it glides through the campfire, blending with smoke. It circles once until the tip of its pinions graze my cheek. Sudden and unbidden memory fills my mind—

The raven found the wolf, wounded and far from the mountains now cold and empty. The raven nursed the wolf to health, to strength, to vengeance.

There were no other ravens; they had flown swift and silent, slipping behind the Moon, gliding between the stars. On each star they passed, they hung a black feather on a silver string to guide whoever followed. The last raven stayed for the wolf.

The raven found the man, too, in the petrified stump forest where it was never dawn.

The raven said to the man, "If you would make amends and have the darkness embrace you, be no more."

And the man said, "I will, lord raven."

I jerk my head back, my heartbeat too fast—the sound will spill from my ribs and betray me. "What do you want?"

The raven lands on the wolf's broad shoulder. Both ghosts wince, white-blue light crackling between talons and fur. The raven nuzzles its beak against the wolf's ear, and the wolf leans into the caress.

"When you killed him," the wolf murmurs, "you left your blood upon his eyes."

The sharp-edged accusation dances like an errant spark in my throat. With living blood blinding the dead, a ghost cannot find its way to rest. It will follow the one who blinded it, helpless and lost until the living cleans away the blood or consecrates the bones. I left the carcass nailed to a tree so the roots would not swallow it and trap its ghost in a cage beneath the forest forevermore.

"I've never blinded the dead."

"You don't remember your own name," the wolf says. "You don't remember what you *did*. Should I show you?"

I flinch backwards. "No. Forgive me, lord wolf." I owe them; the knowledge of that sits heavy in my bones, sudden and weighted with a grief I don't understand. "If I did, it was not by choice."

Muscles ripple under the wolf's pelt, its fur liquid silver and sky-dark by turn. The white on its back glows like the moon. "Unite our bones so we may be at rest."

I dare not move.

The ghost's hollow sockets burn with firelight. Its lips curl back, smile or snarl—one and the same. "Or you will never be named again. Your map will not help you. I know what they did with your name, Man. I will help you, but only if you redress the crime you have committed against us."

I let my breath out slowly, controlled. It's possible to take a new name. But it would have no history, no purpose; it would only mean defeat. I've resisted the map's seductive offers, but my strength will fail, in time. I cannot go on forever not knowing who I am.

I sheath the knives. "Agreed, lord wolf."

Both ghosts smile.

FIRST, I MUST find their bones.

I light a cigarette in the campfire. The heat never burns my skin nor singes the graying stubble on my chin. I don't remember if my hair has been anything more than ash-colored, tied into thick ropes. (It's an odd detail to take irritation with: hair color. I've never thought myself vain.) I inhale smoke, the perfect balance of opium and tobacco, and brace myself to bargain with the map. Then I cut open the scar tissue on my elbow where there isn't any pain and feed a trickle of blood to the vellum.

You won't get what you seek from the dead, the map says.

The ghosts scare me more than the map, and I've owned that map a long time. (I don't remember how long.) "Where are the bones of the wolf and the raven with me now?"

The map's surface is dark. Inverted, paler lines unravel like a detailed woodcut: the three of us in the forest of petrified tree stumps. A line snakes to the east and stops against a picture of the Woods, still living, thick with shadow and lost voices.

The map continues drawing. The line curls lazily through the Woods until it reaches a half-moon clearing. Six shapes, perhaps men, stand in the empty space, and then the map washes the depiction clear.

You can see where they have hidden your name, for a price, the map says.

I grunt in dismissal and roll it up. If you stare too long at the darkness, you'll get a glimpse of the void trapped within vellum. Other men, more curious, have burst at the seams when they looked; some tear out their eyes and go mad; some are simply eaten.

The wolf tilts its head. "You wear pain as a cowl and regret as a shroud."

"Do I?" I haven't looked in a mirror in…well. I don't remember forever, so I'll settle for years.

I kick out the fire and sling my satchel over one shoulder. There's no moon tonight, but I've wandered in the darkness a long time. It settles like a worn, tattered jacket around my shoulders.

"Come," I tell the ghosts. "I'll put your bones to rest."

AT THE EDGE of the Woods, whippoorwills coo minor lullabies while owls sing dirges. Magpies whistle happily of coins in eye sockets and silver in broken teeth. Swallows warble on the taste of ghostly bones.

There are no raven voices.

I crouch, fingers splayed against the ground. The gouged, raw-peeled wood of the tree on which I impaled the raven's carcass stands visible in the night. (How long ago?) The Woods are dense with thick-bodied yews, ancient birch white as bone, buckthorn laden with overripe berries black as liver-blood.

The pungent smell of old, rotting bones under roots fills my nostrils. A shade of half-remembered detail flickers in broken memory: a hand, cool fingers twined with mine, a beautiful face leaning down for a kiss. I can't grasp the context, or find the missing pieces that would make it whole. I grind my teeth in frustration.

The wolf sits at my side and the raven settles on the other flank.

"We cannot enter," the wolf says.

"I can go alone."

"No." The wolf bends too fast and stands before me. "You will not leave us here."

As the ghost's teeth graze the skin of my throat, memory follows.

"Don't," he begged the Sun. "Just let them go. They are no challenge. They only wish to be left in peace."

"You would defy your God? I have created you. Obey."

He had no self or honor to claim as reason to defy the Sun.

That one was *mine*. It carries my scent, hot as smelted metal. I swallow, trembling as my vision clears. For a moment, I wish the wolf's ghost would clamp its jaws around my neck, shake its head until my bones snap and memory fills the holes to drive me mad. But the cold dread holds me still.

When I find my voice, it's coarse and raw. I keep my knives sheathed. "We're not going to waste the night in argument. If you can't enter, I will."

"Where you will be devoured by the dark?" The wolf's eye sockets burn in the dark. "Where you may slip away into the lands beyond and forsake us? You owe us peace, man."

"And I will honor that debt. But not unless you let me pass."

"Give us your eyes," the wolf counters.

I don't blink, tempted as I am. "Why?"

The raven stretches its head back in silent laughter.

"The living may enter the Woods," the wolf says with a smile. "With your life in us, so may we. We will give them back."

They can take what they want without my consent, if they choose.

"Fine, lord wolf," I say, teeth gritted. I brace my arms, fingers curled into the loam.

The raven flaps upwards, hovering on silent wings, and opens its beak.

It hurts. Of course it hurts.

I curse as the raven's ghost plucks first the one eye—given to the wolf—and then the other, which it swallows; the eye resurfaces in its socket.

Ghost-memory doesn't follow, this time.

My vision spins in two opposite directions. Bile sears the back of my throat; blood crusts my cheekbones. The raven cocks its head, spilling half my vision sideways. Slowly, I adjust to this dual sight. I'm staring at my own back with the wolf-eye and my bloodied face with the raven-eye.

Brands knot my back. I've never realized how tattered my clothing is: the shirt barely more than collar and strips of sleeves, trousers sliced into decorative ribbons about my thighs. The brands on my flesh coil in intricate patterns. Bandits didn't mark me like that, yet the sight sends my heart quickening. There's a tug in my gut, a hook threaded on a chain.

The raven scrapes the backs of my knuckles with its talon, unspooling another piece of my own memory, unwanted.

He knelt before the Sun, silent, for he couldn't say he had fallen in love with the darkness. That smooth face made of shadow, the hands curled around his fingers, the caress of lips against his.

But the Sun saw into his heart.

"You would turn from your God?"

He dared not be honest, so he kept his silence. The Sun branded him in punishment—all the words of his blasphemy—and sent him into the mountains.

"Stop this!" I'll crack, fall into pieces, if I must see any more. It could be lies. I long for it all to be lies. "Or our deal is forfeit."

The raven preens its chest plumage.

"You have no weight to bargain with," the wolf says. "We have no wish to wait eternity to see our bones to rest."

Trapped, again. If I hesitate, they'll force memory into me until I obey. I've gotten used to the empty spaces like I've grown fond of the darkness. Perhaps it's better to forget.

You can forget everything you don't want, for a price, the map says.

I step into the woods with the ghosts.

The owls quiet first, and one by one, the whippoorwills and magpies and swallows fall silent.

The wolf's fur ripples, peeling back to show brutal wounds, jagged splashes of bone-white, purpled-red entrails spilling against the ground.

"I died amidst these trees," the wolf murmurs. "I tried to take him home, back to our mountains. He wandered far ahead of me into these lands. I followed, but I cannot run as fast as my love can fly, and when I caught his scent again, you had murdered him, Man."

I turn my face away as sudden pain in my chest I can't name flares bright. The raven-eye watches the wolf, unblinking.

"Who killed you?" I ask finally.

"The same ones who took your name," the wolf says. "They overwhelmed me, in time."

I wish the wolf would make itself as silent as the raven. "We need to keep moving."

The wolf-eye glances at me, but the ghosts make no protest as we stalk deeper into the Woods. The raven flaps languidly at my shoulder, and the wolf prowls at my other side, so, in a manner, I can still see as I once did.

Moonlight lies in congealed puddles like old blood. Broken pieces of starlight glitter sharper from where they hang caught on dark leaves and dead branches. The air itself is heavy, blue-black as it holds the night close.

Between the trees, I catch sight of a face made of darkness, smiling at me. I jerk my head uselessly, but the shadow melts into a formless void once again and is gone. Why is it so *familiar?*

A glimpse of light at my feet attracts the wolf-eye, welcome distraction.

It's a lone sunbeam, shivering under a tree and cornered by shadows. Dawn is far off, not even a whisper in my bones. The pinch of regret startles me as we watch the forsaken sunlight. It will die here.

The most I can do is offer it a warmer burial than the cold ground and damp leaves where the dark curls. A mercy, undeserved, that I desperately need to give it. I kick the shadows aside and cup the sunlight in both hands. It's weak, lukewarm and dimming into ember-red.

"Rest," I whisper to it, and its radiance flickers in a sigh. I tuck it into my vest pocket, a droplet of warmth over the scars along my skin.

"Do you ever question why?" the wolf asks.

I'm tired of riddles. "Speak plainly."

The wolf's shoulders are level with my chest, and the ghost tilts its head to make me stumble, my vision at my own feet. "Why you came to these Woods," the wolf says, "why you have wandered the petrified land of stumps and bones where it is never dawn."

"It doesn't matter." The lie comes with the practiced ease of sliding a knife between sleeping ribs.

"Our pasts matter," the wolf replies. "Would you be here if it did not?"

I won't concede truth to the ghost.

The Woods are tranquil as a newly dug grave. There, against one of the birch, a gash where an ax split the bark. Here, a skeletal bush where a net stripped it of foliage. And there, at my feet, a footprint: my own, bloodied, old. This is the path.

My breath quickens, anticipation braided around dread. I won't turn back now, though some buried instinct begs me to flee, to let the ghosts keep my eyes so long as I escape these Woods.

I scatter the coward's impulse and push forward. Ahead, the trees fall back and we reach the half-moon clearing.

Six man-shapes stand with axes hanging limp in their hands. They aren't ghosts, but they aren't the living, either. Flesh sags from graying bones. Rotted leather garments hang in tatters about protruding shoulder-bones and jutting hips. Their mouths roil with maggots.

"You came back," they say in unison.

Lichen ropes snap from the trees and snare my arms, pulling them above my head. A second forms a noose and snakes around my neck. The ropes heave me backwards, pinning me against a hawthorn. More lichen circles my ankles.

Bound. *Helpless.*

The ghouls lumber forward with axes raised. My heart beats in a panicked frenzy. I strain to lever one arm free as the noose tightens, dragging my chin up.

The ghosts sit back on either side of me and watch.

Pocked, dead skin stretches across the ghouls' faces. Why do I not remember these details, the rotting teeth and ant-chewed eyes—

"We are stronger now." The ghouls raise their axes. "We will not fail you again."

Muscles strain in my shoulders as I pull one arm towards my chest. I feel the warm spot over my heart and hook my fingers inside the vest pocket—last hope. "Burn for me," I whisper, a final plea.

The sunbeam has grown strong on my body heat. The sunlight expands and blossoms, brilliant, terrible, pulling light from high above until it's a miniature sun incarnate. It bursts in a passionate supernova and the echo of a triumphant scream.

Both ghosts shut my eyes so I will not go blind.

The ghouls cry out, their axes dropping to the forest floor. The lichen shrieks and unwinds. Free, I draw my knives and fling myself into the afterimage of the sunlight. Blades meet unresisting flesh.

Pieces of my stolen memory unwind with the crunch of rib and rip of skin, weaving threads back into place.

One.

He remembers the Sun, his God; his purpose is only to obey. He is the Avatar of the Sun, glorious in battle, fierce in peace, merciless in all.

Two.

He was once a man, but when he gave himself to the Sun, it burned away all trace of who he was. He is remade only to serve.

Three.

He takes the map from the body of his predecessor, who looked too long into the abyss stretched dark across vellum. He envies that suicide.

Four.

He stands in a cave, surrounded by wolves—eyes gray, teeth bared, bodies unmoved. Too late he realizes he stares not at living flesh but skeletons, with the ghost-images of life overlaid on bones.

Five.

And he remembers the shadow; the beautiful, cold darkness that soothes the burning in his veins and the unbearable light behind his eyes.

When the sixth ghoul falls, I wait for my name, surely caught like a fishbone within the woodsman's throat.

Only the feel of old blood on my knuckles comes as reward.

I spin in a circle, though the ghosts now watched the clearing and see all. Six bodies. Nothing more. "Where is my *name?*"

"They destroyed it," the wolf says calmly. "You asked them to, after all."

My spine snaps rigid and I turn my head (sightless) until the wolf-eye looks me in the face.

The wolf's ghost smiles cruelly. "Don't you remember, man?" It prowls across the woodsmen's bodies. "Did the dead give you back what you begged them to steal?"

Why would I *ask* for this? "Where are your bones? I will see you buried outside these Woods and at peace and you will *leave me be.*"

"Look down," the wolf says. "You will see."

The raven inclines its head, hooks the eye from its socket with its talons, and pops it back into my skull. The wolf does the same.

Again my vision reels, settles, and I blink against crusted blood on my eyelids.

The ghosts' vengeance falls like an ax blade. Their memories and my own wrap together in my eyes and play out unflinching, unavoidable.

He feeds blood to the map so it will show him where the old huntsmen are buried, cursed into undeath for their failure to save the First Forest from the war between Sun and Moon. Crouched among the petrified tree stumps, agate-colored in the campfire, he uses his knives to dig through ancient soil until he finds the six huntsmen.

(High above, the raven watches him.)

"Why do you disturb us?" the huntsmen wail.

He pulls them from their graves and offers a simple bargain: Follow him to the Woods, which have grown on the blood and bones of the dead left from war. There their axes lie; they will pick up their tools again and kill him. Chop his name into nothing and make his body the same. His bones, full of sunlight, will burn them into ash and they will be free.

(His death is what he promised the raven.)

The woodsmen agree. They take up their axes in the Woods.

(Far away, a wolf races across the land, a rippled blur of silver-black. The wolf raises his head and howls. "Wait, my love! Wait for me!"

But the raven does not hear. The wolf cannot reach the raven in time to save him.)

The huntsmen toss a net over the man, and he waits for the end, waits as they dig his name from his ribs with cold hands, waits as they cut it to pieces, waits—

But the woodsmen's blades are rusted and they have lost the strength in their arms.

It hurts. Of course it hurts.

They fail to kill him, leaving wounds ragged to bone not broken, and they chop away memory. For the undead, memory and flesh are the same—privileges of the living. They cannot tell the difference.

He forgets why he came and who they are, but he never forgets his knives. He cuts himself loose and flees.

A raven flares its wings, blocking the man's path. "Let them finish," the raven says. "You swore to me you would be no more! You swore you would pay for what you did!"

(Far away, a wolf howls.)

He kills the raven.

The memory snaps my head back and the living trees of the Woods rear ancient and hateful above. I drop to my knees.

"You remember," the wolf whispers. "How you, heartblood of the Sun, crawled far beneath our mountains and incited the earth to rupture in fire and ash. You turned our mountains into weapons. You burned our homes, our ships, our people into *nothing.*"

The ache in my gut threads like thorns through every vein. "Yes, lord wolf…"

I sought darkness afterwards so I could forget what I did. But when was I ever honest? I didn't want to forget. I wanted the darkness to devour me, blot out my existence so even the Sun would forget. But the darkness failed.

No…no, I shied away, unable to ask. I fell in love with the darkness, with that face in the shadows, and could not beg for my end that way. The map would only send me back to the Sun. So I found the huntsmen instead.

With the holes in my memory now sewn shut with ash-gray thread woven by ghosts, I look up at the wolf and the raven.

"Your bones aren't here, are they."

The wolf's muzzle crinkles in a sad smile. "You're kneeling on them. The huntsmen buried us together when I was dead. The Woods cannot hurt us."

"You needed no living flesh to come here," I say, numb, the words coming in dull monotone. "And my blood was never in your eyes."

The raven's neck feathers shine blue-black and red. "No, it wasn't."

You cannot trust the dead, says the map.

"You did kill my love," says the wolf.

"And my love died trying to bring me home," says the raven. "Our bones are already together, in these Woods that will never forget."

I kept my word to the huntsmen, then, who will linger no longer, burned by the sunlight and destroyed with knives forged in the Sun. I lift my chin, throat bared, raw hope no different from desperation. *Kill me*, I want to beg. *Let me go.*

"What do you want from me now, lord ghosts?"

Raven and wolf turn their faces together. There is silence between them.

At last, the wolf says, "Once, there was vengeance. But what does it matter to the dead? We only wished you to be held accountable. You do not deserve to live without remembering what you have done."

The raven nods. "And now you will always know. It is why we took your eyes; so you will see forevermore. Even your map cannot take that away."

I stare up at the tree canopy, at the unseen dawn. The sunbeam I freed will bring the Sun news of me. The Sun will wait, as it always does, its wrath unsated.

You can still have your name, the map says. *For a price.*

The map is honest, at least.

"You fled the Sun once," the wolf says. "If you step within its sight again, it will destroy you, and it will not be quick."

"I know," I reply.

"We can find peace now," the raven says. "It is your choice if you do the same."

Wolf and raven turn, side by side, and disappear into the Woods.

I stay on my knees, shivering in the cold.

As I look into the Woods, where the ghosts faded, the shadows curl thickly. For a moment, I catch a glimmer of that face, the one I turned my back on the Sun to find. The darkness is here. It has a name for me all its own.

Will it take me back, even with what I have done?

(I was as bright as the Sun, once. The dark has every right to destroy me as I did the wolves.)

I ignore the map. I will find my own way now; the dawn will always be waiting.

I walk into the Woods in search of darkness.

IRON ARIA

THE MOUNTAIN DREAMS pain. Cold iron vibrates purple-blue deep in the stone while tongues made from rot and rust bite and gnaw and hunger ever deeper.

The dam, buried like a tooth in the mountain's narrow gums, holds back the great burgundy ocean. Otherwise it would pour into the Agate Pass valley and swallow up the mining town at the mountain's toes.

From an owl's eye, the dam is almost as big as the mountain, built five hundred human-years ago. The infesting tongues burrow in from the sea, sent by angry water-memories. The sea cannot see its children in the lakes far beyond the dam. So it sends corrosion into the mountain, into the infinitesimal pores of the dam.

The mountain is being devoured from the inside and it *screams.*

KYRU SQUINTS UP at the mountain in the moonlight.

It slopes massive and muscled against the ice-black sky. The mountain's dream-noise woke him from his own nightmares—the loudness of *steel blood breath*, of his mother's last words—and he shivers in the late autumn night. Snow will come soon, blown in salt-scented gusts from across the ocean on the other side of the dam.

He sits on his windowsill, the shutters thrown open. It is only one floor's drop to the burlap-covered garden below and then twenty steps to the forge, where his heavy boots and thick gloves hang on pegs, where his rucksack, stained from coal dust, waits with his leather apron.

He has never trod up the mountain, so he doesn't know how many steps it would take.

The miners' cart trails are well-worn and wide, easy to walk. He could be gone before dawn and not missed until—

That is where his plan falls to pieces like shattered crockery. His aunt would know he had disappeared within the hour. He apprentices to her in her smithy; and the only routes away from town are up the mountain or down the valley.

He hates the valley. Its floor is littered with unknown graves, mournful bones, his last memories of his mother and sister. He craves escape and does not know how to unearth it.

Dawn chips away the clouds and it is once again too late again to run.

"Kyra?" his aunt calls from the kitchen. "Get dressed. It's a long forge day."

He flinches at the wrong-name, slipped like a needle under his skin. He climbs from the chill window and grabs the heavy leather belts he uses to flatten down his chest before he pulls on his shirt and trousers.

IN THE KITCHEN, his aunt straps on her leather apron as her husband scoops warmed day-old oatmeal into trenchers for the three of them.

Kyru shuffles to the table, his sketchbook under his arm. Mint and honey spice the breakfast. He gulps his warmed cider to keep from having to speak.

His aunt shovels her oatmeal in huge bites, saying around mouthfuls, "We got a big order from Brynu down at the farrier's. He's armoring some new plough horses for hauling ore through the Crags. He doesn't want to take chances on the wolves being hungry this winter."

Kyru nods.

"Kyra," his uncle says with a sigh, "what *are* you wearing in your pants? Another bunch of sackcloth?"

Kyru scoots his chair closer to the table so his uncle can't see his lap.

His aunt shakes her head and shoves her empty trencher aside. "She'll get over it eventually, Dyru. Be glad she's as skilled in metallurgy as her mother, ages rest her memory."

His uncle shrugs and clears the table. "Well, at fifteen I'd hoped she'd be eyeing herself a suitable husband by now. Folk talk more and more, you know."

"Eh, let folk talk. Long as Kyra pulls her weight in the forge, she can put off the men for years for all I care."

He has no interest in marriage, to another man or not. He's never been attracted to other people the way everyone else places such value in.

When he dreams of escape, he pictures himself in his own forge, content with metal-song and the warmth of burning coal, visited only by people who call him by his true name.

His aunt claps her hands, brisk and loud. "C'mon, the farrier's armor won't forge itself."

Kyru's stomach cramps. He leaves his meal unfinished.

The bitter air warbles at his ears. Pleasant gray chill washes the kitchen heat off his skin.

He looks up at the mountain. Over the dam lies the sea. He has never heard of water caring the make of a person's bones and flesh. It all sinks in the end.

"Kyra," his aunt snaps from the smithy door. "Daydream at lunch."

Kyru ducks his head and shoves his hands in his pockets. Even the promise of singing to the metal—when his aunt can't hear—is dulled by her impatience.

He hears the soldiers' swords before the town's alert bells sing.

A REGIMENT OF one hundred soldiers in emerald uniforms and sun-bright armor marches into Agate Pass, the Lord High's brilliant banners snapping in the cold air.

The town of Agate Pass is the last frontier-hold on the mountain. Other towns in the region have withered and crumbled, but Agate Pass holds fast. The dam was supposed to bridge commerce, power great wheels and generate trade and wealth through the valley.

But dour luck has clung here for generations, the dam now only a bridge through the mountain passes to the flatter lands in the empire outside the valley.

Kyru watches, his legs rigid, from behind the cedar fence that corrals the geese into the yard beside the forge. A half-dozen imperial knights, their plumed helmets shaped like roaring lions, stride towards the smithy.

Miners readying for work edge along the road, watching.

"Smith," the knight at the front calls, deep voice rich and thick like the hair that coils down over his breastplate in a thick braid spun with ribbons. The gold leafing along his shoulder pauldrons marks him as a general.

Kyru's aunt shuffles past him, out onto the front stoop of the smithy, and bows low. "Welcome, Hands of the Lord High."

As the knights draw nearer, their armor hums with wariness. Agate Pass has not received a military envoy in two years, since the Summer Census. It's not the town that unsettles the armor's folds and joints, but the dam.

All the knights' armor can feel the wrongness welling from the sea.

A trumpeter, his throat replaced with a gilded cage and thrumming gears, announces that the Emerald Lion General and the Imperial Hands are closing Agate Pass's mines. By the Lord High's order, the mines will be closed until reports of instability in the dam can be confirmed.

As the general strides closer, Kyru notices the general's armor. It is *suffering*. It keens low, stoic. A burning pain lingers from the battlesmithy done on the road, incomplete, which left unseen scars.

Kyru can always hear the voices of metal, like strings sewn through his skin into his heart. He stuffs the cotton strips he uses in the forge in his ears to dull the outside noise.

Can I help?

The armor shivers. *Echoes, stolen breath, wailing dead—*

Kyru flinches and presses his body against the fence, watching through the slats. The armor imprints its experience on his senses: hard angles, scalpel edges, glittering passion, and vicious duty.

Where is your pain?

The armor shows a memory of the dent when an ax caught in the breastplate's folded steel over the sternum. Now metal seams pinch there like crooked nerves.

Dust of kin scattered knife-sharp—buried—blood—stricken—

Kyru rubs his arms above the copper bracers he wears. They belonged to his mother, forged by her hand when he was born. She wrought them with sigils to give light in darkness.

By that light he found his way to Agate Pass the night his mother died.

The general pulls off the helmet and tucks it under one arm.

The general's features are heavyset, highlighted with rouge and eyeliner, lips colored coral-pink. A coiled sigil, whorled threads branching leaf-like from delicate roots, is tattooed on the soldier's temple, just under the edge of hair.

Kyru recognizes the symbol, often painted on skin in the bigger cities: it denotes feminine gender, subtle and elegant.

The general is a woman.

Kyru's heart trips. She is like him, only opposite. He's seen other men with the masculine symbol: waving lines like a river, encircled in a sharp-edged sun. He scratched it on his cheek in charcoal once, but washed it clear before his aunt saw.

"Smith," the general says again, "a word." She strides up the path and into the shop, and Kyru follows as if magnetized.

Two knights wait outside the door, none following the general into the smithy. Kyru slips in like a breath of smoke, scarce noticed.

The general's words hum deeper and richer than his aunt's as the general lays out curt orders. Kyru ignores the two women's voices and sidles towards the general's back.

Can I help? he asks, tentative. *I will be gentle.*

The armor murmurs umber-toned consent. He touches his palm to the breastplate's back; he feels no defensive runes, no static snap of angry magic. He shuts his eyes and spreads his focus out along the damascene plates. With gentle nudges, he unfolds the pinched seam and unweaves the battlesmithy, then smoothes over the wound. The armor's pain ebbs and the breastplate brightens in gratitude—

A hand seizes his wrist and yanks him around. Kyru sucks in his breath, his body taut. He is face to face with the Emerald Lion General.

"Who are you?" the general demands. "And what are you *doing?*"

"It was hurting," Kyru says, scarcely audible.

"Please forgive her, general," his aunt says, twisting her fingers around her forge belt. "She's highly skilled in metallurgy but—"

"'She'?" The general's eyebrows arch. She releases Kyru, who stumbles back, breathing fast. To Kyru, she says, "What's your name?"

"Kyru," he whispers. It is the only word that never hurts.

It was the last word he told his mother ten years prior. She asked him, *What shall I call you, child, when I see you from the heavens?* He told her his name. Then the curse turned her bones into brittle slivers and her skeleton collapsed in on itself.

"And are you a woman?" the general asks.

Kyru shakes his head, his heartbeat like hot gold booming in his ears.

"A man, then?"

Kyru nods, his breath scattered wisps in his lungs.

"I thought as much."

To his aunt, the general adds, "I advise you show your *son* more respect." She flexes her gauntlet and turns for the door. "My lieutenant will pay you for the forge's use and expenses. My smiths will remain here until called for."

She sweeps out; her knights come to attention as she passes. Kyru dashes after her before his aunt can stop him. He catches the door on his shoulder.

He dismisses the bruise. It's a dull sensation, a deep ache he prefers to sharp cuts.

"Wait." Kyru swallows. His tongue itches. The words clink and scrape, wrong angles and too loud against his teeth. "I can help."

The general holds up her first, the steel gauntlet attentive but wary. Her retinue halts. She turns on one heel, a great owl-movement, fluid and terrifying. "How?"

Kyru points up at the mountain. He pushes sounds against his lips despite the pain. "I hear what's wrong."

The general studies him, her dark eyes like mica. "Hearing and helping are not the same."

He lifts his hands. "Your armor. I healed it. Can…do that…with the dam."

It is a chipped truth, not whole. His ribs tighten in fear she will see it and grow angry. He has never touched the dam; he knows its construction only from the architectural drawings housed in the town census hall. As a boy, he sneaked away to lose himself in the drawings of the great dam. He imagined it folding around him and shielding him from the loud, cold world.

After his mother died, after his aunt filed legal claim to raise him, that was all that kept his tears from drowning him.

For the last two months the mountain's dreams have drifted through his thoughts, inescapable. If the dam is not healed, if the mountain is not soothed, everything in the valley will be washed away.

He does not remember where his mother's and sister's bones are, but they should not be churned up and scattered. He does not want to see Agate Pass again, but he does not want it to die.

At last, the general nods once. "Come with me, boy."

HIS AUNT AND uncle protest, but the general hears none of it. In a few terse words, she conscripts Kyru into the Emerald Lion Regiment and tells him that from now on he is in service to the Lord High and Her Holy Empire.

There is no room for sickly, mold-green fear in his chest when he falls in step with the general's silent-footed guard. They head up towards the mountain. The mountain's pain is too vivid, too cold and heavy as it pulls at his thoughts.

Yet even the great vastness of stone cannot erase his worry: will the general send him back when his use is finished?

THE DAY-LONG TRIP up the mountain has brought the regiment to the foot of the Tilted Stairs, a great staircase carved into the stone that leads to the mines and the cave systems inside. From this campsite, Kyru sees the dam in full for the first time.

The Agate Pass Dam expands between the mountain's cleft, as long as hundred wagons, as thick a dozen horses standing nose to tail. Age seeps through the old stone, heavy burgundy teased with gray. He gets only a glimpse before the nauseating swell of mountain-pain washes through him. He sits down on one of the steps, dizzy.

The knights' retinue set up camp, and Kyru wonders why the Lord High would send so many soldiers. He dares to gesture, faint and quick, at the armored men and women around him as he looks at the general in question.

She offers a half-smile. "The last two expeditions sent here haven't reported back," the general says. "I've had reports of maddened animals and crazed bandits. What have you heard?"

He ducks his head. "Hurt."

The general grunts. "Look, boy. I know desperate when I see it. But you're still an unknown element in my plans, do you understand? Your metallurgy will prove useful, but I want you to stay out of my engineers' way when they arrive. Let us do what we've come here to do."

He nods, shrinking inside as he hears: *you cannot help.* Is that his curse? He couldn't save his mother and sister. He can't change his body. He can't heal the mountain and the dam.

NIGHT LOWERS ITS curtains, starless and full of clouds. Kyru keeps the cotton in his ears against the clamor of cheerful pots and sarcastic ladles. The knights' armor is restless, anxious this close to the mountain. Only the Emerald Lion General's mended armor seems calm.

Kyru pulls out his sketchbook and flicks charcoal over the thick paper. The smoothed pulp soothes his fingers while the copper bracelets murmur comfort into his bones from wrists up to his jaw. He hunches over nonetheless, using the slope of his shoulders to hide the awkward bulge of his chest in profile.

He draws what he hears in dreams, what the mountain's nightmares show:

The furious ocean, hurt and mourning children dying far from the parent waters, stripped of salt and memory. The metal cannot see which way to go. Veins of ore twist and writhe while the great iron beams sunk long ago into the consenting stone—

"...we lock down the tunnels in the morning," says the Emerald Lion General. Her name is Tashavis. She sits cross-legged with her boots polished and standing to attention at her side as she paints her toenails a luminous green. "The engineers can examine the dam and find the source of the disturbances. Has Zasa reported back yet?"

"Not yet," one of the soldiers says, her jawline grim. "I've had no word from her since she went up this morning."

Kyru chews the inside of his cheek. Dawn is so far off. He walked in silence beside the general most of the day, but each step deepened the unease in his belly. The mountain's pain is growing worse. He is not sure they *have* until dawn.

He flips through his sketchbook, his fingers tracing familiar pictures as he looks for an unused page. He must illustrate the urgency to the general. There is little space left on the paper.

Tashavis jerks her head at her soldiers. "Set a double watch. Everyone, light rest—we move at dawn."

Kyru sits just close enough to the fire to see his paper and feel the fringe of heat, but not too close to the soldiers. As the knights disperse, he edges closer to the general. Her armor hums welcome and he offers it a tiny smile in return.

"General?"

Tashavis glances at him. "Ah, Kyru. How's your first day of conscription?" She flashes him a smile. "Not quite the excitement you pictured, I imagine."

He hesitates. Despite his aunt's refusal to call him by his true name, they'd developed a useful shorthand in hand gestures when in the forge. He does not have such luxury with Tashavis.

Kyru bites his lip. "No."

"You're an artist," Tashavis says with a nod at the sketchbook. "My brother likes to paint as well. You've heard of the Dragonfly General?"

Kyru shakes his head. He doesn't want to interrupt her—but he needs to make her see. They can't wait until dawn.

Tashavis chuckles. "Well, he didn't earn the title through paints, admittedly. I'll tell you war stories later. What's this one?" she asks, her eye cornering the open page. It's Kyru's self-portrait, the one he made when he first saved his pay from the forge to buy the paper and charcoal. He placed it in the middle of the sketchbook, a single blank page beside it.

Kyru rendered his dream of changing his skin onto the paper: becoming smooth, polished metal—androgynous planes to flatten his chest and hips, his bones wrapped in copper and his skull hairless, domed in bronze. He would have steel mesh fingers, flexible and strong. His ears would be replaced with tiny mechanical doors he could close to keep out noise when he needed silence. Deep iron for his throat and lungs, to lower the timbre and register of his voice. A metal boy, but impervious to heat and sound: a perfect smith. He would train his skin not to feel unpleasant textures so he could dress how he liked. His eyes would be silver, with gold pupils so he could stare into the sun without becoming blind, and see far, far into the night sky to watch the stars dance amid the coal-deep spaces between.

He dares not shut the book and hide it now that she's focused her attention on him. Hesitantly, he points at himself.

Tashavis extends a hand, and Kyru sets the sketchbook on her palm. His fingers shake. She pulls the sketch closer, her gaze sweeping like an unstoppable tidal wave over his true self rendered in charcoal.

"It's beautiful," she says, and hands him the sketchbook back. "You capture your likeness effortlessly."

Kyru blinks, his mouth sticky-dry with surprise. He accepts his sketchbook.

"I'm glad you know yourself, Kyru. I was twice your age before I found the courage to show who I was, even to myself." She adorns her nails with quick, sure strokes. "All persons deserve to have their names and bodies respected."

Pain prickles at the base of Kyru's spine, twingeing the skin of his hips. He stiffens and lifts his chin. It's not *noise*, but he feels old metal, burned and soured with salt, hateful and hurting. He jabs his finger at the far edge of camp where the metal draws nearer. "Someone's coming." The words dig at his gums, splinters under his tongue. He spits them out fast. "Dozens. Angry. Want to kill us."

The general snaps to her feet. Her paints tumble in green-blue pooled stains by the fire.

"Swords ready!"

The camp unfolds like a fierce steel trap, soldiers springing to attention. A gurgle comes from the edge of camp.

A severed hand skitters through the dirt clutching the warning whistle.

The general curses and draws her saber. Kyru claps his hands over his ears.

From the shadows outside the camp, skeletal figures in moldy leathers covered in crustaceans stagger forward, carrying the smell of brine and flotsam in a heavy miasma. Seaweed falls from eye sockets long rotted out. Mouths hang agape, teeth broken like mollusk shells, salt dripping from exposed bones and calcified flesh. The bandits' hands have been replaced with the remains of old swords, hooks, saws. The metal seethes, dragged from the deeps to the stinging air, denied oblivion. Rusted threads corroded by the ocean hold the dead bandits together.

The soldiers crash against the undead bandits. Pulled from the sea, those bodies are fueled with rage and hunger—like the ocean, like the mountain's pain.

Tashavis strides towards the invaders. Her armor brightens with war sigils—fiery green with deeper highlights until her breastplate glows with a rampant lion and the armor roars. "Kyru, *go!* Get to safety!"

Kyru runs the only direction open to him: up the mountain.

He bruises his toes and shins as he scrambles up the steps. The copper armbands glow faint amber to light his path, but it hardly pushes back the dark.

Into the mountain, where the air is damp and cool, he hears the old metal in the stone's veins. Mining tunnels. He read a memoir from one of the first miners in Agate Pass, one of the stone masons who scooped out trenches into the rocks between land and sea with her bare hands—

Kyru keeps the illustrations from that book in his head, traces the woodblock edges with careful memory. His favorite was the one of Mason Irusa, standing on the mountain, holding a great boulder aloft as if about to throw it into the sea. There were maps in the book, too, like worms wriggling through the paper, inky trails to show where the original mines had once been excavated before it was deemed too dangerous and the passages were closed, and new tunnels developed further down the Stairs.

Deeper, he runs.

The metal cries out louder, thundering in his thoughts. His ears begin to bleed, hot itches that crawl down his neck.

PRESSING. DROWNING. WRITHING. BURNING.

Kyru stumbles and lands hard on his knees. Here the tunnel branches, but he can't remember the map. In his memory, the pages keep blurring. Which way?

Instead, he sees his family: himself, his mother, and his sister, with their few belongings, pushing through the forests from the coast up towards the mountain. They fled the ruins of salt-washed boards and icy ropes, all that was left of the shantytown—their home—after the unhappy waves destroyed it.

In the forest, along with the few other persons and broken families who had survived, they came to a wide stream, dark and rippling with unanswered voices.

From those waters rose the old dead, left to rot for so long.

He wasn't near enough when the old dead attacked. He'd been looking for the perfect stick to make a sword, so he could become a guardsman for the Lord High. He heard the screams—his sister's, first—and then his mother's clarion voice invoking a death-curse that would shatter all the dead. His mother saved half the people in their little band of survivors.

He ran back, wielding his stick, terrified, but when he found her, the damage was done. The old dead were no more, and his mother lay dying beside his sister's tiny body.

If he had been there, perhaps the old dead would have gone for him first, not little Zyra.

RAGE SLUICING. THICK, COLD, UNBEARABLE. IT HURTS, IT HURTS, IT HURTS.

Kyru presses his palms against his ears. The metal jars him from memory, from guilt. Too loud too loud too *loud*.

Stop!

IT BURNS, the metal cries. *IT CONSUMES. IT TAKES ALL.*

Kyru fumbles for his sketchbook, rocking on his heels, then realizes he left it in camp. He has nothing to ground himself with. He squeezes his eyes shut, clinging to his copper armbands. Need to think. Need the red noise to go away.

Can't help you when you shout. It comes out a cracked whisper, a thought sent to the metal and stone. *Please. Please. Stop.*

Slowly, too slow, the metal voices dim and settle, pulling the pain inside so it doesn't spark and wash over Kyru in blue-hot waves. Kyru breathes deep, pictures pink copper roses and bronze lilies shaped with touch and heartbeat.

CAN YOU HELP?

Kyru keeps the flowers in front of his eyes, keeps breathing. His neck is stiff, orange-sore, but he can dip his chin. Nod.

Yes. Careful, quiet. Unlike before—with his family, with himself. The metal and the mountain can yet be saved.

Yes, but you need to listen softly. We can't let the rot hear.

KYRU PRESSES HIS hands against the mountain's skin.

He can feel the dam, a mastery of old smithwork: great steel beams, fibrous mesh, and iron braids wound through uncounted tons of stone in a dam that holds back the sea. It's hurting, chewed away by the rot. The dam's umber pain echoes back against Kyru and he bites the inside of his cheek to stop it spilling out into the mountain even more.

Let me help you, he says, desperate. *Please.*

The mountain gives consent.

Kyru shows the new iron where to slip through cracks in the mountain's bones, guides the tendrils towards the dam. The metal follows his will, echoing back into him until there is only a call and response like heartbeats: his to the mountain's, the mountain's to his.

HURRY, rumbles the supports in the wall. *THE WATER PRESSES.*

Kyru's arms tremble. Sweat itches his face, stings his eyes. The blue pain echoes through his gut and up to his jaw until his head feels too heavy to stay attached to his neck.

Pressure like a hundred tons of ore raw to the forge bangs against his bones and his footing slips. No. He must stay—must stand—must—

The dam groans again.

Kyru feels his muscles fray, ligaments cracking, skin seeping iron shavings as he guides the metal ever onwards. It will rip him to pieces, melt him like copper.

The mountain shudders and Kyru wants to scream.

He. Will. Not. Let. GO.

Iron fills the cracks, wraps itself around its siblings worn with rust, binds to stone, nets the dam from the inside until a new web of cold iron stretches between the mountain's gums like a tooth cap and the dam is healed.

Kyru falls into white silence.

THE MOUNTAIN NO longer dreams pain.

It has let the ocean send soft memories through the absence of iron, drifting in stone to flow out in a new waterfall far from the town. The stream will wind through forest land and over dried rock and touch the lost lake-children, the saltless now remembered and able to share dreams with the ocean after so long silent.

KYRU OPENS HIS eyes. He lies on bright sheets, his hands wrapped in gauze, his head brittle-full like a turnip sack filled with glass chimes.

"Don't sit up," says a deep voice, and he remembers it—the Emerald Lion's. "You're a lucky boy. The cave-in we dug you out from almost crushed your skull. The physician says your hands will heal, but it'll take time."

The room drifts into focus as his eyes adjust to the light. Sunlight. He cannot smell the sea, only vinegar and lavender. He hears the contented hum of the general's saber and the twining chirrup of scalpels and bone splints.

"Where?" he manages, lips swollen, the word scraping.

"Shale-Ar," Tashavis says. "About a week's ride from your old town. Whatever you did affected the curse from the dead. They dropped like wet clay, and then we heard the rumbles from the mountain."

The physician, a woman with eyes as dark as water-soaked agate, leans over him and spins a tiny rune between her fingers. "This will numb the pain and help you sleep."

"I…don't…have…to go back?" he manages.

"No." Tashavis smiles down at him, then lays a hand on his shoulder. "We've got another two weeks' journey until we reach the capital. Rest, Kyru. The dam is secured, and you are still under my protection." She shows him his sketchbook, the edges crumpled and the cover dented, and lays it beside him on the bed.

Kyru's ribs loosen, and he pulls in breath.

Through the stone foundations of the physician's house, down into the soil and stretching back through forest roots, Kyru can still feel the mountain again like a whisper in his heart.

The mountain looks over the valley, a truce brokered with the ocean, its skin sharing new memory with the waters as they did once, long ago.

The ocean's wrath has subsided with the tide, and the lakes, reawakened, sing in joy.

Are you all right? Kyru asks.

Yes, the mountain says. *Are you?*

Kyru smiles. *Yes.*

WHAT BECOMES OF THE THIRD-HEARTED

HER SKIN SMELLS of crushed pearls, dried salt, silver fish scales woven into unfinished memories. Her eyes are sculpted starlight, holding the sadness of death a million years ago and a million yet to come.

When she holds out her hand, I turn and run. The sand has turned to glass and my heels crack the shore in tiny percussions like the breaking of my hearts.

THE WORLD'S ENDING was quiet, demure, almost unnoticed.

In sleep, people faded into dreams—leaving behind only the soft remembrance of breath. The ones awake paused in every movement and shut their eyes. No panic, no fear. Gentler, perhaps, than any of us deserved.

I saw a few strangers awake and wandering, caught in their own quests, but none of them were you.

You were two states away and commuting back home when everything stopped. I sent you texts and called you until there was no cell reception and my voice hung in tatters in my throat.

I still whispered your name. *Shelby. Shelby. Shelby.* Until even whispers faded into nothing.

WHERE ARE YOU? I know where you should have been. But the world is a scattered puzzle (ten million pieces, not all there) and I have no box cover to reference what it should look like now.

How do I find you?

THE WOMAN IS everywhere. She drifts at the corner of my vision, watches when I blink, and she never speaks. I turn to face her, and again she slides aside like a mirage. Her footsteps linger, weighted in the land and air alike. I don't know what they will do if I touch them.

I clamber over coral growths thrust up where the highway used to stretch six lanes in both directions; a few pebbles of black, crumbled tar are all that's left of the road.

Like that time Tara was three and she found a Magic Erase marker and scrubbed that cheap thrift store painting of the whales until it was scraps of water enclosed in a frame. You were so furious at my daughter, but as the new step-parent, you tried your best to be reasonable. Did I tell you how much I appreciated that? I know you never quite liked the dolphin painting I replaced the whales with.

The horizon is slabs of darkness like great bricks stacked haphazardly, fire licking the spaces between like mortar. The sky is crumbling at the edges, raining pieces of blackness to reveal a bright, stardust void where clouds once swarmed.

I'm coming, Shelby.

(Am I? Can I, when I don't know how to find you?)

My cellphone turned into a tiny turtle with ruby eyes and *lorem ipsum* painted on its shell after the reception disappeared. I set it loose in the glass sand and it burrowed toward waters that no longer exist.

I haven't slept since the world ended. I can't—if I lie down, if I dream, I will lose what little time I have.

I never thought I'd come to miss the gridlocked traffic roaring past in the distance, our backyard always a little too close to it to let Tara play on the fenced-in grass unattended.

How long will this reality last?

What happens after the end of the world?

M**Y MOTHER TOLD** me we all have three hearts. Not in a physical sense; she clarified that when, at ten, I showed her anatomy photos in a textbook to prove her wrong.

"Your first heart is the smallest and scratchiest," my mother said. "It holds all the wonder and loves you acquire as you grow up. Horseback riding, video games, books, playing in the pool, skating, comics—whatever you love, your first heart can absorb and grow to make room for all of these things. It can become any size you need. Your second heart is made for the people you care for. Your family and friends, your lovers—when you're older—your spouse or spouses."

"Where are pets?" I demanded.

"Second heart," my mother said. "Why wouldn't they be?"

She set her heavy leather gloves on the basement workbench next to her welding helmet. She'd been working on one of her iron sculptures, forged from scrap picked up at junkyards. The basement was cement, empty except for the heavy wood tables and mother's machinery and piles of scrap, smelling always of hot metal and oil and her sweat.

"Your third heart," my mother said, "is a secret."

"Then how do you know it's real?"

She shrugged. "How do you know when anything is real?"

"Ugh, Mom."

She grinned. "Morgan, you'll know what your third heart is one day. It just takes time. No one's is the same."

I glared.

"I don't want three hearts," I yelled, tears in my eyes. I slammed the textbook onto the floor. "And I don't want to look like this."

"What do you want to look like?" my mother asked, confused, but at ten, I didn't have the words I needed.

There's a wall of shale threaded with lady slipper flowers made of papier mâché, tended by ants woven from yarn and silk. It blocks the coral highway now, humming in F-sharp minor with a melody I've never heard. It's not music so much as sensory impressions—blueberries rinsed in the sink, peeling acrylic paint free of your fingers, humid July nights plagued by mosquitoes, jazz horns on the radio, baby powder on Tara's skin, vacuuming the carpet, cuddling in bed after a hot shower, burning popcorn and hiding the taste with too much salt and butter.

The woman is almost at my elbow before I realize the wall is singing to me. Ants are tying minute poison ivy chains over my toes. The sting snaps my focus out of the music. I jump back and stumble down the length of the wall. It has no holes, it has no top. How do I get around?

(Are you on the other side?)

What do you want? I demand of the woman. *Why are you here?*

She extends a hand, inviting. If I touch her skin, I fear I will disappear.

So again I run.

MY MOTHER DIED before we met, but I have one photo left—of when Laura (my ex-wife), Tara (just a toddler then), and I visited her in the hospital. She smiled brighter than all of us, even faded and tired from chemo.

"How can you smile," I demanded, when Laura took Tara out of the room to feed her.

"Why shouldn't I?" my mother responded, squeezing my hand. "I'm going on a new adventure."

"Don't," I whispered. "Please, Mom."

"Honey...I want to tell you a secret."

I pressed her hand against my cheek, hiding my face. She must have felt the tears.

"My third heart is a ship," my mother said. "A beautiful sailboat painted like the sunset. I'm undocking and mastering the rigging. I'm going to sail past the universe and see things never before imagined."

My shoulders shook harder. She pulled my head down against her side and stroked my hair like she did when I was small.

"I named my sailboat *Morgan*," she said. "Because I'll always be with you."

YOU SENT ME a selfie of you and Tara the night before the world ended. You were in a chic little café, Tara with an oversized mug of hot chocolate, you with your black coffee. You both made faces at the camera.

I was too tired to reply. So I just...deleted the text and pretended I'd never received it.

It was the last picture I could have had of you.

THE RAIN RUMBLES towards me. The wall never ends. The ants and spiders follow in geometric patterns, their exoskeletons shifting through the light spectrum and the color wheels I remember from high school art class.

(Are you on the other side? How can I find you?)

The woman watches, her hair coiled like wet leaves about her shoulders.

My knuckles clang like bells when I punch the wall. If you and Tara are behind this wall, I will find a way over or around or through. Somehow. I keep your faces like a tattoo printed against my eyelids, every detail, from your crooked smile to the mole behind Tara's right ear.

I hope Laura is safe. We've always been good friends. When I find you, I'll look for her next. I will look for everyone.

The first drops of rain spatter near my feet. The ground evaporates where the water strikes.

The wall is endless. I don't have rope, or strength to climb.

I run again.

AS A TEENAGER I bound my breasts and wore baggy clothing and demanded people call me he, him, and sir. I cut my hair myself. I dated girls. I was a man.

In my twenties, when I met Laura, I was a woman. We married after college and two years into our marriage I told her I was once more a man. Our divorce was amicable; Laura never questioned my gender, merely said she preferred to be married to a woman who was always a woman. We remained friends.

When I met you, Shelby, I felt like neither. I felt ten again, confused because pronouns fit like jeans two sizes two small, pinching, not fitting all the way.

To you, it didn't matter. You called me "they" like I asked, and I knew I would love you forever.

I can't lose you like this, a deleted selfie before the end of the world.

THERE IS NO break in the wall, no doors or windows or bridges. The higher I climb, the faster the wall arches up towards the red sky. I slide down, covered in ivy and stung by little poems like insect bites.

Shelby! Tara!

Ever silent, the woman watches.

I face her, shaking, exhaustion chewing at every muscle and bone. I sink to the ground. The rain is close again. I don't know how to go on. I don't know where you are.

I'm so sorry, Shelby. Keep Tara safe. (Can you hold her for me?)

I look up at the woman, defeat encroaching like the rain. I can't outrun her. *What do you want?* I whisper, wordless.

She offers her hand again, fingers curled like commas. In her palm is a tiny sailboat made of feather-edged paper, painted like the sunset.

"WHAT'S A HEART, baba?" Tara asked me as I read her a picture book one evening.

I tapped my chest. "It's where you keep all the hugs and kisses and love, like a big balloon that never pops."

Tara giggled. "My heart is as big as the balloon ride!" She stretched her arms as wide as she could. We'd floated up in hot air balloon the week before for your birthday, Shelby. Tara had never been so excited as when she looked out over the countryside and said we were as high as heaven.

"Yes, boo," I told her. "That big."

I STARE AT the sailboat.

My mother smiles—I know her eyes now, beyond the sorrow. She has traveled universes…and she has come back.

And I know, then, why she's followed me.

Morgan is written on the sailboat's side.

My third heart is a compass. I feel it, the hands swinging towards a magnetic north I can't see. I pull it from my ribs, cupping it in both hands. You and Tara smile up at me, painted in photorealistic detail on the compass's face. Your heartbeat and Tara's hum in the compass's smooth, round shape.

I look my mother, at the boat in her hand—

At the rain that is erasing this world—

At the wall I cannot climb—

But perhaps, in a boat, I might sail over it to where you and Tara are, Shelby.

I take my mother's hand and feel the night wind in my face as the sail unfolds around me. She steers while I stand at the helm, compass in hand, guiding our course to find you.

THE GENTLEMAN OF CHAOS

PEOPLE CALL HIM the Gentleman of Chaos, but he is not gentle.

By popular count, he's assassinated thirteen kings, seventy-two princes, one thousand nobles, and five queens.

By popular legend, he's immortal, a god of commoners, a death-demon summoned to feed on corruption, a shadow that devours the unjust. He never unmakes the innocent, it is said.

He is not gentle; I have seen what he does.

But I tell you this: part of his title is true. He is a man. And men can die.

MY BROTHER THE king was cautious. He took the throne when he was twelve, the night after our father was murdered.

With the crown not yet heavy on his head, he called me to his private chamber.

My brother said, "I need your help, sister."

I was six. I said nothing.

He nodded, grim-faced, and sent me away.

Three days later, when I was locked inside the Abbey of Mercy, I heard that I had been declared dead; a tragic drowning accident. My funeral was spectacular, I am told.

THE GENTLEMAN OF Chaos has been painted, illegally, in a thousand different ways: as a winged shadow descending like a hawk against the moon; as a tall, thin wraith cloaked in starlight; as a man with knives for hands and eyes like an owl. He wears armor, or he is naked. He dances across rooftops or rises from the cobbled streets like mist. He smiles or he is faceless.

Always, somewhere in the paintings or the stories, there is blood. Blood on his fingers or in his mouth; blood dripping from his clothing or falling around him like salted rain. Blood that pools for a thousand miles beneath his heels.

He has no name, for it was banished long ago. By royal decree he has no face, for he does not exist. No one has heard his voice, soft like velvet; no one has seen the exhaustion and pain in his eyes; no one has felt his hand, scarred and callused, on their cheek in an apologetic caress.

No one has heard him whisper, "Not yet, child. Not tonight."

BECAUSE HE KNEW how our father died, my brother laid his plans in delicate layers over slow years. I did not see him again in person until I was twelve, when he visited once to ensure I was what he had commanded I become, but I always knew his voice, his words, his will. It wrapped around me like iron cords. Not a day had passed in six years that I did not know my brother's wishes.

My brother shaped me, built me into the perfect bodyguard—skilled in lies and unable to lie to him; deadly in the arts of poison and steel; loyal only to him; unremarkable in looks but my body trained until I had exacting control over every muscle, every breath. I had no title and no name. My brother called me She.

I was forged with one purpose: to serve my brother, to protect his body and soul, so that he might reign long.

THE GENTLEMAN OF Chaos has no past. Or perhaps those in power wronged him, had his lover murdered, imprisoned his child, broke and reshaped his body, strove to take away his will and identity.

It doesn't really matter, because he doesn't exist.

"I DREAMED ILL omens last night, sire," I told my brother.

The king clutched his goblet until his knuckles paled. "What omens?"

"The Gentleman of Chaos is coming for you."

He scoffed. "With you, She, I am always safe. Isn't that true?"

"Yes, sire," I said. I did not lie.

MY BROTHER THE king married twice, yet both wives died in childbirth, their stillborn infants strangled with bloody umbilical cords. Courtly tongues spun rumors of sorcery, a curse carried in the king's seed.

"Did you do this, She?" he asked me, tears glistening in his eyes.

I told him no.

"Then how?" he screamed. "Who did this?"

"The Gentleman of Chaos," I said.

The king did not remarry.

ON THE DAY I was released from the Abbey of Mercy, my brother the king summoned me to his side. He held a slim iron collar engraved with old magics.

"It cost a fortune to have this made by the reclusive wizards to the north," my brother said, "and even more to have them killed afterwards. But it will be worth any price. This is yours, She."

I held motionless as he snapped the collar about my throat.

"She," he said, "will obey all orders from my lips. She will never harm me or let me come to harm. She will never lie to me. She will serve until death."

The collar was unbreakable, permanent.

I did not let the king see my hatred; it was private, mine alone. Though tempted, I did not ask him, *If you had a brother, would you be as merciful?*

I simply bowed and said, "What do you command, sire?"

AT SIXTEEN, MY brother gave me an ultimatum: by my eighteenth birthday I must have given birth to a healthy child. He did not care who I bedded. I was to have my pick of any man not of noble breeding, and as many of them as I liked.

Not a tiresome order as I enjoyed the company of men. I fucked a dozen of them, experimenting in what I liked, what I didn't. They were tools, just as I, and I used them as such. I never learned their names; they were guardsmen or bakers or stable keeps or scribes.

At seventeen, I was pregnant.

THE FIRST PUBLIC attempt on my brother's life came during the autumn ball when I was eighteen. The Count of Dunfly, an unambitious cousin twice removed, hosted the masquerade. My brother had crushed the Redgrove Rebellion in the spring, prevented the Ishzaven from uprising on the northern border with carefully executed genocide the winter before, and eradicated the Musavo from within the kingdom that summer.

A very successful legacy in so short a time, said the court, a reign worthy of celebration. He would continue to do great things, his advisors told him. He made examples of commoners who dared to insult him and call him the Bloody Prince. ("I am king!" he told me as we watched the executioners make public spectacle with screams and gore.)

My brother the king was invincible so long as She was there to guard him.

As my brother danced with the Countess of Dunfly, a woman twice his age, I drifted in the shadows of gaudy gowns and pleated suits, gilded masks and lace-scoured hats. As always, I wore black: trousers and a tight-fit vest that flattened my chest; no loose threads or stray fabric that might be used against me.

I smelled the sweet rot of lilac before I saw the assassin, dressed in a beautiful lavender suit and carrying a fan sewn from dyed swan feathers. I threaded between the dancers and caught the assassin by the wrist before the fan, tipped in needles, could brush against my brother's skin.

"Dance with me," I whispered, and spun the assassin away.

"You will never protect him," the assassin said between clenched teeth. "You will fail one day."

"No," I said. "I never fail."

Fifteen steps later, at the end of the waltz, the assassin slumped in my arms, the fan's needles embedded between his fingers. I let him fall like a drunk beside a marble pillar and continued to watch my brother.

I KNEW WHAT the baby was. Leverage, a thing to hold over me.

My brother the king, who thought he had a sister, was not so arrogant that he did not fear me. I was with him always. I shadowed him when he went hunting, when he held court, when he danced, when he fucked whores and married duchesses alike.

I could not become soft, so I did not nurse the baby. She was given to a wet woman and I could only visit her once a month, under guard, in my brother's presence. He watched me, all but unblinking, as I stood with arms folded at my back, staring down at the thing I had pushed from my womb.

She looked like me, the baby did: she had my eyes, brown and wide, and my nose (but not broken yet). Her complexion was lighter, like the man who had fathered her. I thought, one day, she might grow up and smile.

I did not ask what name my brother had given her.

THE GENTLEMAN OF Chaos is not cruel.

He is a sadist. He tortures his victims and rips out their souls.

He kills them painlessly, quickly, and they never know they are dead.

He says rites over the corpses; he curses them before life flees their eyes.

He wears the trophy-teeth of his victims and he leaves a black-dyed rose with each.

No one has ever conversed with him and lived to speak of it.

"THERE'S TOO MUCH inconsistency!" my brother spat. "How can he be a sadist and also show mercy? You're lying to me, She."

I pointed at the collar. "She can't, sire."

He paced in his bedchamber, empty tonight of female companionship. I sat like a bird of prey, a great vulture, on the leather ottoman at the foot of the bed.

"Then tell me how all these stories can be true!"

"All stories contain truth, sire," I said. "One must be willing to see it."

THE GUARDSMAN'S NAME was Vyren. He was stationed in the outer city, keeping nebulous order in the streets in the aftermath of the unsuccessful coup against my brother's throne.

I asked him if he wanted a child with me. My brother, after all, did not care who fathered my offspring. When Vyren agreed, understanding it would be some years before he could know who the child was, I fucked him for weeks until I knew the seed caught and I conceived.

Vyren was a good man. He wrote me notes and left them where only I might find them. He cared for his younger brothers and his elderly mother with his wages as a guard. He smiled, for he still knew what happiness was—warm food, sleep, laughter with others, sex, watching the rising sun, defending his family from injustice.

"What if I told you I don't see myself as a woman?" I asked him one night, as we lay together in the dusty hallway, away from spying eyes and wagging tongues.

He propped his head up, elbow crooked, and looked down at me. "I'd tell you I like you just as well."

"You wouldn't be lying?"

"No," he said, and kissed me. "I like *you*, Vessai. Man, woman, something else—it doesn't make me feel different. I like all of you."

Something in my chest cracked, like glass beneath a booted heel. Not a physical rending of muscle or bone, but as painful, as vivid.

"I fear I love you," I whispered. He laughed, but I couldn't join him. "I've never loved anyone since…my parents."

"Not even Free?" He used our daughter's name with care, for that was what he thought we should call her, no matter what the king decreed.

"I don't know how to love her yet," I said.

Vyren pulled me closer to his chest, his sweat and mine mixed into pungent musk. He stroked my shaved head; hair was a liability and a vanity. "One day, Vessai, things will change. I don't know how or when, but they will. We'll see our daughter again."

I shut my eyes, a luxury I did so seldom. His heart beat steady and sure against my ear. "I need you to do me a great favor," I said.

THE GENTLEMAN OF Chaos visited me in the Abbey of Mercy when I was ten. He stood in the high, narrow window, a silhouette of death against the moonlight that lit the chapel vestibule.

I knelt inside the granite penitence circle, my wrists chafed bloody by ropes, my back aching from the Mother Superior's cane. I had not been fast enough; the cloth and clay mannequin representing my brother had been stabbed before I could put myself in the knife's path.

"What do you need?" asked the Gentleman of Chaos.

"Nothing," I said. "I need nothing."

"Be careful with that word," said the Gentleman of Chaos. "It holds more than you imagine."

I glared at him.

He drifted down from the window, with rope or silent, unseen wings, and prowled toward me. I saw no weapons; I saw only death.

"No," he said, and sat cross-legged at the edge of the penitence circle, a band of iron inlaid in the floor, with razors set against springs that would snap at the slightest pressure. With one finger, one smooth caress against the iron, I would die, pierced by a thousand razors. "It is not your time, Vessai."

That was my *name*. Not the one bestowed at birth, but the one I called myself.

I gritted my teeth. "Why not?" I was the only one in my family save for my brother. My mother, so my brother wrote, had died of grief after I left. The weight of two lives bore into me heavier than the Mother Superior's cane.

"You are nothing yet," he said. He reached out, his hand long, but only his shadow touched my cheek. "Be patient, child."

Then he stood and vanished again through the window.

"HE COMES CLOSER every year," I told my brother. "I feel him. I hear whispers from the vultures and the ravens."

"Hunt him down," my brother said. His voice cracked in tension.

"I would," I said, "but She cannot leave your side, sire. I will be ready, however, when he arrives."

He stared at me, his teeth grinding.

In the end, he did not send me away.

MY BROTHER THE king was not a kind man.

The guardsman and I stood before my brother in a small, private study left to spiders and dust on royal decree. It was where my father had been killed so many years before, where I had once played under the table with toy soldiers and horses.

"You've consorted with an assassin," my brother said.

"Sire," the guardsman said, still at attention, "I would never—"

"She." My brother gestured at me. "She is an assassin."

The guardsman swallowed and glanced at me sidelong. I remained motionless. When I'd spoken with him, roughening my voice, meeting his eye as men do, he'd never known my brother called me She. It was an odd-fitting word, one that chafed like the collar.

"Do you know what assassins do? They target royalty. They target *me*." My brother paced. "You've slept with her. You gave her a daughter. You would turn her against me."

The guardsman backed away. I'd already taken his sword when we entered the study. "No, Sire, I've never—"

"Kill him," the king told me.

I slit the guardsman's throat and lowered his body, half-shielding his face from my brother's sight. His blood spurted over my tunic and I tasted salt. His gaze never left me, even as he choked.

"I'm sorry," I murmured in his ear, and it was not a lie. He had died in Vyren's stead; a man who looked similar, one with whom I'd let myself be seen around so my brother would suspect.

I was a vulture, circling the dead.

When I was twenty-one, my daughter asked to see me. Ever benevolent, my brother allowed me a visitation. He watched us from the balcony as we sat on the garden bench by the fountain.

"Do I have a father?" the girl asked.

I watched her, emotionless. "Everyone does."

"Yes, but who is *mine*?"

I did not respond. She had inherited my shrewdness; she would know if I led her astray.

"The king says he's my father," the girl said quietly. "But he's lying."

"Do you know who your mother is?" I asked her.

She shook her head. "He says she died when I was born."

We stared into the fountain. Our eyes were so alike.

"Maybe she did," I said. "But if a king is your father, that makes you heir to the throne, doesn't it?"

"I guess," my daughter said.

"And that means one day you will be queen."

She kicked her heels against the fountain's rim. "Could I be a good queen?"

"Yes, child, you can."

THE GENTLEMAN OF Chaos lives in nothingness. The dark of the moon is his bed, the twilight his dawn. He appears to the wicked in their time of destruction.

By popular account, he never fails when he chooses a target.

Popular legend is a lie.

"SIRE," I SAID to my brother as we ate in private. He had taken a fancy to the old study; I had left several tiny bloodstains from the guardsman's murder on the stone. "It's time we acted."

"No one gives me orders!" He grabbed my throat. I watched him, unmoved, and waited until he loosened his hold, leaving the imprint of the collar pressed into my skin. "I am king. I! I decide when it's time!"

He sat back, breathing hard. His eyes were bloodshot. He had not slept well in weeks, haunted by nightmares. Every sound startled him; every footstep made him twitch. I tasted his chamomile tea each night before bed, and never had it been poisoned; he did not understand why he could not rest without waking in a sweat, screaming.

The nightmares were delicate beasts, carved from lace and feathers, bright teeth dripping and cold. They paraded the faces of the dead before his eyes, skeletons wearing the masks of murdered innocents.

"Your word is law." I tilted my head. "What does the law command?"

He threw his plate across the room. The shattered glass made him flinch. "I want the Chaos man dead. Do you hear me, She? Dead. In torment, damned forever! See it done!"

"Of course, sire."

When he retired to his bedchamber, I tasted his tea, let the dreambane wash off my tongue into the warm chamomile, and gave him the cup.

I SAT IN the steam bath adjacent to my brother and considered my body. Hardened, scarred, shaped with binding leather straps and cloth to give it a more masculine profile. I was indifferent to my breasts; they would never nurse, and I had no sensation in my nipples from the hardening agents injected into sensitive flesh by the Sisters. It was only on my brother's orders that they had not sewn shut my cunt, because he wanted me to bear a child one day.

Every time I sought out men to fuck, for enjoyment, for *myself*, I pictured the Mother Superior's face and laughed. The Sisters made competent assassins out of girls who were deemed undesirable.

I never admitted to the Mother Superior that she had been tricked into training a man.

AT FOURTEEN, ON the eve before I was released from the Abbey of Mercy, the Gentleman of Chaos returned to me.

He slipped through the window, a shadow against the dark I lived in, and I leapt upon him. I laid a blade against his throat as he did mine.

"Is it time?" I whispered. "For our deaths?"

"That is your choice."

Temptation ached inside my chest. "Why didn't you kill my brother from the beginning? You could have spared me all this."

His eyes were filled with sorrow. "When I calculated the cost, I could not. If he died that night, so would you. Your mother would have her throne usurped. There have been jackals in the courts for years, ones your father barely kept in check. The king has eliminated them now. But then? War would have overrun the land. I hoped that if you lived, one day, you would take the throne and restore balance."

"All this?" I hissed, leaning closer. His knife broke the skin of my throat and I did not care if it cut to bone. "For a hope?"

"I have made worse mistakes," he said softly. "And so will you."

He lowered his arm. I did not.

"You could have saved him!" My hand shook. "You could have saved my father."

"We all fail," said the Gentleman of Chaos. "You know your brother the king; you know what he will do."

"Then end him," I said. "Fix your failures."

"I am dying, Vessai. I have been for years, since you came here. I ask you to take my name, become the next Gentleman of Chaos, as I did once, as the one before me did so long ago."

"Why?"

"Because now," he said, "you are nothing."

He caught my wrist and guided my hand. I slit his throat and let him fall.

His blood was no different than mine, spread along the stone floor.

It was the only time, since my father's death, that I cried.

"SIRE," I TOLD the king, "my ravens whisper that the Gentleman of Chaos is here."

His bloodshot eyes were wild. "Tell me where!"

"He will come to the palace chapel, below where your father died. He will come alone."

"I will have an army waiting, then!" cried the king.

"Sire," I said, "I have lured him here with the rumor that on the full moon, you pray alone and will be unguarded. If he sees soldiers, he will disappear again and haunt you longer. Allow me to finish this."

The king stared hard at me, his jaw working. "It will end?"

"Yes," I said, and it was not a lie.

THE GENTLEMAN OF Chaos glided from the shadow, through moonlight patches that danced from the stained glass windows in the palace chapel.

My brother knelt in a show of prayer, unarmored, unarmed, exposed, trembling as his ragged breath filled the chapel.

"She?" the king called. "Protect me!"

She was gone. She had been fading for years, piece by piece, eaten away by time and realization that She had never been a woman.

There was only the Gentleman of Chaos.

THE NIGHT MY father was murdered, I was hiding under the heavy table, my toys clutched in tiny hands. Blood spread under the tablecloth and stained my feet.

I'd watched my brother stab our father again and again after Father told him, quietly, in private, that he would not be named heir.

"You have no heart, my son," Father had said with great sadness. "A king cannot rule without heart."

"Lies," my brother had shouted.

Neither of them had known I was under that table, because I was always a quiet child.

"I hear your grief," the Gentleman of Chaos murmured, his hand drying my tears.

"Can you save Father?" I asked.

His eyes held all the sadness in the world. "I'm sorry. I can't."

I grabbed his hand and held on so he would not vanish and leave me alone. "Then will you kill my brother?"

"Not yet, child. Not tonight." He kissed my forehead and whispered a promise, "But I will show you how."

THE KING LOOKED at me, wide-eyed, gasping without breath. I, the Gentleman of Chaos, carefully set the king's heart in his own hands.

Impossible, formed on the king's lips. His heart dripped and stilled in his fingers.

The Gentleman of Chaos unclasped the useless collar that had controlled She. It had never bound Vessai—it had bound a lie, and I had laid that lie to rest at last. I was not She. I was not the sister of the king. I was Vessai, and now the Gentleman of Chaos.

"Magic only binds the true self," I told the king.

I would see my daughter on the throne, for the king had named her heir. She would always be safe, with Vyren at her side to guide her, and the Gentleman of Chaos would always be her shadow.

I would spread my vulture wings and I would haunt the world, as my predecessor had, and all those who had come before him.

THE GENTLEMAN OF Chaos is not a gentle man.

His hands are red, his eyes are dark, and his heart is heavy.

He serves a just queen from shadow, and no assassin will touch her. She will bring balance; she will rule well. This loyalty, this service, the Gentleman of Chaos shows his queen is born from love.

He will never again let a king bind him.

HOW TO BECOME A ROBOT IN 12 EASY STEPS

How TO TELL your boyfriend you are in love with a robot:

1. Tell him, "I may possibly be in love with a robot," because absolutes are difficult for biological brains to process. He won't be jealous.

2. Ask him what he thinks of a hypothetical situation in which you found someone who might not be human, but is still valuable and right for you. (Your so-called romantic relationship is as fake as you are.)

3. Don't tell him anything. It's not that he'll tell you you're wrong; he's not like his parents, or yours. But there's still a statistical possibility he might not be okay with you being in love with a robot.

ON MY TO-DO list today:

- Ask the robot out on a date.
- Pick up salad ingredients for dinner.
- Buy Melinda and Kimberly a wedding gift.

The robot is a J-90 SRM, considered "blocky" and "old-school," probably refurbished from a scrapper, painted bright purple with the coffee-shop logo on the chassis. The robot's square head has an LED screen that greets customers with unfailing politeness and reflects their orders back to them. The bright blue smiley face never changes in the top corner of the screen.

Everyone knows the J-90 SRMs aren't upgradable AI. They have basic customer service programming and equipment maintenance protocols.

Everyone knows robots in the service industry are there as cheap labor investments and to improve customer satisfaction scores, which they never do because customers are never happy.

Everyone knows you can't be in love with a robot.

I drop my plate into the automatic disposal, which thanks me for recycling. No one else waits to deposit trash, so I focus on it as I brace myself to walk back to the counter. The J-90 SRM smiles blankly at the empty front counter, waiting for the next customer.

The lunch rush is over. The air reeks of espresso and burned milk. I don't come here because the food is good or the coffee any better. The neon violet décor is best ignored.

I practiced this in front of a wall a sixteen times over the last week. I have my script. It's simple. "Hello, I'm Tesla. What may I call you?"

And the robot will reply:

I will say, "It's nice to meet you."

And the robot will reply:

I will say, "I would like to know if you'd like to go out with me when you're off-duty, at a time of both our convenience. I'd like to get to know you better, if that's acceptable to you."

And the robot will reply:

"Hey, Tesla."

The imagined conversation shuts down. I blink at the trash receptacle and look up.

My boyfriend smiles hello, his hands shoved in his jeans pockets, his shoulders hunched to make himself look smaller. At six foot five and three hundred pounds, it never helps. He's as cuddly and mellow as a black bear in hibernation. Today he's wearing a gray turtleneck and loafers, his windbreaker unzipped.

"Hi, Jonathan."

I can't ask the robot out now.

The empty feeling reappears in my chest, where it always sits when I can't see or hear the robot.

"You still coming to Esteban's party tonight?" Jonathan asks.

"Yeah."

Jonathan smiles again. "I'll pick you up after work, then."

"Sounds good," I say. "We'd better go, or I'll be late."

He works as an accountant. He wanted to study robotic engineering, but his parents would only pay for college if he got a practical degree (his grandfather disapproves of robots). Computers crunch the numbers, and he handles the people.

He always staggers his lunch break so he can walk back with me. It's nice. Jonathan can act as an impenetrable weather shield if it rains and I forget my umbrella.

But Jonathan isn't the robot.

He offers me his arm, like the gentleman he always is, and we leave the coffee shop. The door wishes us a good day.

I don't look back at the robot.

A BEGINNER'S GUIDE on how to fake your way through biological social constructs:

1. Pretend you are not a robot. This is hard, and you have been working at it for twenty-three years. You are like Data, except in reverse.

2. (There are missing protocols in your head. You don't know why you were born biologically or why there are pieces missing, and you do not really understand how human interaction functions. Sometimes you can fake it. Sometimes people even believe you when you do. You never believe yourself.)

3. Memorize enough data about social cues and run facial muscle pattern recognition so you know what to say and when to say it.

4. This is not always successful.
5. Example: a woman approximately your biological age approaches you and proceeds to explain in detail how mad she is at her boyfriend. Example: boyfriend is guilty of using her toiletries like toothbrush and comb when he comes over, and leaving towels on the bathroom floor. "Such a slob," she says, gripping her beer like a club. "How do you manage men?" You ask if she has told him to bring his own toothbrush and comb and to hang up the towels. It seems the first logical step: factual communication. "He should figure it out!" she says. You are confused. You say that maybe he is unaware of the protocols she has in place. She gives you a strange look, huffs her breath out, and walks off.
6. Now the woman's friends ignore you, and you notice their stares and awkward pauses when you are within their proximity. You have no escape because you didn't drive separately.
7. Ask your boyfriend not to take you to any more parties.

JONATHAN AND I lounge on the plush leather couch in his apartment. He takes up most of it, and I curl against his side. We have a bowl of popcorn, and we're watching reruns of *Star Trek: The Next Generation.*

"I have something to tell you," he says. His shoulders tense.

I keep watching the TV. He knows I pay attention when he tells me things, even if I don't look at him. "Okay."

"I'm…" He hesitates. The Borg fire on the *Enterprise* again. "I'm seeing someone else."

"A guy?" I ask, hopeful.

"Yeah. I met him at the gym. His name's Bernardo."

I sigh in relief. Secrets are heavy and hurt when you have to carry them around all your life. (I have to make lists to keep track of mine.) "I'm glad. Are you going to tell anyone?"

He relaxes and squeezes my hand. "Just you right now. But from what he's told me, his family's pretty accepting."

"Lucky," I say.

We scrape extra butter off the bowl with the last kernels of popcorn.

We've been pretend-dating for two years now. We've never slept together. That's okay. I like cuddling with him, and he likes telling me about crazy customers at his firm, and everyone thinks we're a perfectly adorable straight couple on the outside.

The empty spot in my chest grows bigger as I watch Data on screen. Data has the entire crew of the *Enterprise*. Jonathan has Bernardo now. I don't know if the robot will be interested in me in return. (What if the robot isn't?)

The room shrinks in on me, the umber-painted walls and football memorabilia suffocating. I jerk to my feet.

Jonathan mutes the TV. "Something wrong?"

"I have to go."

"Want me to drive you home?"

"It's four blocks away." But I appreciate his offer, so I add, "But thanks."

I find my coat piled by the door while he takes the popcorn bowl into the kitchen.

Jonathan leans against the wall as I carefully lace each boot to the proper tightness. "If you want to talk, Tesla, I'll listen."

I know that. He came out to me before we started dating. I told him I wasn't interested in socially acceptable relationships, either, and he laughed and looked so relieved he almost cried. We made an elaborate plan, a public persona our families wouldn't hate.

I'm not ready to trust him as much as he trusts me.

"Night, Jonathan."

"Goodnight, Tesla."

How to tell your fake boyfriend you would like to become a robot:
1. Tell him, "I would like to be a robot." You can also say, "I am really a robot, not a female-bodied biological machine," because that is closer to the truth.
2. Do not tell him anything. If you do, you will also have to admit that you think about ways to hurt yourself so you have an excuse to replace body parts with machine parts.
3. Besides, insurance is unlikely to cover your transition into a robot.

I have this nightmare more and more often.

I'm surrounded by robots. Some of them look like the J-90 SRM, some are the newer androids, some are computer cores floating in the air. I'm the only human.

I try to speak, but I have no voice. I try to touch them, but I can't lift my hands. I try to follow them as they walk over a hill and through two huge doors, like glowing LED screens, but I can't move.

Soon, all the robots are gone, and I'm all alone in the empty landscape.

11 REASONS YOU want to become a robot:
1. Robots are logical and know their purpose.
2. Robots have programming they understand.
3. Robots are not held to unattainable standards and then criticized when they fail.
4. Robots are not crippled by emotions they don't know how to process.
5. Robots are not judged based on what sex organs they were born with.
6. Robots have mechanical bodies that are strong and durable. They are not required to have sex.
7. Robots do not feel guilt (about existing, about failing, about being something other than expected).
8. Robots can multitask.
9. Robots do not feel unsafe all the time.
10. Robots are perfect machines that are capable and functional and can be fixed if something breaks.
11. Robots are happy.

IT'S SATURDAY, so I head to the Purple Bean early.

The robot isn't there.

I stare at the polished chrome and plastic K-100, which has a molded face that smiles with humanistic features.

"Welcome to the Purple Bean," the new robot says in a chirpy voice that has inflection and none of the mechanical monotone I like about the old robot. "I'm Janey. How can I serve you today?"

"Where's the J-90 SRM?"

Robbie, the barista who works weekends, leans around the espresso machine and sighs. She must have gotten this question a lot. The panic in my chest is winching so tight it might crack my ribs into little pieces. Why did they retire the robot?

"Manager *finally* got the company to upgrade," Robbie says. "Like it?"

"Where's the J-90 SRM?"

"Eh, recycled, I guess." Robbie shrugs. "You want the usual?"

I can't look at the new K-100. It isn't right. It doesn't belong in the robot's place, and neither do I. "I have to go."

"Have a wonderful day," the door says.

How to rescue a robot from being scrapped: [skill level: intermediate]
1. Call your boyfriend, who owns an SUV, and ask him to drive you to the Gates-MacDowell recycle plant.
2. Argue with the technician, who refuses to sell you the decommissioned robot. It's company protocol, he says, and service industry robots are required to have processors and cores wiped before being recycled.
3. Lie and say you only want to purchase the J-90 SRM because you're starting a collection. Under the law, historical preservation collections are exempt from standardized recycling procedures.
4. Do not commit physical violence on the tech when he hesitates. It's rude, and he's only doing his job.
5. Do not admit you asked your boyfriend along because his size is intimidating, and he knows how to look grouchy at eight a.m.
6. The technician will finally agree and give you a claim ticket.
7. Drive around and find the robot in the docking yard.
8. Do not break down when you see how badly the robot has been damaged: the robot's LED screen cracked, the robot's chassis has been crunched inwards, the robot's missing arm.
9. Try not to believe it is your fault. (That is illogical, even if you still have biological processing units.)

Two techs wheel the robot out and load it into Jonathan's car. The gut-punched feeling doesn't go away. The robot looks so helpless, shut down and blank in the back seat. I flip open the robot's chassis, but the power core is gone, along with the programming module.

The robot is just a shell of what the robot once was.

I feel like crying. I don't want to. It's uncomfortable and doesn't solve problems.

"What's wrong, Tesla?" Jonathan asks.

I shut the chassis. My hands tremble. "They broke the robot."

"It'll be okay," Jonathan says. As if anything can be okay right now. As if there is nothing wrong with me. "You can fix it."

I squirm back into the passenger seat and grip the dash. He's right. We were friends because we both liked robots and I spent my social studies classes in school researching robotics and programming.

"I've never done anything this complex," I say. I've only dismantled, reverse-engineered, and rebuilt the small household appliances and computers. No one has ever let me build a robot.

"You'll do fine," he says. "And if you need help, I know just the guy to ask."

"Who?"

"Want to meet my boyfriend?"

NECESSARY QUESTIONS TO ask your boyfriend's new boyfriend (a former army engineer of robotics):
1. You've been following the development of cyborg bodies, so you ask him if he agrees with the estimates that replacement of all organic tissue sans brain and spinal cord with inorganic machinery is still ten years out, at best. Some scientists predict longer. Some predict never, but you don't believe them. (He'll answer that the best the field can offer right now are limbs and some artificial organs.)
2. Ask him how to upload human consciousness into a robot body. (He'll tell you there is no feasible way to do this yet, and the technology is still twenty years out.)
3. Do not tell him you cannot wait that long. (You cannot last forever.)
4. Instead, ask him if he can get you parts you need to fix the robot.

BERNARDO—SIX INCHES shorter and a hundred pounds lighter than Jonathan, tattooed neck to ankles, always smelling of cigarettes—is part robot. He lost his right arm at the shoulder socket in an accident, and now wears the cybernetic prosthetic. It has limited sensory perception, but he says it's not as good as his old hand.

I like him. I tell Jonathan this, and my boyfriend beams.

"They really gut these things," Bernardo says when he drops off the power cell. (I want to ask him how much I owe him. But when he says nothing about repayment, I stay quiet. I can't afford it. Maybe he knows that.)

We put the robot in the spare bedroom in my apartment, which Jonathan wanted to turn into an office, but never organized himself enough to do so. I liked the empty room, but now it's the robot's home. I hid the late payment notices and overdue bills in a drawer before Jonathan saw them.

"Getting a new arm might be tricky, but I have a buddy who works a scrap yard out in Maine," Bernardo says. "Bet she could dig up the right model parts."

"Thank you."

I'm going to reconstruct the old personality and programming pathways. There are subsystems, "nerve clusters," that serve as redundant processing. Personality modules get routed through functionality programs, and vestiges of the robot's personality build up in subsystems. Newer models are completely wiped, but they usually don't bother with old ones.

Bernardo rubs his shaved head. "You realize this won't be a quick and easy fix, right? Might take weeks. Hell, it might not even work."

I trace a finger through the air in front of the robot's dark LED screen. I have not been able to ask the robot if I have permission to touch the robot. It bothers me that I have to handle parts and repairs without the robot's consent. Does that make it wrong? To fix the robot without knowing if the robot wishes to be fixed?

Will the robot hate me if I succeed?

"I know," I whisper. "But I need to save the robot."

How to tell your pretend-boyfriend and his real boyfriend that your internal processors are failing:

1. The biological term is "depression," but you don't have an official diagnostic (diagnosis) and it's a hard word to say. It feels heavy and stings your mouth. Like when you tried to eat a battery when you were small and your parents got upset.

2. Instead, you try to hide the feeling. But the dark stain has already spilled across your hardwiring and clogged your processor. You don't have access to any working help files to fix this. Tech support is unavailable for your model. (No extended warranty exists.)

3. Pretend the reason you have no energy is because you're sick with a generic bug.

4. You have time to sleep. Your job is canceling out many of your functions; robots can perform cleaning and maintenance in hotels for much better wage investment, and since you are not (yet) a robot, you know you will be replaced soon.
5. The literal translation of the word "depression:" you are broken and devalued and have no further use.
6. No one refurbishes broken robots.
7. Please self-terminate.

I WORK ON the robot during my spare time. I have lots of it now. Working on the robot is the only reason I have to wake up.

I need to repair the robot's destroyed servos and piece together the robot's memory and function programming from what the computer recovered.

There are subroutine lists in my head that are getting bigger and bigger:

- You will not be able to fix the robot.
- You do not have enough money to fix the robot.
- You do not have the skill to fix the robot.
- The robot will hate you.
- You are not a robot.

Bernardo and Jonathan are in the kitchen. They laugh and joke while making stir fry. I'm not hungry.

I haven't been hungry for a few days now.

"You should just buy a new core, Tesla," Bernardo says. "Would save you a lot of headaches."

I don't need a blank, programmable core. What I want is the robot who worked in the Purple Bean. The robot who asked for my order, like the robot did every customer. But the moment I knew I could love this robot was when the robot asked what I would like to be called. "Tesla," I said, and the blue LED smiley face in the upper corner of the robot's screen flickered in a shy smile.

Everyone knows robots are not people.

There's silence in the kitchen. Then Jonathan says, quietly, "Tesla, what's this?"

I assume he's found the eviction notice.

REASONS WHY YOU want to self-terminate (a partial list):

1. Your weekly visit to your parents' house in the suburbs brings the

inevitable question about when you will marry your boyfriend, settle down (so you can pop out babies), and raise a family.

2. You don't tell them you just lost your job.
3. You make the mistake of mentioning that you're going to your best friend Melinda's wedding next weekend. You're happy for her: she's finally marrying her longtime girlfriend, Kimberly.
4. That sets your dad off on another rant about the evils of gay people and how they all deserve to die.
5. (You've heard this all your life. You thought you escaped it when you were eighteen and moved out. But you never do escape, do you? There is no escape.)
6. You make a second mistake and talk back. You've never done that; it's safer to say nothing. But you're too stressed to play safe, so you tell him he's wrong and that it's hurting you when he says that.
7. That makes him paranoid, and he demands that you tell him you aren't one of those fags too.
8. You don't tell your parents you're probably asexual and you really want to be a robot because robots are never condemned because of who they love.
9. You stop listening as he gets louder and louder, angrier and angrier, until you're afraid he will reach for the rifle in the gun cabinet.
10. You run from the house and are almost hit by a truck. Horns blare and slushy snow sprays your face as you reach the safety of the opposite sidewalk.
11. You wish you were three seconds slower so the bumper wouldn't have missed you. It was a big truck.
12. You start making another list.

"WHY DIDN'T YOU tell me?" Jonathan asks, more concerned than angry. "I would've helped out."

I shrug.

The subroutine list boots up:

· You are not an adult if you cannot exist independently at all times.
· Therefore, logically, you are a non-operational drone.
· You will be a burden on everyone.

- You already are.
- Self-terminate.

"I thought I could manage," I say. The robot's LED screen is still cracked and dark. I wonder what the robot dreams about.

Bernardo is quiet in the kitchen, giving us privacy.

Jonathan rubs his eyes. "Okay. Look. You're always welcome to stay with me and Bern. We'll figure it out, Tesla. Don't we always?"

I know how small his apartment is. Bernardo has just moved in with him; there's no space left.

"What about the robot?" I ask.

How to self-destruct: a robot's guide.

1. Water damage. Large bodies of water will short-circuit internal machinery. In biological entities, this is referred to as "drowning." There are several bridges nearby, and the rivers are deep.
2. Overload. Tapping into a power source far beyond what your circuits can handle, such as an industrial grade electric fence. There is one at the Gates-MacDowell recycle plant.
3. Complete power drain. Biologically this is known as blood-loss. There are plenty of shaving razors in the bathroom.
4. Substantial physical damage. Explosives or crushing via industrial recycling machines will be sufficient. Option: stand in front of a train.
5. Impact from substantial height; a fall. You live in a very high apartment complex.
6. Corrupt your internal systems by ingesting industrial grade chemicals. Acid is known to damage organic and inorganic tissue alike.
7. Fill in the blank. (Tip: use the internet.)

BERNARDO'S FAMILY OWNS a rental garage, and he uses one of the units for rebuilding his custom motorcycle. He says I can store the robot there, until another unit opens up.

Jonathan has moved his Budweiser memorabilia collection into storage so the small room he kept it in is now an unofficial bedroom. He shows it to me and says I can move in anytime I want. He and Bernardo are sharing his bedroom.

I don't know what to do.

I have no operating procedures for accepting help.

I should self-destruct and spare them all. That would be easier, wouldn't it? Better for them?

But the robot isn't finished.

I don't know what to do.

How to have awkward conversations about your relationship with your boyfriend and your boyfriend's boyfriend:

1. Agree to move in with them. Temporarily. (You feel like you are intruding. Try not to notice that they both are genuinely happy to have you live with them.)
2. Order pizza and watch the *Futurama* marathon on TV.
3. Your boyfriend says, "I'm going to come out to my family. I've written a FB update, and I just have to hit send."
4. Your boyfriend's boyfriend kisses him, and you fistbump them both in celebration.
5. You tell him you're proud of him. You will be the first to like his status.
6. He posts the message to his wall. You immediately like the update.
7. (You don't know what this means for your façade of boyfriend/girlfriend.)
8. Your boyfriend says, "Tesla, we need to talk. About us. About all three of us." You know what he means. Where do you fit in now?
9. You say, "Okay."
10. "I'm entirely cool with you being part of this relationship, Tesla," your boyfriend's boyfriend says. "Who gives a fuck what other people think? But it's up to you, totally."
11. "What he said," your boyfriend says. "Hell, you can bring the robot in too. It's not like any of us object to robots as part of the family." He pats his boyfriend's cybernetic arm. "We'll make it work."
12. You don't say, "I can be a robot, and that's okay?" Instead, you tell them you'll think about it.

I WRITE ANOTHER list.

I write down all the lists. In order. In detail.

Then I print them out and give them to Jonathan and Bernardo.

The cover page has four letters on it: H-E-L-P.

REASONS WHY YOU should avoid self-termination (right now):

1. Jonathan says, "If you ever need to talk, I'll listen."
2. Bernardo says, "It'll get better. I promise it does. I've been there, where you're at, thinking there's nothing more than the world fucking with you. I was in hell my whole childhood and through high school." He'll show you the scars on his wrists and throat, his tattoos never covering them up. "I know it fucking hurts. But there's people who love you and we're willing to help you survive. You're strong enough to make it."
3. Your best friend Melinda says, "Who else is going to write me snarky texts while I'm at work or go to horror movies with me (you know my wife hates them) or come camping with us every summer like we've done since we were ten?" And she'll hold her hands out and say, "You deserve to be happy. Please don't leave."
4. You will get another job.
5. You will function again, if you give yourself time and let your friends help. And they will. They already do.
6. The robot needs you.
7. Because if you self-terminate, you won't have a chance to become a robot in the future.

"HEY, TESLA," JONATHAN says, poking his head around the garage-workshop door. "Bern and I are going over to his parents for dinner. Want to come?"

"Hey, I'll come for you anytime," Bernardo calls from the parking lot.

Jonathan rolls his eyes, his goofy smile wider than ever.

I shake my head. The robot is almost finished. "You guys have fun. Say hi for me."

"You bet."

The garage is silent. Ready.

I sit by the power grid. I've unplugged all the other devices, powered down the phone and the data hub. I carefully hid Bernardo's bike behind a plastic privacy wall he used to divide the garage so we each have a workspace.

We're alone, the robot and I.

I rig up a secondary external power core and keep the dedicated computer running the diagnostic.

The robot stands motionless, the LED screen blank. It's still cracked, but it will function.

"Can you hear me?" I ask. "Are you there?"

The robot:

I power up the robot and key the download sequence, re-installing the rescued memory core.

The robot's screen flickers. The blue smiley face appears in the center, split with spiderweb cracks.

"Hello," I say.

"Hello, Tesla," the robot says.

"How do you feel?"

"I am well," the robot says. "I believe you saved my life."

The hole closes in my chest, just a little.

The robot's clean, symmetrical lines and tarnished purple surface glow. The robot is perfect. I stand up.

"How may I thank you for your help, Tesla?"

"Is there a way I can become a robot too?"

The robot's pixelated face shifts; now the robot's expression frowns. "I do not know, Tesla. I am not programmed with such knowledge. I am sorry."

I think about the speculative technical papers I read, articles Bernardo forwarded to me.

"I have a hypothesis," I tell the robot. "If I could power myself with enough electricity, my electromagnetic thought patterns might be able to travel into a mechanical apparatus such as the computer hub."

(Consciousness uploads aren't feasible yet.)

"I believe such a procedure would be damaging to your current organic shell," the robot says.

Yes, I understand electrocution's effects on biological tissue. I have thought about it before. (Many times. All the time.)

The robot says, "May I suggest that you consider the matter before doing anything regrettable, Tesla?"

And I reply:

The robot says: "I should not like to see you deprogrammed and consigned to the scrapping plant for organic tissue."

And I reply:

The robot says: "I will be sad if you die."

I look up at the frowning blue pixel face. And I think of Jonathan and Bernardo returning and finding my body stiff and blackened, my fingers plugged into the power grid.

The robot extends one blocky hand. "Perhaps I would be allowed to devise a more reliable solution? I would like to understand you better, if that is acceptable." The blue lines curve up into a hopeful smile.

The robot is still here. Jonathan and Bernardo are here. Melinda and Kimberly are here. I'm not a robot (yet), but I'm not alone.

"Is this an acceptable solution, Tesla?" the robot asks.

I take the robot's hand, and the robot's blocky fingers slowly curl around mine. "Yes. I would like that very much." Then I ask the robot, "What would you like me to call you?"

How to become a robot:
1. You don't.
2. Not yet.
3. But you will.

PUBLICATION HISTORY

CPSIA information can be obtained
at www.ICGtesting.com
Printed in the USA
LVOW08s1916270517
536107LV00001B/2/P